LORE & LUST

QUEER VAMPIRE ROMANCE SERIES BOOK ONE

KARLA NIKOLE PUBLISHING

LORE & LUST

KARLA.NIKOLE

KARLA NIKOLE PUBLISHING

First Karla Nikole Publishing Edition, October 2020

ISBN: 978-1-7355898-0-0 (paperback)

ISBN: 978-1-7355898-1-7 (ebook)

Library of Congress Control Number: 2020916075

Cover illustration by Thander Lin

Contact@LoreAndLust.com

www.LoreAndLust.com

Printed in the United States of America

10 9 8 7 6 5 4 3 2 1

*For all of my beautiful, clever and hilarious
friends who encouraged me along the way.*

EARLY NOVEMBER

ONE

England in winter—darkness, bitter cold and rain. Haruka shivers from the frigid damp. Everything about this situation is miserable.

Tiny droplets and long streams of water speckle the glass of the car window. Sitting in the back seat of the parked vehicle, the dark vampire shrugs deeper into his long wool trench coat. He closes his eyes. *Stay calm*, he thinks. Haruka hasn't been outside his home to engage the vampire aristocracy in ten years. Put simply, he is a little stressed.

His manservant's voice cuts through the silence from the driver's seat. "Just so we're clear, I don't like this."

Haruka doesn't like it either, but what are his options? Ignore the formal request being made of him? Lose his feeding source and become an object of derision within the British vampire community? Or...

Haruka peeks one eye open. "We could go home... pack up the house—"

"No. We're not running away *again*."

"Then what would you have me do, Asao?"

"I would have you find a new purebred source." Asao turns to watch him from the driver's seat, his salt-and-pepper hair briefly illuminated by the glow of headlights from a passing car. "You've been drinking first-gen blood and it doesn't give you optimum nourishment. You're not strong enough for this—to be exposed this way in a house full of vamps we've never met. I'm dreading this damn bonding ceremony next month for the same reason."

Haruka sighs, closing his eyes again. "As long as no one challenges me, I should be fine." Finding a purebred source isn't easy. It isn't like quickly finding a pencil when you need to write something down. It's more like searching for a rare gemstone across a vast cavern. Tanzanite or black opal.

Haruka has tried to secure a new purebred source in the past, but it's never worked out. Too many demands, too much required in exchange. *This* is his life now. His manservant needs to accept it.

"If someone challenges you tonight, then what?" Asao asks. "You can't keep the lure of your aura enclosed like this *and* fight someone off. Once your aura is exposed, every vampire in the house will be drawn to you... like a bunch of stupid frat boys to a keg. You need both defenses and offenses, Haruka, and feeding from a purebred will give you the strength—"

"I *know* this, but what will the purebred require of me in return?" Haruka scowls, his voice louder. "I have tried before—the price has always been too high. I will *not* form another bond. This discussion is pointless... What the hell is a 'frat boy'?"

Asao turns forward in the dark silence, shaking his head. Raindrops tap loudly against the vehicle. "This other purebred that we'll meet in London tomorrow... Just let me ask if he'd be willing to send you bags of his blood—"

"*No*," Haruka breathes. It is undignified to make such

blatant requests, and it would only expose him in his vulnerable state—making him an easy target. "You are concerned for me. But I will manage. I've been fine for more than ten years now. Shall we go inside and get this over with?"

Asao is still for a long moment, then hesitates at the door handle. "You are living a life *significantly* beneath your capabilities." He steps outside. Shuts the door.

Haruka rolls his eyes. How is this statement helpful right now? Besides—his life, his choices. Somewhat... when he isn't being forced to do something because of his bloodline and ranking.

The back door opens. A rush of damp, wintery air caresses Haruka's face. Asao is holding a large black umbrella overhead as Haruka takes in the elegant brick structures surrounding them. The streetlights cast silver rays down the length of the dark road like spotlights on a dramatic stage. It's quiet—only the peppery sound of rain on pavement.

They ascend the steps to the Duke of Oxford's residence. Traveling the long distance from their home in Devonshire, they'll be spending the night here. Tomorrow, they'll travel to London to confront the purebred. The only other pureblooded vampire living in England aside from Haruka.

Civil wars and the Great Vanishing have wiped out every last purebred of British descent.

The tall blue door to the apartment swings open. Yellow light pours over them, making Haruka wince at the sudden contrast of bright illumination against darkness.

One manservant rushes out to relieve Asao of the large umbrella while a second stands at the door. He lifts his arm in a sweeping gesture. "Gracious master to the House of Hirano, welcome to Oxford. The duke and his family are in the banquet hall. Everyone is anxiously awaiting your arrival. This way, please, my lord."

Haruka discreetly sniffs the air as he walks past the formally dressed servants. Their scents are unembellished—the smell of dried earth. They're vampiric in nature but very low level. The human blood within their ancestry supersedes the vampiric.

The hallway is cool as he steps inside the residence and onto the polished marble floor. The walls are patterned with green Victorian-style wallpaper and the large chandelier above casts sparkling flecks of white light against every surface. The air is still. A smattering of voices echoes down the long hallway as Haruka breathes in the faint scent of salty meats and baked bread.

One manservant glides behind him to take his coat. Haruka obediently shrugs out of the long garment. The second manservant is standing in a daze and staring at Haruka with blue irises the color of summer skies. Haruka furrows his dark brow—he knows this particular look *very* well. It's the look of someone hungry for something that registers as primal... not in the stomach. Below the waist.

The manservant holding Haruka's coat walks around and discreetly smacks his colleague in the arm. The blue-eyed male blinks and smiles weakly, the trance broken. "My apologies, your grace, please follow me." The manservant turns, hastily moving down the hallway as if trying to outrun his embarrassment.

Well, we're off to an inauspicious start. He hasn't been in this house five minutes and already a manservant is stupefied by his stifled aura.

Haruka exhales a breath, massaging the back of his neck with his palm as they walk down the narrow hallway. It's going to be a long night.

SECRETLY, Haruka had hoped for a quiet evening between himself and the Duke of Oxford. What he receives is an extravagant feast with fifteen other dukes and duchesses seated within an elaborate ballroom.

When he enters, everyone stands at attention—perfectly still. Their vivid eyes are watching him. They remind Haruka of statues as he walks toward the empty seat at the head of the table just beside the Duke of Oxford. Each vampire tilts their head down in reverence as he passes, like dominoes. Even from a vampire's perspective, the scene is eerie. The blood-red, dramatic baroque décor of the room certainly doesn't help. *Interesting*, he observes. *They enjoyed the eighteenth century to the extent that they refuse to leave...*

After receiving a humble bow from the duke, Haruka nods politely and sits down. Everyone follows his lead and the duke proceeds with long-winded introductions for each of his guests. When a glass of red wine is placed in front of him, Haruka breathes a sigh of relief. *Thank God.* Merciful provision to aid him through the long evening ahead. He curls his fingers around the glass and brings it to his lips.

With the introductions finished, the Duke of Oxford tilts his round head, blatantly sniffing. "My gracious lord, the scent of your aura is truly exquisite. Why do you keep it so strictly enclosed?" The first-generation vampire reminds Haruka of a marble bust he'd once seen in the British Museum of the Greek philosopher Antisthenes. Or perhaps a plump, short Zeus?

Haruka takes another sip from his wine glass before answering the invasive, awkward question. He smiles kindly, setting his glass down. "My aura can be exceptionally distracting. It is with consideration for those around me that I restrain it." Consideration for others. Protection for himself. Two birds, one stone.

"Oh no." The duke shakes his head, making the ringlets of

his curly white beard sway like a curtain. "I can only just sense the nature of it, but it seems *divine*. I envy you pureblooded ones and your ability to radiate such alluring energy—born immaculately vampiric. Even with it stifled I can sense the unique composition of it. Your blood must be extraordinarily old. Have you ever needed to feed from a human?"

"No." Haruka brings his wine glass to his lips again. He'll need a refill very soon. Perhaps his own bottle?

He's never fed from a human, and as far as his family record states, neither had his father, grandfather nor anyone in his extensive ancestry. His vampiric bloodline is extremely old —clean. His clan had been among the first to discover the intrinsic benefits of feeding from other vampires rather than humans.

"My mother was the purebred in my parents' coupling," the duke explains, his British accent heavy. "Unfortunately, she fed from humans as a child. The act weakened our bloodline. I still experience difficulties as her offspring."

"The sun, my lord." Amelia, the duke's daughter, lifts her chin to address Haruka. She's strategically seated just beside him. "Father has designated our realm as nocturnal because of his strict aversion to sunlight." She has straight blonde hair and sharp, green-iridescent eyes set in a round face similar to her father's. When Haruka focuses his senses on her and breathes in, she smells of peppermint.

"Although I am second-generation, *I* am able to withstand sunlight like you, your grace." Amelia casually reaches up to brush her long hair behind her ear. "Because my father and mother have never fed from humans, it has helped to deconta- minate our bloodline from human biology. I could... potentially walk beside you in the light."

Haruka narrows his eyes. *Where exactly are we walking?*

"Your grace, will you partake of table food?" the duke asks

just as the wait staff begins placing baskets of cottage loaves, small bread and crumpets throughout the table. "I understand you do not strictly require it, however some of my guests are of lower-ranking bloodlines."

"I will," Haruka assures him. "I greatly enjoy the taste of human nourishment."

The duke beams. "Splendid. You are much unlike the purebreds of old. Your grace, may I humbly ask, what is your age?"

"I am one hundred and one."

"So young..." the duke's mate gushes. The Duchess of Oxfordshire is seated at the duke's opposite side. She's the spitting image of her daughter, but with delicate creases etched into her lean, angelic features. "Our Amelia has just reached eighty this year. Why are you unbonded, your grace? It is rare to cross paths with a purebred in this modern age, particularly one that is so beautiful and without a mate."

More flowery compliments, uncomfortable questions and talk of bonding. As beings who live for centuries, the conversational topics at their disposal run vast and compelling: arts and philosophy, the curious passage of time and subsequent shifts in modernity within their culture, the intricacies of colloquial language, Brexit, the weather.

"I have not yet found a vampire that I am compatible with," Haruka says, defaulting to his socially couth answer. Truthfully, he has no desire to bond. Stating this would create more commotion than he is willing to manage.

"Please spend some time with our Amelia at the ceremony next month," the duke says, reaching for a biscuit. "We also have an elder son that is currently traveling for business. I am certain that you will find one of them pleasing enough to consider forming a bond?"

Everyone stares at Haruka expectantly, as if he's a magician about to perform a trick. He clears his throat. "My apologies.

The matter of the ceremony next month and speaking with the purebred in London take precedence. My mind is focused on the tasks set before me."

"Of course, your grace," the duchess coos. "Do you have any explanation as to why this purebred would callously ignore the Duke of Devonshire's formal request? Does he think himself better than us?"

Haruka has no idea. As for himself, he absolutely *does not* want to participate in this archaic ceremony. But outright ignoring a formal request from a lower-ranked vampire is like committing social suicide—especially in a foreign realm. He is a guest within the British aristocracy. Purebred vampires are the dignity and peacekeepers of their race. Not instigators of societal turmoil.

"I am uncertain," Haruka demurs. "I will appeal to the purebred directly tomorrow." Quietly, Haruka prays he'll oblige. Misery loves company.

The duke sits back, absently twirling a thick curl from his beard in his fingers. "The Duke of Devonshire told us that you held the position of Historian when you oversaw your realm in Japan. I'm certain that much detailed research is necessary for the ceremonial contract."

Haruka freezes—dread washing over him like a dark ocean wave rushing ashore. He's been avoiding working on the ceremonial contract: the legal document outlining each bonding vampire's family lineage and the conjoining of their assets. Truthfully, he's ignored the entire ordeal, hoping it might be called off. He needs to start the contract as soon as he returns home. His appalling habit of procrastinating has officially gotten the better of him.

The Duke of Oxfordshire smoothly leans forward, his voice low. "And how interesting that the duke's son would choose a creature from Brazil to bond with. I mean, my word, of *all* places, considering the trouble there right now."

Nodding politely, Haruka remains silent, not wanting to encourage the duke's prejudice. Although the environment of the Brazilian aristocracy is indeed in chaos, it seems unfair to cast sweeping generalizations upon its vampires.

Haruka discreetly casts his gaze sideways when he feels the gentle pressure of fingertips grazing his thigh underneath the table. Amelia is watching him with her iridescent eyes, smiling seductively. Her incisors slowly elongate into sharp white points.

TWO

By the time Haruka has taken a hot shower and collapses onto his back in bed, he's exhausted. Throughout dinner, Amelia had focused all her affection and conversation in his direction.

What are you looking for in a mate? You're so very stunning. When do you think you'll be ready to bond? Your eyes are lovely, but are they normally this color? What's the aristocracy like in Japan? Do you have a physical source? Do you find me desirable? I find you incredibly desirable.

Somehow, he graciously weaved through the barrage of questions. Before tonight, he'd worried that he might come across as socially awkward from years of isolating himself in the English countryside. Whether he's inept or not, it doesn't seem to matter. He is *desirable* and apparently this is sufficient. Physical prowess supersedes any deeper character failings. A pretty face will do.

The look and feel of the guest chamber flow in rhythm with the rest of the house: moody lighting with dark baroque décor. Tapered candlesticks dripping with wax. Even his bed is an excessively large four-poster monstrosity that occupies most of the room's square footage.

Haruka turns onto his side, burrowing his body into the soft comforter. He's finally alone, feeling somewhat at ease for the first time in hours. When there's a soft knock at the door, his eyes flicker open. He rolls onto his back, concentrating. Stretching his mind and vampiric senses toward the door, he sniffs the air. It is definitely the ogling, blue-eyed manservant from earlier in the evening. He stares blankly at the low ceiling, exhaling a heavy sigh. "And so we begin."

He drags his body upright, eventually moving toward the door to crack it open. The servant blinks his large, baby-doll eyes as Haruka peers through the gap. He is much shorter than Haruka in stature, his vampiric bloodline weak. Essentially, he is a human clinging to the edges of modern vampire culture. A human-vampire. Low-leveler.

The manservant's hair is sandy-brown, cut short to complement his heart-shaped face. A splattering of light freckles graces his nose and cheeks, like careless flecks from a paintbrush. Although he seems fairly young, he is an undeniably attractive male and Haruka knows what he wants. The sultry, admiring look he gives with his cerulean gaze is unmistakable.

"Your grace, is everything well within your chamber dwelling?"

My chamber dwelling. The longer Haruka stays in this house, the more he feels he's being swept back in time—or as if he's part of some human-conceived, literary stereotype of his culture. He half expected an extravagant coffin in his guest room in lieu of an actual bed.

"All is well," Haruka assures him. "Thank you for your concern."

"Of course." A warm smile slowly forms on the manservant's thin lips. "Do you wish for me to come inside to review the apartment? It is my sincere desire for you to be pleased while you abide with us. I would do *whatever* is necessary to ensure you are satisfied, my beautiful and gracious lord."

God help me. Haruka politely returns his smile. "I appreciate the kind offer. But I would like to rest tonight."

"Are you certain? I am quite skilled—"

"I am."

"I understand. It is my great loss." He bows his head, then looks up at Haruka from beneath long brown eyelashes before turning and walking away. When the door is closed, Haruka switches the lock for good measure.

As soon as he's back in bed with his eyes closed, there is another knock at the door.

Haruka remains still this time, stretching his senses and inhaling once more. It is the second-generation female with the lovely brown skin tone. She'd been one of the silent twelve in attendance during dinner. They'd literally said nothing all evening—only laughed and smiled on cue like stiff actors in a community theater troupe.

The door is locked, so Haruka decides to play possum. After a few minutes she gives up, her subtle essence fading away.

When the third knock comes, Haruka is asleep. He lazily opens his eyes. Exhaustion is settled heavily in his mind as he yawns, but before he can discern who is outside his bedroom, there's a loud click in the silence. He turns his head. The lock mechanism has shifted. He watches in confusion as the door creaks open.

Yellow light from the hallway precedes Amelia as she steps into the room and swiftly closes the door behind her. The female is already walking toward Haruka as he hastily sits upright in bed. He rubs his palm down his face in a weak attempt to shake his disoriented state. "What are you—"

She launches herself forward. She moves fast but Haruka is faster—quickly blinking and making his eyes burn bright as he wills the power of his nature from within his body. The sensation is a tight knot deep in his core, unraveling and rushing fiercely outward like a blazing river. As it moves, it grows and expands. Haruka intentionally sends the force of it toward Amelia and she gasps, suddenly frozen, wide-eyed under his subjugation.

Haruka's chest heaves as he holds her in place. He subdues her in totality, not even leaving her consciousness free to communicate with him. He hasn't willed his nature outward like this in at least a decade, and now he's done it sloppily—indiscriminately and without true focus or his usual finesse. The scent of his unique aura permeates the room like a cloudy haze of smoke from a fire, but crimson and supernatural. If he doesn't absorb it within himself soon, it will stir the inhabitants of the house, drawing them in like a beacon.

"Asao?" Haruka speaks into the still silence, his eyes fixed on the frozen form of Amelia in front of him. To his great relief, Asao soon opens the door. He closes it, then moves to stand behind Amelia.

Once her arms are secured behind her back, the manservant lifts his chin. "I'm ready. You can release her."

Haruka inhales, mechanically absorbing the weight of his energy back within his body. He mentally stuffs it into a knotted hold deep inside himself. Amelia sucks in a breath as if she'd been underwater, her eyes bulging. She bucks and thrashes her voluptuous frame against Asao to free herself, but the solid manservant easily restricts her.

"You—you have actual *powers*," Amelia breathes, her voice

ragged from the impact of subjugation. "I *knew* it. I could smell —and your blood. Incredible!"

"*Amelia.*" Haruka uses the weight of his deep voice to calm her. Being lower ranked, she is more vulnerable to his words after direct exposure to his aura. "You *cannot* break into some-one's room. I am a guest in your home and it is extremely rude... I should not need to say these things."

"I—I apologize, your grace." She sways in Asao's grasp. She almost falls over, but he holds her steady. "I wanted to feed from you—to *please* you... to release... your... aura." She sleeps. Asao rearranges her in his arms to properly support her. He looks down at her sagging frame and shakes his head.

"First of all, I *told* you."

Haruka rolls his eyes.

"Second," Asao continues, "poor kid barges in here and she can't even handle you. 'Pull your aura.' Yeah, right. Did you need to fully subjugate her?"

Haruka takes a deep breath and scratches the back of his head. "No... However, she startled me and I'm out of practice. You came quickly—were you listening?"

"Yeah. I heard you when she first came into the room. They have my bedroom so damn far away that it took me a while to walk over here. This place is creepy."

Haruka yawns. It has been a day. "I am grateful for your unique ability."

"You're not grateful for it when you're trying to sneak wine from the kitchen in the middle of the night." Asao smirks.

Haruka breathes a laugh. "True."

"What the hell should I do with her?"

There is a knock on the bedroom door. Haruka smirks. *Ask and you shall receive.* He focuses and sniffs. "Perhaps the young manservant on the other side of the door can help?"

Sitting down hard on the bed, he watches as Asao grapples

with a peacefully sleeping Amelia. The freckled manservant timidly peeks his head into the room. He's dumbfounded as Asao speaks, staring past him to uncomfortably gawk at Haruka on the bed. Soon, Asao awkwardly hands Amelia over to him and shuts the door.

"You've had quite a few admirers tonight." Asao grins, walking toward the bed as Haruka settles back down. He pulls the sheets up to make himself comfortable while his manservant sits along the side. "It's a good thing she was second-gen," Asao continues. "What if she'd been higher ranked?"

Haruka closes his eyes, mumbling against the sheets. "What if you help me pack up the house?"

"*Haruka*. How long are we going to do this? Ignoring your true responsibilities and stifling your nature? You've avoided talking about this for years now... This whole mess started with Yuna. Your bond—"

"Asao, *please*." Haruka turns to look at him, imploring. He's exhausted from rapidly pushing his aura outward, annoyed about the upcoming bonding ceremony and frustrated that he has irresponsibly procrastinated over the start of a major cultural document. The last thing he wants to do is have a heart-to-heart about the ghosts of his unfortunate past.

"My apologies, your grace," Asao says stiffly. "Do you want me to stay here with you while you sleep?"

Haruka shifts his head against the pillow, his body and mind rapidly shutting down for the night. He has overexerted himself. "You don't have to."

"Need I remind you that the vampires of the Oxford realm are nocturnal?"

Perfectly still, Haruka opens his eyes. Blinking. Considering.

"That being said," Asao goes on, "everyone will be awake while *you* are sleeping."

Haruka turns to meet his manservant's eyes. There is a distinct moment of pause before Asao grins and points. "I'll sleep on that couch in the corner."

"If you think it is best," Haruka says, closing his eyes with a grin. "I will not argue with you."

THREE

Using his innate powers takes a heavy toll on Haruka, so he sleeps late into the next day. By the time he wakes up, gets dressed and wanders into the dining room in search of table food, it is late afternoon.

Practically everyone in the duke's estate is asleep due to the nocturnal mandate. The house is eerily quiet. *Full of sleeping, old-fashioned vampires*, Haruka ponders. *Like a crypt.* Only a skeleton crew of attendants oblige Haruka and his manservant with a late lunch before his departure.

When they're done, Asao stands from the table with a look of conviction set in his square jaw. "Let's get the hell out of here before these weirdoes wake up." Haruka agrees wholeheartedly. Soon after, they quietly leave the Duke of Oxford's home.

They reach London at sunset. Haruka stares blankly out the window as they drive, watching the orange-and-pink gradient of the early evening sky.

"Is your awareness of this purebred growing stronger as we

get closer?" Asao asks from the driver's seat. "I hope this address is right."

"Mm. The duke says that his business is located in Camden Lock. That information corresponds with my innate sense of him."

"He owns a bar, right?"

"Yes."

Asao sighs. "Alright. We'll have to walk when we get near that area. I don't think I can drive down the market streets."

Haruka rubs his palm down his face. Walking in a public area filled with a myriad of humans and vampires on a frigid winter night. *God help me.*

IT'S dark when they finally arrive at Camden Lock. They navigate the narrow cobblestoned streets and alleyways, eventually standing in front of a bar with an illuminated sign. It shines brightly in white, like a second moon against the deep indigo sky. It reads *Scotch & Amaretto* in relaxed cursive script.

Haruka reaches out to pull the bar door open, but pauses at the sound of his manservant's voice. "Now... what if this purebred is some kind of crazy pervert and attacks you?"

Standing straight, Haruka genuinely considers the possibility. He can handle a lower-ranked vampire in his weakened state. Another purebred, or even a particularly strong first-generation would be much more challenging. "Most purebreds have exceptional control over their natures, and my primal aura is enclosed. I doubt he would wish to create havoc within his place of business."

"True." Asao nods. "I'm suddenly reminded of that one very pushy purebred we met in Montreal. Remember that? What year was that, eighty-three?"

Haruka remembers. He wishes he didn't. He's met more than his share of pushy, selfish and entitled vampires. "Why are you reminding me of that right *now*?"

"It's better to be prepared."

Again. Not helping. Haruka tugs the heavy wooden door open (a little harder than necessary).

When he steps inside, he's immediately tense. The luscious smell of the purebred consumes him. The aroma is clean, woodsy and with a hint of something spiced—mahogany but somehow intermingled with cinnamon. The lighting is low, and in combination with the smell, the intimate space feels perfectly warm and inviting.

He glances around, taking in the refined details of the bar. Several tall dark-oak tables with high stools are thoughtfully placed throughout the main floor. Jewel-toned, orb-shaped candle holders sit in the center of each table, creating soft flickers of light throughout the room. The stone walls are adorned with burning lanterns and sconces, giving the overall impression of a romantic, very trendy Renaissance castle basement... if such a juxtaposition can exist.

Even with all these wonderful elements for the eyes to behold, the farthest wall from the entrance is clearly the focal point of the room.

A full bar glows softly in the darkness. The wall is filled with multi-colored bottles of alcohol, interspersed once more with bright candle holders and other curious, antique-looking artifacts. Haruka likens the wall to an apothecary's pantry filled with exotic potions and mysterious elixirs.

The bar hosts a comfortable crowd of people for a weekday night. Naturally, they have all stopped and are now staring at him. Haruka sighs. *To hell with a discreet entrance.*

He scans the length of the bar. Empty. The purebred is

nowhere in sight but Haruka can feel his energy. He is definitely here.

"He smells nice," Asao says brightly, standing behind
Haruka. "I'll stay by the door?"

"Fine."

Haruka walks forward, ignoring the blatant stares as he
skillfully moves his tall body between the tables to follow the
narrow path to the bar. As he approaches the counter, a male
ducks out from behind a heavy velvet curtain covering a doorframe on the opposite side of the bar. Their eyes meet. Haruka
stops dead. The purebred pauses as well—rigid as he stares.

The knot of Haruka's enclosed aura pulses in his core. It's
subtle, but it independently shifts as if to untie itself from the
forced hold. His nature has never done this before. It's bizarre.
Surprised, he almost takes a step back and away from the male
gawking at him.

With his pulse racing, he takes a deep breath to gather
himself and steps forward again. His action sets the creature
behind the bar into motion, and he too cautiously shifts closer
to the counter between them. Before Haruka can introduce
himself, the purebred speaks.

"Hi... It's Haruka, right? Haruka Hirano?"

Haruka pauses again, blinking. "How... Why do you know
my name?"

"I think every vampire in the UK knows who you are.
You're pretty famous. I had no idea you were this young
though." The purebred shifts his golden-amber eyes to the side,
then runs his fingers into his thick hair—coppery-brown in color
and styled in a modern trim with wavy length in the top. His
honeyed skin practically glows under the soft lighting of the bar.

He flickers his eyes back toward Haruka, sulking. "Am I in
some kind of trouble? Is that why you're here?"

Haruka softens his expression, oddly wanting to put him at ease. "Not in trouble. May I sit?"

"Of course, please. Would you like a drink?"

"Merlot, please," Haruka says, making himself comfortable atop the closest bar stool.

"No problem." The purebred turns away, then briskly turns back toward Haruka. For the first time, he offers a timid smile. "I'm Nino, by the way. It's nice to meet you."

"Likewise."

Nino runs his fingers through his hair again, hesitating before making himself busy behind the bar. He pulls a bottle from the illuminated shelf, then glasses and a handled corkscrew from underneath the bar. His movement is fluid now, like a fish swimming underwater.

"Nino, what is your full name?"

Nino abruptly pauses, his vivid eyes wide. "Excuse me?"

"Your full name," Haruka repeats. "It is proper in new introductions like this."

Nino works the cork, then twists and smoothly pulls it from the wine bottle. "It's sorry—I mean, *I'm* sorry, for not..." He takes a deep breath. "My name is Nino Bianchi."

"And what is your age?" Haruka asks.

"One hundred and twelve." Nino focuses, pouring the dark burgundy liquid and generously filling both glasses. Haruka keeps his expression even, but he is surprised. Nino's manner presents as fairly juvenile, like that of a vampire well below a century. Not only is he over a century, he's older than Haruka by eleven years.

Nino carefully lifts the wine glass and places it in front of Haruka. "So... what's your age? May I ask?"

"Of course." Haruka gently wraps his fingers around the glass. "I am one hundred and one."

Nino's haunting eyes brighten, his smile open and genuine.

"We're pretty close. I've never met another purebred near my age before. Where I'm from they're all old or scary."

"Where are you from?" Haruka lifts his glass, taking a sip.

"Milan, Italy. My father's clan still has firm control over the city, but everyone in my mother's clan was killed during the First World War—starting at the Qingdao conflict."

Haruka considers, scanning his memory like the pages of an old reference book in the expansive library of his mind. Qingdao had primarily been a conflict between Japan, Germany and the UK over a German port in China. To his knowledge, the Italian military had not been involved. "I am sorry for your loss... In what way was your mother's clan entangled in the siege?"

"They were major players in the Japanese navy. My grand-father was the commanding officer on the *Kawachi*."

Haruka blinks, processing the information. Nino finishes a long sip of his wine and smiles timidly. "You're thinking I don't *look* half-Japanese."

"No." Haruka stares into space. "I was having difficulty remembering when the *Kawachi* sank. Was it 1918?"

"Yeah, that's right. I'm surprised you would know such an arbitrary fact right off the top of your head."

"It is essentially my job to know many arbitrary facts."

Nino leans with his elbows against the counter slightly off-center from Haruka. He makes himself comfortable and gently twists his wine glass with his fingers at the stem. "Historian?" he asks.

"Correct."

"I *knew* it." Nino beams in his open, genuine way once more. "My family specializes in roles related to business and social affairs, so I've never met a proper vampire Historian before... I always imagined them as these cultured, intelligent people. Looks like I was right."

Haruka's knotted aura independently shifts again, a distinct warmth gently bubbling up his spine. He discreetly stretches his lower back and sucks in a breath. *What the hell is this?*

"How many languages do you speak?" Nino asks. "You're a polyglot, aren't you?"

Distracted and tense from this abnormality of his aura suddenly having a mind of its own, Haruka picks up his glass. "What evidence do you have that warrants this assumption?"

"Am I wrong?"

Haruka pulls his glass to his lips, shifting his eyes sideways. "No..."

Nino laughs, the sound warm and bright and accentuating the energy rolling off of his delicately sculpted body. There is an undeniable wholesomeness—perhaps goodness—in his vampiric aura as he comfortably lets it rest outward. He is like a creature derived from the sun.

Haruka drains his glass. He can't remember the last time he had a conversation with another high-level vampire that wasn't centered around his physical appearance or bonding. It is a pleasant surprise, but he needs to cut to the chase. "Nino, have you been receiving the invitations to the confirmation ceremony next month?"

Standing up from the bar, the amber vampire straightens his spine. His posture stiff. "I knew I was in some kind of trouble."

"It is not trouble," Haruka assures him. "However, your presence has been formally requested, so it is proper for you to respond and attend. The requesting family wants us to officiate the ceremony... the admittedly archaic and invasive ceremony. Nonetheless, will you attend?"

Nino visibly exhales while shifting his eyes away. "Listen... to be honest with you, I don't know anything about officiating a bonding ceremony. I would rather not be part of it, if possible."

"How can you not know anything about it? You are a one-hundred-and-twelve-year-old purebred vampire—"

"I know how old I am, and what I am," Nino says, watching Haruka. "But I'm not—It's not something I want to do."

Haruka pauses, dumbfounded. They are *purebreds*. Part of their station in life is doing things they don't want to do. It is simply how their culture works—especially at the behest of lower-ranked vampires. The strong help the weak, the haves support the have nots.

Unless you run away. No one can ask you to do something if you aren't there to do it. Haruka has discovered a loophole. However, in light of his manservant's apparent defiance, Haruka can no longer use his loophole. He needs Nino to participate. Simply "not wanting to" isn't an acceptable excuse.

Keeping his voice calm, he appeals to the vampire behind the counter. "If times were different and there were more pure-breds within this country, perhaps you could dismiss your responsibility. There are only three of us in the UK, and the purebred in Edinburgh has other obligations. If you feel inse-cure about your knowledge..." Haruka hesitates, wondering if he is truly so desperate to have another purebred in attendance that he would open his home to a complete stranger.

Yes. Yes, he is.

"I have a library at my estate in Devonshire, off the coast in Sidmouth," Haruka explains. "In my collection, there is a book that specifically details the process of bonding. If you wish, you can spend a few days researching with me as I prepare for the ceremony, then we can travel there together?"

Nino pauses a beat, giving Haruka a false sense of hope before he ultimately shakes his head. "I'm sorry, Haruka. It's... I can't. But I appreciate the kind offer. I'm really sorry."

Indignant, Haruka stands from the bar and pulls his wallet from his coat pocket. He takes a breath to squash his incredulity. This is the modern age—the twenty-first century. If this purebred desires to live his life as an outcast of the aristocracy, who is Haruka to persuade him otherwise? To each their own.

Haruka will handle the ceremony alone, somehow. He manages every disappointing thing life throws at him.

He removes a twenty-pound note from his wallet and places it on the counter. "Understood. I won't trouble you any further—" Nino reaches out, his hand firmly resting over Haruka's fingers. The physical contact abruptly shifts Haruka's knotted aura again and he inhales sharply. Startled, he snatches his hand away from Nino's grasp.

Nino is completely still. His shoulders drop when he exhales a breath. He closes his eyes as he runs his fingers into the top of his thick hair. "You—you don't need to pay... The wine is on me."

Haruka takes a step back, smoothly sliding his hands and wallet into his coat pockets. He straightens his spine. "I insist. Good luck with your future business endeavors."

FOUR

Later the same night, Nino closes down the bar, counts the register, does some light cleaning with his employees and stops by the bank before returning to his flat in Tufnell Park. When he finally sits down on his bed, he *still* has weird chills running through his body. He's never been electrocuted or struck by lightning (thankfully), but he imagines the aftershocks feel something like this. Odd jolts and jitters racing up his spine.

He stares absently out the window across from him. Glittery snowflakes dance against the deep blue backdrop of the night sky—or is it morning? The pointed rooftops of St. George's Church across the street are lightly dusted with winter white. He picks up his smartphone beside him and presses it on. 4:25 a.m. He checks his messages to see if there's a response from his best friend. Nothing. She's definitely asleep by now.

It is late (or early) but he needs to talk with someone. His brother will be irritated by his calling, but Giovanni is almost always irritated with him anyway. Nino hits his number and brings the phone to his ear, waiting.

"What's wrong?" His brother's husky voice immediately fills the line.

"Nothing is wrong, per se—"

"Then why the hell are you calling me at three-fucking-thirty in the morning?"

Nino leans down, resting his elbows against his thighs and running his hand into his hair, stressed. "Aren't you flying to Russia today?"

"Yes."

"*Right.* I wanted to ask you something before you're on a plane for six hours and then in business meetings all weekend." Nino vigorously massages his hand against his scalp, creating a frenzied mess of his coppery hair. The line is suddenly silent. He abruptly sits up straight like an anxious meercat. "G?"

"I'm waiting for you to tell me what you want," Giovanni says. "You only call me when something is wrong, so what is it?"

Nino takes a deep breath. Whenever he speaks with his older brother, he feels like one of those people on a spinning wheel at an old-timey circus. The ones that got knives thrown at them. "I didn't tell you about this, but I've been getting these weird invitations from one of the vampires of the aristocracy here."

"What kind of weird invitations?"

"They say something about confirming a bonding ceremony—"

"Shit," Giovanni breathes. "They still do those in England? Fucking weird. We haven't done one of those in Milan since the early 1800s. Gross."

"Is this thing what I think it is?" Nino asks. "I tried to Google it but nothing specific to 'bonding confirmation' came up."

"Kiddo, you're not going to find deep-rooted aristocracy

vampire shit on the Internet. Look up 'bedding ceremony.' It's fairly close, objective wise."

Nino hunches his body down again, stifling a groan. He already looked that up.

"Did you accept the invitation?" Giovanni asks.

Here come the knives. Nino takes a deep breath. "No."

"*Why?*"

"G... I don't want to—"

"You told me you were going to England to be more independent and learn. You told me you weren't just following behind Cellina—that you wanted to change. If you're going to keep avoiding everyone like a child and only thinking about yourself, you might as well come back home and do that shit. We can find you a new source."

Nino falls back against the bed, his phone still pressed to his ear as he throws his arm over his eyes. He doesn't want to run away or be selfish, but he also doesn't want to be in an ancient castle in the middle of nowhere, full of strange vampires he's never met.

And he *definitely* doesn't want to watch them have sex.

"British purebreds became extinct sometime after the Vanishing," Giovanni says, shuffling against the phone. "Is it only you they're asking?"

"No..." Nino sighs. He hates it when people casually reference the Great Vanishing—when several purebreds across the world literally vanished into thin air one hundred and fifty years ago. He hadn't been alive at the time, but even reading stories about it deeply disturbs him. Until this day, there is no explanation as to why or how it happened.

Nino rolls his shoulders. "There's another purebred in England. I heard there was one in Scotland too, but she can't go. The one in England came to talk to me today, at the bar."

"Oh yeah?" Giovanni asks. "Bonded?"

"No," Nino says.

"Male or female?"

"Male."

"Were you scared?"

Nino flops his arm down against the bed and stares up at the ceiling, thinking about his encounter with Haruka. He'd sat at his bar—dark, utterly calm and never taking his eyes off Nino. He reminded Nino of a black panther, or something else very elegant and mysterious. Restrained. His eyes were a deep shade of brown, not vivid and bright like most purebreds' irises. Regardless of color, the eyes are always a telling sign of a vampire's strength and bloodline quality.

When their gaze had met, Nino's nature had helplessly burned brighter, almost reaching out toward him. Just thinking about it makes Nino shiver again.

"No," Nino says. "I was nervous and I thought he might be angry with me... but he was actually nice."

Giovanni continues in his grilling. "Old or young?"

"Young. We're only eleven years apart, and he's a Historian. He even offered to let me research the ceremony in his home library."

Although Nino is slightly older, something about Haruka feels very different. Wiser? More experienced? Their interaction was short, but Nino keeps quietly revisiting the idea of Haruka's offer. While the ceremony itself is wholly off-putting, learning more about Haruka and spending some time with another purebred so close to his age... That might be nice.

"Old blood or new blood?" Giovanni asks.

"His bloodline feels old... very clean. Definitely older than ours. He's that *regal* type. The only weird thing is he keeps his aura enclosed inside his body, and the color of his skin is odd— like, faded. Something feels off about him. I don't know exactly what it is, but I'm not afraid."

Vampires with very old blood like Haruka have successfully kept their lineage free of human DNA for centuries. Their ancestry is unmarred because their descendants learned early on to feed exclusively from other purebreds and high-ranked vampires as opposed to humans. Some clans were slower to catch on. When they did, it was as if their bloodline restarted completely—sharper senses, enhanced physical prowess and an improved quality of life. Like hitting a reset button for the subsequent generation.

It's clear that Haruka's bloodline hasn't been reset for a very long time.

"Take him up on his offer," Giovanni asserts. "Go to him. Do the ceremony."

Nino breathes a laugh, shaking his head. "Just like that?"

"Just like that. You sound like you instinctively trust him, so go learn from him. Try not to get yourself ostracized in this new aristocracy. You need this."

"Alright, G." Nino smiles weakly, scratching his head. "Sorry for waking you up."

"No you're not."

"Love you."

"Love you, too."

He hangs up the phone and moves across his bedroom to his desk. He opens a drawer, then pulls out an elegant silver invitation, flipping it over in his hands. The return address is for an Emory Alain, Duke of Devonshire. He needs to return the RSVP, and then figure out how to let Haruka know that he's changed his mind. He is accepting his offer.

EARLY DECEMBER

FIVE

Haruka sits at his desk in his library, nervously drumming his fingers against the dark, polished wood and sincerely questioning his decision to allow an unknown purebred into his nest.

It has been four weeks since his initial encounter with Nino. In that time, he has conducted some research on the Bianchi Clan of Milan through primary and secondary sources. Haruka's father had traveled abroad in his youth with the sole intent of researching their vampiric culture and the shared practices spanning indigenous civilizations. He recorded his own first-hand accounts, as well as bartering for original historic chronicles and journals.

One such acquisition contains many documents focusing on western Europe, including a short registry of prominent vampire families in Italy. Using this and a common search of the Internet, Haruka has acquired many details regarding the Bianchi Clan.

The mother of the family is deceased, which Nino had previously disclosed. The father, Domenico, has surprisingly survived his mate's passing, but is very ill as a result. The death of a mate in a bonded couple almost always leads to the demise of both vampires, which had been the case with Haruka's parents.

The Internet search on the eldest Bianchi son, Giovanni, resulted in much modern news coverage under both vampiric- and human-owned outlets: personal interviews, acquisition announcements, business analyses and even some innocuous tabloid articles. Giovanni is largely regarded as an impressive businessman. He is a well-known analyst and strategist, with reputable clients spanning multiple industries across the European continent.

As much information as there is on Giovanni and his achievements, there is as little on Nino. Haruka found practically nothing, as if the younger son has been hidden away from the bright spotlight of his family's prestige. It strikes Haruka as odd, and as the hour of Nino's arrival approaches, he wonders if he's made a mistake in extending this private invitation.

During his investigation, Haruka briefly considered searching for himself online, or at least his name in juxtaposition with "Yuna Sasaki." Ultimately, he decided against it.

The advent and popularity of the Internet over the past couple decades have been positive from an information accessibility standpoint, but increasingly negative in terms of validity and the loss of privacy. Nino had said that Haruka is "famous" among vampires in the UK. Whether that statement is hyperbole or if details of his life have been exposed in some undesired fashion, he can't discern.

He sits back against the cool leather of his chair, folding his arms. "Where ignorance is bliss, 'tis folly to be wise. Asao?"

A minute later, his manservant pokes his head in the door frame. "I'm not bringing you any wine right now, Haruka. You can have some tonight—"

"Did I ask you for wine?" Haruka snaps, frowning. "What time did Nino say he'd arrive?"

Asao leans with his shoulder against the doorframe. "He said he's leaving his bar early, so around eight tonight. The guest bedroom is already made up. I'll have dinner ready by the time he gets here."

Asao shifts his eyes down to the floor surrounding Haruka's desk, his expression suddenly that of someone facing a complex riddle. "Why do you need twenty different books and ten stacks of papers to accomplish *anything?*"

Haruka smirks. "There is a discreet system in place."

"It's a mess." Asao shakes his head in awe. "You're just like your father."

Taking that as a compliment, Haruka sits back in his chair. "Have I made an error in judgment? Was I somewhat hasty in extending this offer to Nino?"

Asao folds his arms. "I'll admit I'm pretty damn surprised by it, but I think it's okay. He seems harmless. And let's be honest, you have an affinity for these bronzed European males. Like that big one in Greece—"

"I do *not*." Haruka's eyes widen in disbelief. "Never mind. Just go away."

Asao breathes a laugh through his nose. "Alright, your grace. By the way, you got another letter in the mail today. From Japan. This is the tenth one she's sent this year."

Haruka swallows hard, his throat tight. The simple mention of her still makes his body tense. He looks back down at his journal to resume his work. "Send it back, please."

Asao nods. "My pleasure." He turns and disappears from the doorframe.

A MINUTE BEFORE EIGHT O'CLOCK, the doorbell to Haruka's estate rings. He is waiting in the kitchen, knowing that Asao will first show his guest to his room on the second floor, then allow Nino to settle his things before coming downstairs for dinner.

Even now, Haruka is anxious—his knee nervously bouncing underneath the table. What had gotten into him? For the past ten years, his primary objective has been to avoid other people at all costs, *not* invite them into his home. He can already smell Nino's woodsy, cinnamon-laced essence gently floating throughout his nest like an alluring spell. Haruka's own nature shifts in response, but he's prepared for it now, so he easily stifles the sensation.

Ten minutes later, Asao precedes their handsome guest into the kitchen. Nino looks around, taking in the space. Asao has made sukiyaki for dinner—the air is warm and accentuated with the scent of simmered beef, vegetables and sweetened soy sauce. Haruka watches Nino from the wooden breakfast nook tucked into a corner along an exposed brick wall. Industrial-style pendant lights hang down from the low ceiling, giving the space a modern yet homey feel.

Haruka stands from the table, taking a deep breath to prepare for whatever he's gotten himself into. "Hello, Nino. Welcome to my home."

Nino responds with a slight bow. "Thank you... I appreciate you letting me do this. Your house is beautiful. Picturesque."

"You're very kind." Haruka gestures toward the bench. "Please sit. I hope you like Japanese food?"

"Is this sukiyaki?" Nino blinks in awe. "Holy—I haven't had this in forever. It looks incredible."

"Everything is ready." Asao turns toward the door, grinning. "I hope you enjoy. Call me if you need anything."

"Thank you," Nino calls, his gaze settled on Asao's back as he leaves. When the manservant is gone, Nino turns to face Haruka. "Asao is third-generation, isn't he?"

"He is," Haruka confirms, grabbing an empty bowl for the soup.

"It's unusual for a ranked vampire to be a servant. How did that come about, if I may ask?"

Lifting slightly from his seat, Haruka grasps the ladle from the large pot. He generously fills the bowl and hands it to Nino, then fills a second bowl for his own helping. "Asao was my father's best friend as a child. I do not know the story in its entirety, but he willingly pledged his loyalty to the Hirano Clan. When my parents passed, he was named as my guardian."

"How old were you when they died?"

"Twelve."

"Jesus." Nino pauses. "You were young. I'm sorry for your loss."

"Thank you, Nino." Haruka sits, brings a spoonful toward his mouth and blows before carefully tasting the warm broth.

Already, Nino has surprised him. Haruka hadn't realized it until this moment, but he'd been waiting for the shallow, elaborate compliments on his appearance. For the awe over the stifled power of his nature or worse, for the blatant sexual advances.

They simply eat in comfortable silence. When Nino speaks again, his question is once more unexpected. "I meet a lot of funny humans while I'm working in my bar," he says, a certain fondness in his expression. "Do you have human friends? Or do you interact with them at all?"

"I personally do not," Haruka says. He places his chopsticks and soup spoon beside his empty bowl. "While I feel strongly that we should protect and maintain our unique culture, I also feel that some integration with humans is healthy and necessary."

"I think so too," Nino says. "I think positive relations should be encouraged among all beings, regardless of their inherent nature. My older brother, Giovanni, focuses on that in business. He wants to get more vampire and human companies working hand in hand instead of exclusively for their respective audiences."

"You achieve this on a local level at your bar, yes?"

Nino takes a quick sip of his wine. "I guess you're right. I have both human and vampire patrons. My vampire customers are inherently drawn to me, you know? On a fundamental level. They're always pretty low-ranking, so they don't ever cause me any trouble. The humans are the ones I worry about."

"In what way?" Haruka asks, bringing his own glass to his lips. He has a fairly strong impression of humans from literature and news, but the quiet truth is that he's almost never had any personal interaction with them. The existence of his race has long been exposed to humans. There are exceptions, but most higher-level vampires remain secluded.

Life for vampires in the contemporary era presents itself as a wide spectrum, where the old world of aristocratic vampire ways comfortably co-exists beside human society.

Nino sits back, making himself comfortable. "Well... they almost always drink too much, then one of three things happens—they get angry, they get sloppy or they become overconfident. Sometimes all three, but those are the worst cases and fairly rare. Angry and sloppy I can deal with easily. Overconfident is probably the most... exasperating? They're not doing anything wrong per se, so I just have to tolerate their advances. And it almost always starts with the 'If you were human' game."

Haruka tilts his head to the side, a frown creasing his brow.

He is wildly intrigued by this insight. To him, Nino is like an anthropologist who has deeply researched and exposed himself to a precarious species—a species that has shown much fear and discrimination toward vampires in the past. "What does this game entail?" Haruka asks.

"It starts with 'How old are you?' Usually out of the blue, with no context whatsoever. They've probably been sitting there watching me and thinking about it all night. So I tell them, then I get a long stare. Eventually I hear, 'If you were human, you'd be...' Insert random age. It's like they need to establish some frame of reference so that I fit into the mold of their understanding of life. They can't just accept that I'm a hundred and twelve. Then, depending on the person, I start getting random cultural questions—'Did you know Mussolini?' or 'What about Pompeii?' And I'm like, what *about* Pompeii? Did you not hear me say I'm only a hundred and twelve?"

Haruka frowns in disbelief. "So what human age do they typically assign you?"

"Usually something between thirty and thirty-five? Believe it or not, thirty-two is what I get most often. If I opened a bar for every time a human gave me that number, I'd be franchised all across Europe."

Haruka shakes his head in amazement. "Such an arbitrary and pointless exercise... Pompeii." *Are they drunk when asking these ridiculous questions?*

"I know." Nino shrugs. "But they enjoy that kind of stuff. These playful little games. And they tell me as if it's something clever—like I don't have a human do that to me multiple times each week."

"It sounds exhausting." Haruka tilts his head back, finishing his drink.

"There are worse things." Nino smiles, mischievousness

sprinkling his expression. "So… if I'm thirty-two, I guess that means you look twenty-nine?"

Haruka's jaw drops in naked shock. "I *do not* present as some weak, twenty-something infantile *human*." When Haruka was still under a century, that had been frustrating enough. Vampires over a century have the irritating habit of treating younger vampires as if they're children—as if they understand nothing about life and the complexities therein.

"It's just hypothetical, for fun." Nino grins. "So how old do you think you look?"

Flickering his eyes to the side, Haruka briefly considers. "One hundred and one."

Nino holds his palms up, apprehension set in his amber eyes. "Okay, I'm sorry. I didn't mean any offense—"

"You have cast great insult unto the House of Hirano."

Nino freezes, blinking. Serious. "I'm so sorry, I—"

Haruka smirks as he reaches to pour himself another glass of wine. Registering the jest, Nino sits back and runs his fingers through his hair. He closes his eyes in a broad smile. "Jesus."

"You will be flogged forthwith and sent to the dungeons."

The golden purebred laughs openly, the warmth of it filling the dimly lit kitchen.

SIX

The following morning, sunlight pours in through the guest bedroom window like soft lamplight—yellow and with a distinctly hazy quality. Nino lies perfectly still in bed, blinking with his back against the fluffy down bedding. He calmly assesses his surroundings in the tidy room.

He is in another purebred vampire's house.

For the next three days, he'll be researching the process of bonding.

Then, he'll travel to East Sussex to oversee an archaic ritual at Hertsmonceux Castle.

"What the living hell am I doing? Whose life is this?"

Nino takes a deep breath, inhaling the rosy, subtle scent of his new purebred acquaintance. Haruka's essence saturates every space of his home, which is comfortably nestled between a thick forest at the front of the estate and a wide, open moor at the back. The exterior is comprised of gray stone and white trimmings. It looks like something from a wholesome Christmas fable. Except the halls aren't decked and there's no mistletoe.

He doesn't know how all of this will work out, but he's here.

No turning back. His brother was right. Nino left home with the intention to grow and become more independent, and a perfect (albeit weird) opportunity is staring him in the face. He needs to make the most of it. He will.

Nino gets out of bed, dresses casually in jeans and a warm sweater then heads downstairs. He needs coffee. After being blessed by Asao with a cup, he carries it back upstairs to find Haruka already in the library.

Asao had given Nino a brief tour when he'd arrived the previous night, but seeing the impressive space in the daylight is vastly different. The rest of Haruka's house is cozy and fairly modest, but the library is much more extravagant.

It's filled with natural light and the walls are lined with dark-oak bookshelves crammed with literature. One area features a cushioned bay window that overlooks the open expanse of the moor. The ceiling is high with warm, modern light fixtures and there's a black, spiraled iron staircase leading up to a second floor full of books.

Once upstairs, a path lined with the same decorative iron railing wraps around the perimeter of the hollow room. For a touch of character, white candlesticks are mounted in antique-looking sconces strategically placed along the bookshelves.

Haruka is sitting at a handsome cherrywood desk. A wall of colorful, weathered book spines is perfectly arranged behind him. His cable-knit sweater is deep burgundy. When he looks up at Nino, the color reveals subtle flecks of red in his rich brown irises.

"Good morning," Haruka says.

"Hi." Nino moves toward him, feeling tense. Their conversation during dinner the previous night was surprisingly easy. They talked about everything from current events in the news to their favorite musicians. Haruka had gone on at some length about classic jazz, particularly John Coltrane and Red Garland.

The reality of being in a stranger's house still creates a jumbled mess of nerves in Nino's stomach—like he's stumbling along blindly in unknown territory or a dark room. At any moment he could easily fall flat on his face.

"Did you sleep well?" Haruka asks.

"I did, thank you. The bed was soft and the room is nice. Everything in your home is so clean and organized."

"That I cannot take credit for." Haruka smiles, a certain warmth in his expression. "Asao is the instigator of any tidiness you observe. Left to my own devices, perhaps things would be more... spontaneous."

Nino laughs, scratching the back of his head. "Is 'spontaneous' a euphemism for being messy?"

Haruka grins as he stands from his desk. "To each his own. Do you desire breakfast?"

"No, coffee is good. I'm fine."

The stately vampire moves toward a small, beautifully crafted live-edge coffee table near a sofa in the middle of the library. There is a thick manuscript bound in tawny leather on the table's surface.

"If you need something, please do not hesitate to let me or Asao know," Haruka says, standing beside the table. "I am grateful that you have decided to join me in this antiquated endeavor. So I truly wish for you to feel at ease while staying here."

"You don't need to say thank you... I should be apologizing to you. It's something I should help with anyway. I'm sorry I initially refused. That was selfish of me."

"Tabula rasa." Haruka bends to pick up the oversized manuscript. "The slate is clean. This reference guide will help prepare you for the ceremony."

After quickly placing his coffee cup on the table, Nino takes the reference from Haruka's grasp. It's heavy and stuffed to the brim with yellowed pages. Nino moves around the low table to plop himself down on the soft couch. Once settled, he runs his fingers across the embossed leather. The material is cool and smooth underneath his fingertips.

Lore and Lust

Hirano Hatakemori | Hirano Hayato | Hirano Haruka

Evidence and analysis of vampiric bonding.
Cases collected starting Kennin 1201, March 22 to Shōwa 1973, December 23.

"Lore and Lust?" Nino reads. He looks up at Haruka from the couch. The purebred is seated back at his desk. "A little tongue in cheek for an ancient vampiric reference book, no?"

Haruka shuffles papers atop his desk. "Not so ancient. I finished compiling it in the 1980s. And the title is my father's doing. He was... indisputably coquettish."

"Wait—*you* wrote this?"

"With research primarily compiled by my grandfather and father, yes. I simply summarized, typed and organized the material."

"Incredible." Nino blinks. "So... it sounds like your dad was fairly good humored and playful. Like father like son?"

"Not particularly," says Haruka, keeping his eyes on his papers as he begins writing.

"Don't let him fool you."

Nino whips his head toward the doorway. Asao is standing here. He walks into the library carrying a bamboo tray with a black lacquer tea set on top. He moves closer and Nino can see that the inside of each cup is coated in bright gold. Intricate pink cherry blossoms are painted on the outsides.

"Haruka definitely has his mother's calmer, more patient demeanor," Asao goes on, setting the tray down on the small table directly in front of Nino. "But his eyes and that sultry, 'come-hither' nature of his are all Hayato, if he'd ever let it out—"

"Asao—*urusai*. Damatte kudasai. Sonna no iranai." Haruka's frown is focused on his manservant as he switches to his native tongue. But his gaze isn't angry, more like pleading.

Please stop talking. Nobody needs that. Nino's smile broadens as he translates Haruka's admonition in his mind. He's wildly intrigued by this sudden, candid turn in their conversation.

"So Haruka's aura is like his father's?" Nino asks, keeping in English. "My mother's vampiric essence was dominant in my parents' coupling, although my brother and I physically favor our father."

"Right." Asao nods. "Your mother was Japanese. Do you speak and read it fluently?"

"I can speak it fluently, but reading is hard." Nino sighs. He probably should have practiced more growing up. He probably should have done a lot of things in his life.

Asao raises his eyebrow, coyly looking toward the desk. He switches to Japanese. "Maybe Haruka could give you some tips while you're with us? Have some tutoring sessions?"

Haruka instantly lifts his head, frowning yet again at his manservant but speaking in English this time. "He is not here to take Japanese lessons from me. He needs to review the reference—and I have to finish this arduous contract to finalize the confirmation. If we need something, *I'll call you.*"

Nino bites his lip to hide his smile. Clearly, this is Haruka's euphemism for "get the hell out." Asao winks at Nino in a knowing way as he turns and moves toward the door.

"I hear you, your grace," Asao says, openly grinning. "Nino, would you like me to bring a pot of coffee in lieu of tea?"

"No, this is perfect. Thank you very much."

"Of course. Such a polite young purebred you are... Maybe *you* should be the one giving lessons."

Haruka's nose is upturned as he watches the older vampire leave the room. Once he disappears through the doorframe, Haruka drops his expression, studiously focusing on the papers in front of him as if nothing happened. Nino stifles a laugh. *What an interesting male...*

Opening the leather manuscript cover, Nino skims over the table of contents and other technical notes. He starts reading the first major section.

Article I. Blood

The foundation of all vampiric bonds is consensual, mutual blood exchange through feeding. Both beings must feed intimately from each other, i.e., direct consumption of blood from flesh. Location of consumption is inconsequential. Blood cannot be consumed indirectly or without consent, e.g. violence, force, medical extraction, etc.

Cases of empirical data collected: 11,203
Compilation summary: Shōwa 1973, December 23

Section 1. Ashikaga Tomoyoshi, Matsunaga Chiyo | Pure-bred | Nagoya, Japan: Successful bond activation after two months of mutual, consensual feeding as confirmed by Hirano Hatakemori, Chosokabe Morihiro, et. al. Genkyū 1205, February 27.

Nino curiously reads through each account. It's interesting, but many of the entries are similar. His eyes start glazing over from reading so many archaic Japanese names. He shakes his head to rouse himself.

The library is silent. Bright sunlight warms the space, quietly marking the subtle shift from morning to afternoon. With his hot cup of tea in hand, Nino feels surprisingly peaceful, occasionally stealing a quick glance across the room at Haruka. The dark purebred is focused on writing the confirmation contract at his desk. Aside from the occasional shuffle of papers, he doesn't make a sound.

> Section 5,495. Tanaka Miya, Aisha Patel | First-Generation, Purebred | Tokyo, Japan | Successful bond activation after six months of mutual, consensual feeding as confirmed by Devya Khatri, Nakagawa Rei, et. al. Taishō 1912, October 1.

"Hm." Nino tilts his head, hesitantly breaking the long-established silence of the room. "Based on this reference book, you get a firm sense of when Japan started integrating with vampires from other countries. That's pretty neat."

"All of my grandfather's entries through the year 1523 are from those vampires of Japanese descent," Haruka says, his eyes cast down as he writes. "My father's entries are much more diverse. He also traveled abroad for a short time and collected accounts from various mated couples internationally. He seemed to have a genuine passion for this research."

Despite himself, Nino chuckles. "Or maybe he just liked watching?"

Haruka abruptly stops writing and looks up at him, his brown eyes flat. "May I emphasize that not all accounts in the book are first-hand."

"I'm sorry, I honestly just meant that as a joke—not funny.

Sorry." Nino scratches his head and returns his gaze to the book, flipping further along in the section. *Stupid, Nino. Nice job, you ass.*

"No apology is necessary," Haruka assures him, offering a little smile. "Later, the research becomes undeniably... detailed? Even I questioned my father's motives at times. It is valuable information—though inelegant."

Grateful for the reassurance, a subtle warmth slowly fills Nino's chest. "Do you have first-hand accounts written in here?" he asks.

Haruka sighs and sits back in his chair. He stares vacantly across the room. "Only one. Afterward, I discontinued the practice of formal confirmations under my realm. I firmly believe that vampires should bond privately and at their own discretion. *Not* in a fishbowl."

"Couldn't agree more," Nino says, scanning another entry. "I wonder what that was like back then? Even though our culture is non-discriminate about race and gender, humans during that time definitely were—still are. How did those vampires manage? Especially couplings of the same gender."

Haruka folds his arms, his brow furrowed. "I imagine it was extremely difficult. Our presence as creatures genetically contrasted with humans was a myth until the 1800s—something only expressed among humans as folklore or through the hysterics of an escaped victim. Our *existence* was still hidden at that time, let alone the added, complex layers of race and sexuality."

"Sounds like hell. I'm grateful to be born in this era where we can be free."

"I echo your sentiments," Haruka says. "But many humans still face these challenges in certain geographic areas, although they have made undeniable progress as a race overall."

Nino flips another page, then exhales a frustrated sigh. He can't hold it in any longer. "Haruka... can I ask you a question?"

Haruka pauses, guarded in his expression as he returns Nino's gaze. "Yes?"

"Wouldn't it have been more convenient to arrange this information by chronological order, and then by each couple's bloodline rank?"

Haruka blinks. "What?"

Standing, Nino walks to meet him at his desk, book in hand. He lowers the manuscript to Haruka's field of vision. "If I wanted to know data for all purebred couples—meaning a purebred mating with a purebred, versus a first-gen coupling or a third-gen coupling—it'd be impossible to tell with the way you have this set up. How can I know for certain if the success rate among first-gen couples is any better than between a first-gen and purebred couple? What if someone asked a question about a particular mated couple in a time span? It'd take forever to find them this way."

In Nino's analytical mind, it makes the most sense: organize the information in one overarching way, then another within it to create even more specific, streamlined results.

Haruka's confused expression slowly morphs into one of indignation. When his dark eyebrow dramatically arches up his forehead, Nino instinctively takes a step back.

"Are you criticizing forty years' worth of detailed work, organization and translation?" Haruka asks, his gaze steady and his deep voice eerily calm.

Nino opens his mouth, then shuts it. He moves toward the couch and tries again. "No, I was just... It was an observation."

"Both my grandfather's and father's research were in Japanese, so I had the added task of translating it into English so that it could be understood by a larger audience if necessary. Ultimately, I decided not to have it reprinted due to the sensitive nature of the information. I apologize that it does not meet your organizational and analytical standards."

Nino runs his palm down his face. *Why am I so stupid?* Hesitant, he looks up from beneath his lashes, wondering if Haruka might show him grace yet again. "Do you want me flogged and thrown in the dungeon?"

Haruka unexpectedly breathes a laugh as he shakes his head. "No. This offense would have you thrown in the stocks."

Nino grins. "With raggedy peasants hurling tomatoes at my head?"

"Potatoes."

"Ouch."

"Your suggestion is valid." Haruka draws his long body up from the desk, stretching his arms. "Albeit dilatory. Shall we break for lunch?"

"Sure. As long as there are no potatoes involved."

SEVEN

Article II. Intimacy

In conjunction with consensual, mutual blood exchange through feeding, an act of sexual intimacy* is necessary to activate a vampiric bond. As noted in Article I, sexual intimacy cannot be violently forced in forming a bond, nor can it be achieved through non-consensual means.

Section note: sexual intimacy is defined as intentional actions resulting in the release and exchange of bodily fluids, or the act of penetration in some unspecified form.

"You were right. This is starting to feel like voyeurism." Nino rolls his shoulders. Day two at Haruka's estate. Nino is sitting on the floor of the library, his legs comfortably folded against the carpet as he reads.

Haruka is standing at a nearby bookshelf, his back facing Nino as he searches for something. "Agreed. But keep in mind these individuals requested to have their bonds confirmed by purebreds. And the information is paramount. Bonding is a cardinal aspect of our culture, but it is typically steeped in ambiguity and conjecture. This book helps to cleanly decipher the process."

"Absolutely, the research is impressive," Nino agrees, but discreetly, he flips through as many pages as possible and toward the next section, only skimming as he turns. A minute later he stops and turns back. He reads through a couple's entry.

"Holy shit—this couple bonded after feeding from each other for only *two weeks*?" Nino blinks up at Haruka, who is casually resting with his back against the bookcase, an open manuscript in his hands.

"Mm," Haruka says. "As you read, you will find that those cases are rare. Bonding in general is a challenging task and choosing a mate is *not* absolute. There can be more than one vampire that is suitable for your individual nature. But there are undoubtedly some vampires whose inherent vitalities might prove more compatible than others."

Nino turns the information over in his mind. "So intrinsically, this two-week couple was uniquely compatible? Their natures immediately clicked, like soulmates?"

Haruka scoffs, the sound abrupt in the quiet calm of the library. "That assessment is highly unlikely."

"You don't believe in soulmates?"

"I believe in making a thoughtful, intentional choice," Haruka says. "Not being forced into something significant as a result of mystical, unseen ideals beyond my control."

"So that's a 'no,' I take it?" Nino wiggles his eyebrows. Haruka smirks as he swaggers toward his desk with his newly acquired book, his posture perfectly straight and tall. When they walk side by side, Nino notices they're the same height—but Haruka's body is leaner, as if he prefers swimming to

Nino's running (Haruka doesn't exercise at all though. He hates it. Especially running. He told Nino that running should be strictly reserved for emergencies.).

Up close, Haruka has a tiny mole just off the bridge of his nose, underneath his eye. It stood out to Nino the first night they had dinner because it's unusual for vampires to have any blemishes on their skin.

They've spent almost two full days together, talking and sharing opinions about every subject under the sun. Considering their objective though, Nino is beginning to feel like they're ignoring the elephant in the room. It isn't his business, but his curiosity is getting the better of him.

"Haruka, why aren't you bonded? You're especially high-bred and knowledgeable. You seem like the type to be properly mated with someone."

"Do I?" he asks, taking his place behind the desk once more. Silence hangs in the air between them.

"Yeah, absolutely," Nino finally says. "And you literally wrote the book on it."

"The irony." Haruka's deep voice is flat. He resumes writing. When he says nothing more, Nino shrugs and looks back down at the manuscript. He knows when to quit—lest he be threatened with imaginary stocks, potatoes and dungeons.

A moment later, Haruka speaks. "Why are you unbonded, Nino?"

He meets his gaze. Nino thinks for a moment, because in truth, he never really has. Not in any sincere depth, anyway. In his mind, bonding feels like something far away... like squinting across the turquoise expanse of the ocean to catch the spout of a whale or the tail of a dolphin. He recognizes it as something incredibly special, but well beyond his scope.

"I'm not ready," he says honestly. Nino doesn't know why he always makes these naked, awkward confessions to this vampire he hardly knows. It's probably a sign that he's lacking in something: friends, proper social skills. A hobby. "And I haven't met anyone that I would want to be with like that, and that would want to be with me."

Haruka is watching him with his deep brown eyes, nodding quietly. Finally having diverted his attention from his books and papers, Nino meets his eyes, playful. "But at least I'll be armed with lots of information when the time comes?"

"Indeed." Haruka mirrors his grin. "Valuable research."

"Lots of sex positions."

"Some may inevitably yield a higher success rate than others," Haruka notes thoughtfully. "I'll leave the analysis and research to you."

"Wow, thanks a lot." Nino chuckles, and Haruka's deep, throaty laugh soon echoes within the space as well.

EIGHT

It's windy on the third day. Nino turns, absently looking out the window above the padded sill. The breeze is so strong that he can hear the whistling howl of it rattle the glass. Gray, hefty clouds stretch endlessly across the sky—a promise that some form of precipitation is coming.

He glances back down at the oversized book resting in the hollow of his folded legs. It's been a lot to take in, but Nino is especially intrigued by this particular section of the book.

Article III. Intrinsic Compatibility

The third and least scientifically discernible component of forming a vampiric bond is the natural compatibility of a couple's conjoined natures. While compatibility cannot be outwardly measured to any quantifiable extent, this section examines the specific number of attempts made before successfully activating a bond. Thus, fewer attempts presupposes that a couple is "highly compatible."

"There's a couple here that bonded after three tries," Nino says, scanning the entries. "That seems pretty good compared with the rest. Looks like the average number of attempts for higher-ranked couples ranges from five to ten?"

"Correct," Haruka confirms from his desk. "Cases lower than five are exceptionally rare. The lowest documented is twice. In section eight thousand twenty-four, a couple in France attempted twenty-seven times over the course of six months."

Nino's mouth gapes open, his eyes wide. "*Twenty-seven?* God, I hope we don't have to watch that many times."

Haruka laughs in his deep, throaty way as he writes, not stopping to look up.

"Well..." Nino continues. "I guess... it's not as if they weren't enjoying themselves?"

"It was quite literally a labor of love."

Nino runs his palm down his face. After three days of reading through the reference book, he understands its fundamental value. To have research that uniquely details, tracks and analyzes bonding is unprecedented within their culture. Pioneering. It's shocking that Haruka has kept something so valuable to himself.

But the manuscript is also pretty invasive. *Our ancestors were perverts.*

"If it takes twenty-seven times to activate a bond," Nino says, flipping through multiple pages to view the final sections of the book, "maybe that's their intrinsic natures telling them *no*, this isn't a good idea?"

Haruka rests his chin in his palm as he leans with his elbow on the desk. "On the contrary, perhaps it shows their genuine conviction to each other?"

"Maybe. I can respect sheer will and determination, but I think things like this should happen naturally, you know?"

"You are a romantic," Haruka declares, standing from his desk and moving toward the door. "Some of these vampires were mating for economic gain and social status. My grandfather and father did not thoroughly document the surrounding circumstances of each couple's mating."

"That's a *huge* gap in the research, Haruka. Who was mating for love and who was mating for business? The rate of activation might be vastly impacted based on the couple's intent."

"Says the obvious romantic," Haruka teases in his roguish way. "Lunch should be ready. Shall we gratuitously indulge in table food?"

"Sure—" Nino pauses when he comes to the final heading in the book. He frowns, reading the oxymoronic title. When he turns the pages within the section, they're completely blank. "Haruka, why do you have a section here called *Broken Bonds*? Bonds between vampires can't be broken once they've been established."

It is fact. Nino might be ignorant about the deeper mechanisms of forming vampiric bonds, but everyone knows they can't be broken.

Haruka shrugs, his eyes emotionless as he returns Nino's gaze. "Or so they say. I believe curry is on today's menu. Chicken katsu, to be precise."

"Chicken katsu curry..." Nino whispers, mesmerized as he stands and follows Haruka out the room.

Walking beside him, Nino realizes that the nervousness he'd felt a few days earlier has dissipated. He's calm—comfortable with Haruka now. But his nature deep within him is still restless and twisty, like a small child throwing a tantrum. It's an odd juxtaposition.

He discreetly glances at Haruka's profile. He doesn't know

why his instincts are reacting this way toward him, but Nino is very glad that he accepted Haruka's generous offer.

"WE'LL LEAVE for Hertsmonceux tomorrow afternoon. Do you feel more prepared after reading through the research?"

"I do," Nino confirms. It's true. He feels intellectually equipped for the confirmation. Emotionally, his anxiety is stirring. An isolated castle full of high-level vampires is *not* his idea of a fun-filled weekend. "You're already finished with the confirmation certificate, right?"

"I am," says Haruka, stretching his arms up and rolling his neck. "The rest of today will be spent reviewing my work and making certain I have the names, titles and rankings of each vampire's lineage correct. It is tedious, but not wholly unpleasant. Scripting the legal verbiage within the document was much more monotonous."

Nino shakes his head in amazement. "I can't even imagine." He's never met anyone like Haruka. Just as he'd suspected, simply being around him has exposed Nino to new ideas and deep cultural insight.

Haruka is smart, but not condescending. Sophisticated but not arrogant. When Nino is confused about something, Haruka approaches him with patience. Kindness. When Nino speaks, he listens. He counters his opinions and challenges him, but with respect (except for those odd times he's being threatened with corporal punishment tactics from the Middle Ages). Haruka has been timidly playful too, and Nino is always surprised by his wry, discreet sense of humor.

Aside from his best friend, Nino hasn't ever met another ranked vampire that he's felt this comfortable with. Going into the confirmation event this weekend, Nino decides he needs an ally. He needs someone who understands him—someone he can open up to about his past should any issues arise. It's only been three days... but he wonders if Haruka could become a genuine friend?

Nino grips the edge of the bench. He cautiously looks up at Haruka, deciding to trust his instincts.

"Can I tell you something personal?" Nino asks. "About me, I mean."

Haruka is leaning against the table with his elbow, his chin resting in his palm and his eyes closed. Finishing the official confirmation document has clearly been challenging. Arduous. Even when Nino has gone to bed at night, Haruka usually remains in the library, busily writing and focused on his notes.

Haruka lazily opens his eyes to look at him. "Sure."

Nino takes a deep breath, his hands trembling. He holds the bench a little tighter. As a general rule, he never talks about this. He doesn't usually need to, because everyone he's grown up with already knows. "When I ignored the invitations to the confirmation, it was because I was scared."

The dark vampire is perfectly still and calm as he watches with heavy lids. "Scared of...?"

"Being around so many ranked vampires in an isolated place. One of the benefits in my moving to England was that there weren't as many high-level vampires here. I... I know that sounds weird because *I'm* a high-level vampire, but—"

Nino takes another breath. He's dawdling. He needs to get to the point. "When I was little, my uncle used to force feed from me."

Haruka doesn't move at all, but something in his expression shifts. It's subtle and Nino can't quite read it, but it's there. "He —he did it pretty often," Nino goes on, keeping his breathing even. "I think I was five? Maybe six. The way he did it, he was manipulating me and telling me it was okay for him to do it. I didn't know any better. But it hurt like *hell*, him biting me like that."

Nino rakes his hand through his hair. Haruka slowly sits up straight to lean back against the bench, as if Nino's movement has given him permission to move as well.

"I know it was more than a hundred years ago..." Nino shakes his head, feeling shamed that he's *still* so deeply impacted by the event. "But... I just want you to know before we go to Sussex that I don't mean to be selfish, or a coward—"

"I would not perceive you in that way," Haruka says, his eyes more alert. Focused. "Nor have I ever. On the contrary, I feel that you are exceptionally brave... and selfless, given your history. To willingly attend this event and accept my invitation knowing nothing substantial about me. I am impressed by your courage."

Nino's chest warms, making him smile. He wishes his brother would see things that way. "When we met, I don't know... I felt like I could trust you."

Haruka lifts his hand to rub the back of his neck, shifting his deep brown irises away. If Nino didn't know any better, he would swear that Haruka was... embarrassed?

"I would never harm or create distress for you," Haruka says, still avoiding Nino's eyes. "And thank you... for—for the honor of confiding in me."

He finally flickers his gaze back at Nino. The hesitation there is so endearing that it only makes Nino's heart warmer. This sudden, candid shift in Haruka's otherwise unruffled, diplomatic mask. Nino playfully bumps his knee against Haruka's underneath the table, making the dark vampire jump about a mile high.

"Thank you for listening." Nino smiles, relaxed. "You don't need to be so formal. It's awkward."

Haruka hunches and rubs both palms against his face. Nino laughs. Until now, Haruka has always been so perfectly poised, courteous and composed.

It's nice... seeing him a little unraveled for once.

NINE

The lake surrounding Hertsmonceux is frozen over, covered with a thin white layer of dusty snow. The slanted rooftops and cylindrical towers reaching up toward the overcast sky also wear a blanket of white. In summer, Haruka imagines the landscape to be beautiful—sweeping green forests, flowers and lively birdsong set against the idyllic brick castle. All of it perfectly reflected within the lake.

But now, the castle feels inhospitable and cold. Watching the imposing structure slowly appear before him makes Haruka wish for nothing more than to turn around and head back to the familiar warmth and comfort of his own home. He sighs. "Grande responsabilité est la suite inséparable d'un grand pouvoir."

"What does that mean?" Asao says from the driver's seat, slowly bringing the car to a stop.

"Where there is great power, there is great responsibility."

Haruka glances out the window at the group of vampires huddled around the grand entrance to the castle.

Asao looks back at him, his brow furrowed. "Why are you quoting Spider-Man in French?"

"Who is 'Spider-*Man*'?" Haruka asks, returning his scowl.

Asao slowly shakes his head as he steps out of the car. "You need to get out more—it's like you do this on purpose. I'm going to find Emory's manservant to ask if they have blood bags for you. Nino is parked behind us."

Asao shuts the door. In the muffled silence of the car, Haruka sinks a little lower into his seat. "Nino..."

The pit of Haruka's stomach had dropped when Nino confided in him about his abuse. The emotional transparency of it caught Haruka off guard.

Verbal consent is vital in order to feed from another adult vampire. One cannot use their incisors to pierce another vampire's skin without first receiving permission.

Vampire children are still emergent in their unique natures until they reach the age of sixteen, which is when their skin fully hardens. Prior to that, their skin is soft and they are not capable of giving formal consent. Any adult committing this forbidden, gruesome act does so forcefully and purely for selfish, perverse gain.

Nino comes across as a charming, kind and optimistic male. Haruka would never have guessed that something so cruel and dark lies hidden within the complex fabric of his being. The thought of a young, bright Nino experiencing such abuse makes Haruka's chest ache.

There is a tap on the glass beside Haruka's head and he jumps, startled. When he looks, Nino is staring back at him with his bright eyes the color of amber stone. He's wearing a stylish olive-green parka well suited for his tall frame—the color perfectly offsetting his creamy, honeyed skin tone. He smiles openly with his natural ease and affection as he pulls the door from the outside, gesturing for Haruka to step out of the car.

"You're not having second thoughts about this, are you?" Nino asks. "Because if you are, I'll drive the getaway car."

EMORY ALAIN II, FIRST-GENERATION DUKE OF DEVONSHIRE,
AND CATHERINE ALAIN, FIRST-GENERATION DUCHESS OF DEVONSHIRE,
FORMALLY WELCOME YOU TO

The Bonding Confirmation of
Oliver James Alain and Gael Silva

Order of activities is as follows

Reception & Cocktails from 6:00 p.m.
Dinner from 7:30 p.m.
Formal Certification Reading from 9:00 p.m.
Commencement of Bonding Rituals from 10:30 p.m.

Please leave all gifts and celebratory offerings with Geoffrey
in the servants' quarters near the east entrance to the gardens.

"THEY LITERALLY HAVE the sex scheduled and written on a piece of paper." Nino points, leaning into Haruka's side as they stand together in the midst of old wealth and opulence.

Haruka's body tenses from his woodsy, cinnamon scent and nearness. "Yes, I see that," he says, distracted.

"I can't imagine how much it cost to rent this entire castle out for the weekend. I looked this place up online and it's not even supposed to be open to the public this time of year."

"Vampire owned," Haruka says simply. Within the modern framework of their ancient culture, exceptions are often made for vampires, by vampires. Several years ago, when he'd been living in Paris, Haruka had attended a centennial celebration at the Louvre for a purebred turning four hundred. The event was private and had begun at midnight.

"Hm, that makes sense," Nino says. "Do you think it'll take you an hour and a half to read through the contract?"

"That is *not* my plan." Haruka straightens his posture, stretching his spine as he takes in his surroundings. Emory, Duke of Devonshire and father of one of the grooms, has truly outdone himself with this venue.

The ballroom they currently occupy is surprisingly cozy despite its grandiose nature. Beaded crystal chandeliers hang from the high ceiling, casting warm light against the milky-white marble of the floors and stone walls. The east wall has two stacked rows of stately, arched windows offering views of the snowy forest. The west wall is dominated by an oversized, burning fireplace.

Including himself and Nino, there are at least twenty high-level vampires in attendance. However, only the two purebreds will have the "honor" of overseeing the private confirmation.

"Is this normal?" Nino asks, his voice low. "For everyone to be subtly watching us like this? I feel like an animal at the zoo."

"The vampires of the British aristocracy do seem a bit fervid in their behavior," Haruka says, bringing his drink to his lips. They're halfway through cocktail hour, having arrived early to settle and change clothes in preparation for the evening. Haruka casually glances at Nino beside him. He looks handsome in a pewter-gray suit well tailored to his frame. His shirt is starched white and his tie black satin. When Nino catches his eyes, he grins. "What is it?"

"How... are you feeling?" Haruka asks quietly. "You expressed much apprehension in coming to this event. Are you uncomfortable?"

"No, I'm okay. I think... us being here together helps."

"I am glad." Haruka sighs, glancing down at Nino's suit once more. "You look very nice."

"Thank you. You do too."

Haruka calmly looks away. Internally, he feels anything but calm. His restrained aura keeps pulsing of its own volition. He shifts his spine again in a discreet stretch. *What the hell is wrong with me?*

A moment later, he turns his head to the side to watch a young first-generation female with brown, shoulder-length hair approach him. She is short—pixie-like in stature. She is Elsie, the Duke of Devonshire's youngest daughter and Haruka's feeding source.

"Good evening, your grace." Elsie bows deep, her hair falling forward as she keeps her hands clasped behind her back. "You look quite handsome tonight."

"Hello, Elsie. You are very kind. May I introduce Nino Bianchi of Milan. He will also oversee the ceremony tonight."

Elsie bows toward Nino, but when she speaks there is no warmth in her expression. "Are you the purebred that adamantly ignored our invitations?"

"That... would be me," Nino says, his smile strained.

"He is here, nonetheless," Haruka points out. "We wish to support Oliver and Gael in their desire to bond their natures."

Elsie lifts her chin. "Tonight marks the third, so we believe it will be a success. While they have not been feeding from each other for as long as you have been consuming *my* blood, the timing should be sufficient."

Haruka maintains a tactful façade, but inside, he is fuming. "Elsie. I would greatly appreciate it if you kept the nature of our arrangement private. It is a very personal matter."

She coldly flickers her eyes up at Nino, then politely grins when they rest on Haruka. "Absolutely. I understand, your grace. But I do wish to tell you that my father has forgotten the bags we prepared. I heard that your manservant has been asking after them? Bloody shame... no pun intended."

Haruka blinks, feeling as if the floor has dropped out from underneath him. "Excuse me?"

Elsie sighs, a nearly convincing look of disappointment painted on her angelic face. "In all the commotion of preparing for this event, I think it simply slipped his mind. But do not fear, my beautiful lord, I am more than happy to intimately provide for you. I look forward to it, in fact. Perhaps I should visit your quarters later this evening? Through my sources, I have acquired a copy of *The Aeneid* in its original Latin form. I thought you might enjoy it. I can deliver this to you as well? Two birds with one stone and all that."

Haruka's mask is cracking. He brings his fingers to the bridge of his nose, shocked at the blatant entrapment. To make matters worse, he's already overdue to feed.

"Um, Elsie?" Nino hesitates. "I think maybe Haruka isn't feeling well."

She raises her eyebrow in suspicion toward Nino, then shifts her gaze toward Haruka and offers a polite nod. "Your grace, let us discuss this later. *Privately.*" She turns, flipping her hair as she walks away. Haruka closes his eyes and massages his forehead. The circumstance is inconceivable to him, like a rope is slowly tightening around his neck.

"Jesus... you're as white as a sheet," Nino says quietly. "Let's take a break, yeah?" He gently places his hand on the small of Haruka's back, then silently guides him out of the crowded ballroom.

TEN

Nino pushes the door to Haruka's bedroom closed once they're both inside. When he turns, the dark vampire drops himself down hard on the side of his bed. He hunches over in his tailored black suit, crisp white shirt and black tie, his fingers plunging into his silky hair. The longer they stood in that ballroom, the more miserable Haruka became.

They've only been at Hertsmonceux for a few hours, but it's already overwhelming. Nino has been asked at least three times why he isn't bonded (which seems like a personal question to ask within the first five minutes of a conversation). At least once, he's pretty sure he was openly propositioned to try changing his unmated status during this weekend.

What Nino experiences is nothing compared to other vampires' reactions to Haruka. He's lost track of how many times someone has called Haruka "exquisite," "beautiful," "gorgeous" or "stunning." What is his age and "my, how young" he looks. His lovely vampiric nature and "why on earth does he keep it enclosed?" It's one thing to be showered with compliments, but Haruka is being drowned.

Nino thought he had it bad in his bar with humans playing guessing games and flirting with him about his age, but that seems like child's play compared to tonight. When they had spent time together in Sidmouth, Nino wondered why Haruka chose to isolate himself in the English countryside. The reason is becoming painfully apparent.

"What's going on?" Nino walks toward him. "I feel like I'm missing something. What bags is she talking about?"

Haruka is quiet, massaging his fingers against his scalp with his head down. Just as Nino is about to tell him never mind and that it's none of his business, Haruka's deep voice cuts through the silence. "Elsie is my source, but I do not feed directly from her. I ask that they medically bag her blood for me."

Nino sits in a tufted armchair close to the bed. "Okay, why do that?"

"Because it keeps me from being strictly beholden to her, and to Emory and his family," Haruka sighs, his gaze cast downward. "If I feed directly from her, it constitutes intimacy—which means I should spend time with her. If I monopolize her time and am intimate with her, then I am expected to eventually form a bond with her. I do not wish to form a bond with anyone, under *any* circumstances."

Nino mentally unpacks everything Haruka has just expressed. He doesn't want to bond. Very strong feelings there. He doesn't want to be obligated toward Elsie, but her father has forgotten the bags of her blood. Now, Haruka needs to feed directly from her, intimately, in order to survive the weekend.

Haruka is distraught. He's old blood—ancient, purebred blood. The restart of Nino's familial bloodline can be traced back to the late 1800s, but he's certain that Haruka's blood origins reach back much farther.

It's evident in the hidden strength of his aura, in the way he smells and how he carries himself. Old blood keeps detailed documentation going back five centuries. Old blood employs outspoken, steadfast third-generation vampires as servants. And old blood requires pure, high-level sustenance in order to function at optimum strength.

But Haruka is drinking the blood of a first-generation vampire who would attempt to corner him into submission. To put his well-being at risk.

Like a sack of potatoes, Haruka falls back hard against the bed. He exhales an exasperated breath. "Everything will be fine. I simply need to be careful to not over-exert myself for the next two days. Then I can return to my home."

"Then what? Will you still keep feeding from Elsie? Even though she doesn't seem trustworthy?"

Haruka's chest quietly heaves up and down underneath his dress shirt, his black tie askew. "I'm not sure—I will figure it out later. It will work out."

How? Nino sits back against the chair, his breathing shallow and his heart rate climbing as he grips the soft, faded upholstery underneath his palms. A thought slowly forms, pressing to the forefront of his mind.

Could I be his source?

Nino has never offered himself to anyone before. Not once (not even to his best friend—and she wouldn't accept anyway). He's never wanted to. The simple thought of it has always sent his mind into a dark place filled with painful memories. Images of his uncle's large hands clasping Nino's small shoulders, his thick fangs biting down hard into the base of his neck and hungrily pulling from him as if to wholly consume his life-force.

Nino shakes his head to rouse himself. He looks at Haruka again. The dark purebred drags his body up to sit on the edge of the bed, then adjusts his jacket and tie. He squares his shoulders. His grayish skin tone makes him look tired. His dark hair is rumpled from the impromptu scalp massage.

Haruka smiles. It's a charming little expression that reaches his deep brown irises. "I sincerely apologize, Nino." He lifts his arms to pat his hair, combing the mess of it through with his fingers. "It is... truly unseemly for me to behave this way in front of someone—"

"You don't always need to be perfectly composed and polite," Nino assures him. "I hope... that after all this is over, you would consider me as a friend? With friends, you can let your guard down."

Unexpectedly, Nino's heart is in his throat. Haruka is blinking at him and Nino doubles back in his mind. Does he sound like an idiot? Like a child? Why does he keep saying these emotive, revealing things to this vampire?

But when Haruka offers a little grin again, Nino breathes a silent sigh of relief.

"I would genuinely like that," Haruka says.

"Good." Nino nervously rubs his hands against his thighs. "So... what can I do to help you? Let's brainstorm."

Haruka shakes his head, still grinning. "You do not need to do anything. Just being here and having the camaraderie of speaking freely with you is more help than I could have ever imagined."

But you need more than that. He can't say it. When he'd first met Haruka, he knew that something was off. After spending time with him and learning the subtle nature of his blood and his enclosed aura, Nino can see it plainly.

Haruka is malnourished. Secretly weak. He isn't in any immediate danger and he isn't starving. But he is constantly in a state of being underfed. His ancient bloodline requires higher-quality sustenance that matches his own. Purebred blood.

Blood exactly like Nino's.

ELEVEN

"I overheard Elsie tell you they didn't bring the bags," Asao says, his voice a furious whisper. "*What the hell?* They've been giving me the runaround about this since we got here."

"Wait," Nino says quietly, confused. He's sitting beside Haruka at a large rectangular dinner table within the busy banquet hall. Asao is crouched down on his haunches and behind their chairs. "How did you hear that?" Nino continues. "You weren't even close by."

Haruka is sipping water. He stops, leaning in toward Nino and keeping his voice low. "Asao has exceptional hearing. It is a skill that is unique within his family bloodline, so he can hear anything within a walled space if he focuses—no matter how large."

Both Haruka and Asao watch Nino as his entire face scrunches. He draws back.

"*What?*"

"*Shh,*" Haruka admonishes him. The last thing they need is to draw even more attention to themselves.

"Why the hell wouldn't they bring the bags?" Asao directs his exasperated whisper toward Haruka. "What are they playing at? This isn't some kind of damn game—"

"Hold on," Nino says. "Are you telling me that for the three days I stayed with you both in Sidmouth, you were always *listening* to us?"

Asao shrugs. "Not always. I have my own life, you know. But yes, I needed to make sure you weren't some kind of crazy pervert vampire, so I listened fairly often."

"*Crazy perv—*"

"*Shh.*" Panicked, Haruka presses his fingertips against Nino's soft lips. But the second Nino's wide amber eyes meet his own, Haruka removes his hand. "I—I sincerely apologize."

"It's okay..." Nino grins timidly. "I didn't mean to raise my voice like that. Sorry."

Silence. It's as if they're temporarily frozen in the awkward moment. Haruka's heart is beating like a drum in his chest. He shifts his gaze down toward Asao, still crouched on the floor in between their chairs. The manservant's eyes are flickering between them.

He smirks. "Cute."

"Asao, can we *please* figure this out later?" Haruka asks, the heat of embarrassment rushing up his neck. "Now is not the time."

"The schedule is packed full," Asao says. "We won't have time tonight."

"Morning is fine. I will survive."

Asao pauses again, this time staring directly at Nino. Thankfully, Nino has shifted his attention away and is taking a bite of something from his plate. Asao looks at Haruka, his face flat and his voice low. "*Ask him—*"

"*No.* Goodnight, Asao." Haruka turns forward in his chair.

"Your grace?"

He blinks, looking up. Elsie's older brother, Oliver, is sitting across the table from him. His intended mate, Gael, is at his side. Oliver favors his younger sister. He has the same slight build, but is taller. His thick, short chestnut-brown hair has an elegant curl to it as it lies swept back for the formal event.

Gael is tall and strong. Burly—like someone whose profession is exclusively lifting very large objects. He has wavy black hair and a square, handsomely stubbled jaw. When Haruka introduced himself earlier, Gael towered over his five-foot-ten frame. When they shook hands, he'd lingered. It was subtle, but just an uncomfortable second too long.

"I am *absolutely* looking forward to your reading of the certification after dinner," Oliver says, his proper English accent bright with excitement. He truly seems pleased about Gael and the prospect of being bonded with him. "It's such an honor to have both our family legacies recognized as we bring our bloodlines together—fingers crossed, anyway! Isn't that right, darling?"

He leans into Gael, prompting him to speak. His heavily accented English booms from his large body. "Yes, we are grateful for you, Senhor Haruka Hirano. Senhor Bianchi."

"Aren't you excited to watch him read?" Oliver asks brightly.

A slow smile spreads across Gael's mouth. "Eu poderia passar horas assistindo esse gostoso fazer qualquer coisa."

Oliver laughs, laying his head on Gael's large shoulder. "Love, you know my Portuguese isn't where it should be. We spent the summer together in Brazil—thank *God* we got out of there before the uprising."

I could spend hours watching this hot guy do anything. Understanding Gael's words, Haruka takes a long pull from his water. He briefly wonders if he should pour it over his face to drown himself (although he has drowned once before by accident—terrible experience).

"The uprisings have been getting worse the past six months," Nino says, stepping in where Haruka has faltered. "This is strictly an aristocracy issue, right? No humans are directly involved."

"Right." Oliver nods, concern resting on his angelic brow. His appearance and demeanor are those of a male who has never wanted for anything in his entire life. No hardships whatsoever. "The aristocracy in Rio de Janeiro is unraveling. I think the steady decline in the purebred population is making everyone behave irrationally. The loss of purebreds means the inevitable end of our race."

"The purebred leader of Rio de Janeiro is pretty famous, isn't he?" Nino comments. "What's his name again?"

"Ladislao Almeida," Haruka says. The Almeida Clan took control over Rio de Janeiro a century ago, traditionally ruling under a strict, classist-driven system. Purebreds mating only with purebreds, first-generations with first-generations and so on. A dogmatic attempt to keep bloodlines from mixing.

Six months ago, the very ancient clan leader overseeing the region died. His eldest son, Ladislao, has since taken control. So far, he's cast their society in the complete opposite direction of his father—and to a fault. Many lesser vampires within his realm oppose his "extremist views."

"My darling used to work closely with the Almeida Clan." Oliver looks up at Gael, his eyes practically twinkling. "Didn't you?"

"Yes," Gael confirms. "But after the death of Senhor Almeida... many things changed. Foi terrível. I do not like Ladislao's way, so I quickly leave there."

"And I fell right into his muscular arms." Oliver swoons.

"Tonight is the third, so I'm absolutely positive we'll be successful."

"Many factors contribute to forming a bond," Haruka rationalizes. Oliver is so excitable, Haruka feels he should temper his expectations. "It typically takes time and much patience, so please be prepared."

"What kinds of factors? How do you know this?" Oliver asks. Gael stares as well, curious. The existence of *Lore and Lust* isn't a secret, but Haruka rarely brings it up in conversation. As if ranked vampires need one more reason to obsess over the topic of bonding.

"My family has privately conducted much research on mating and which factors are necessary to establish a successful bond. It is the legacy of my father and grandfather."

"It's an entire book," Nino chimes in proudly. "The information is incredible."

"A *book* on bonding?" Oliver says, his eyes wide. "Oh my God—"

A light bell rings out. Emory is at the head of the long table, announcing that it's time to start the certificate reading. Somehow, Oliver perks up even more. He reminds Haruka of an untrained puppy.

"It's time!" Oliver squeaks, smiling from ear to ear and turning to Gael. "Are we ready?"

Gael looks directly at Haruka, his gaze suddenly intense. "*Very* ready."

"Por favor, señor," Nino begins, his expression stern. "No coquetee en frente de su prometido. Es *asqueroso*."

Without another word, Nino stands and leaves the table. Haruka briefly glances at a scowling Gael before standing, offering a polite nod and following Nino out of the extravagant dining hall.

When Haruka catches up to him in the hallway, he grins,

pleasantly surprised by Nino's assertive behavior. "I did not know you spoke Spanish? Do you think Gael understood you?"

"I don't know," Nino fumes. "I understand a lot of Portuguese but I can't produce it well, and I didn't want to upset his fiancé by saying it in English. What an *asshole*. Why is he blatantly flirting with you in front of this male that he's about to bond with? We're here for *them*. Because they're supposed to be in love."

They turn down an empty corridor in the castle and Nino stops to breathe, running his hands into the top of his wavy, coppery hair. Haruka leans with his back against the wall beside him. "I mentioned before that bonding is not always about love. A vampire can have a multitude of intentions and hidden agendas when wishing to activate a bond."

"That's disgusting," Nino says.

"You are a romantic—"

"And you're not? You don't believe in bonding for love, Haru? Because you feel innately and naturally drawn to another vampire?"

Nino's intense gaze is expectant, making Haruka pause. He shifts his eyes away. "I—I'm... not sure."

"Is this how things are for you?" Nino asks. "Vampires wagging their fangs at you, creepily staring and making lewd remarks in multiple languages?"

Haruka breathes a laugh. "Yes. But today has been particularly unpleasant... You cannot imagine how much more unbearable it would be if I allowed my aura to rest outward—"

"But that's *their* problem, isn't it?" Nino says, his voice rising and echoing in the chilly hallway. "Not yours. You shouldn't have to physically contort yourself to have some semblance of a normal life and interactions. Everyone should just fucking control themselves."

Nino stops. He presses his back into the wall opposite

Haruka so that they're facing each other in the narrow space. He lowers his head. "I apologize for my language."

"You can swear in my presence."

"But I don't want to." Nino closes his eyes. He leans his head back into the wall. "Everything about you makes me want to be better. Just being around you... I *know* I can do better."

The hallway falls silent, save for the nearby echoes of vampires moving back into the main ballroom for the certification reading. For the briefest moment, Haruka has a strong urge to step into him. He doesn't know what he would do afterward, but something deep inside him is urging him forward—drawing him toward this warm, amber and honey vampire.

He stifles it, then stands from the wall and turns. They need to head to the ballroom. "Please do not try so hard to alter yourself," Haruka says. As he speaks, Nino lifts his head and opens his vivid eyes. "I feel that you are lovely now. Just as you are."

A warm smile brightens Nino's handsome face, like the sun gradually peeking over a cloudy horizon. It makes Haruka's stomach flip, so he shifts his gaze forward.

"Come," he says. "You must listen to me read this tedious document."

Snickering, Nino pushes himself off the wall to move beside him. "I meant to ask you... Elsie and Oliver said something about tonight being 'the third.' What did they mean by that?"

"Remember from the reference book that almost all bonds become activated sometime after three attempts, if all other factors are in line? So tonight will be the third time that Oliver and Gael have engaged in some form of intercourse while also exchanging blood."

"Oh," Nino says. His face sours as if he has swallowed

something distasteful. "I don't know why, but I assumed they were virgins—like we were watching their first time."

"You are disappointed by this?" Haruka grins, raising his eyebrow. "You wish to watch from the beginning? Perhaps they are the type to use recordings—" Haruka's breath catches when Nino playfully bumps into his shoulder as they walk.

His friend smiles. "You think you're funny?"

TWELVE

It's dark. Only the light of the moon pouring in through the large window illuminates the space. It practically glows—soft, blue and ethereal. Nino watches the heavy snowflakes descend from the night sky, but he sucks in a breath from Haruka's warm tongue dragging up the length of his neck.

Nino's chest tightens. The ache in his groin and belly flashes with heat. Haruka slides his long fingers up and into Nino's hair, against his scalp. He bites down into his flesh and Nino moans from the pleasure of his incisors piercing his skin.

Haruka pulls, gently sucking against his neck. Nino can feel the warmth and wetness of his tongue as he feeds. Knowing that he's providing for and nourishing this divine male—this elegant, enigmatic creature—makes Nino's heart swell.

He wraps his arms around Haruka's waist, tightly securing their embrace. Nino never imagined this. That despite the deep pain and fear he's felt in the past, he would enjoy this feeling—giving of himself. Offering himself and being willingly vulnerable to another vampire.

When Haruka finishes feeding, he lifts his face and looks

into Nino's eyes. Nino tilts his head and slowly leans into him. Across his entire existence, he's never wanted to kiss another creature so badly…

Nino inhales sharply, his eyes flashing open and burning brightly from the vivid dream.

He can't catch his breath. Wild confusion grips his mind until he registers his surroundings. He's inside his private guest room at Hertsmonceux, lying on his back against the cool sheets as his heart beats wildly in his chest. His shaft is fully erect. Painfully.

He slows his breathing and carefully shifts onto his stomach. Once there, he relaxes. His face pressed into the pillow, he groans—the loudness of it effectively muffled in the silent room. Turning his head to the side, he closes his eyes and continues breathing in and out. After a moment, his body unwinds.

While he lies there surrounded by cold stone walls, old portraits of strangers and dusty, intricately woven tapestries, his mind drifts back to everything that happened in this singular day. Calling it eventful feels drastically insufficient. Like calling the Taj Mahal a "nice building."

He thinks back to the image of Haruka in his classic black suit, standing with perfect posture at the head of the ballroom as he reads the confirmation contract. The chandelier lights are cast low, creating soft shadows all around. The audience is silent, hanging on to his every deep, eloquent word as if he were singing a soothing lullaby. It was mesmerizing, not boring like Nino had genuinely anticipated.

"Old blood," Nino sighs, shifting his belly against the mattress. Ancient vampire blood does something. It has an impact. The deep, genetic origins of their race call out, demanding reverence and submission. But in Nino's eyes, that cannot be used as an excuse for acting like a mindless pervert.

When Haruka had completed his reading and sat down

beside Nino, the dark vampire had been unexpectedly modest. "Do you think it was sufficient?" Haruka had asked, blinking his chocolate-brown eyes.

Nino had smiled, amazed at his quiet uncertainty. "I think it was perfect."

But then a barrage of syrupy compliments were poured over Haruka. Remembering it now makes Nino's skin crawl.

And there was yet another circumstance that had dramatically turned his stomach earlier tonight.

Gael had watched Haruka. *During* the bonding ritual. While he was supposed to be making love to his intended mate, his focus had been on the dark purebred at Nino's side. The whole thing was as uncomfortable and invasive as Nino had anticipated, but the added element of Gael's misplaced eye contact had made Nino want to scream from outrage. He could barely hold it together by the time they left the failed ceremony. Nino didn't dare ask Haruka if he'd noticed. Of course he had.

The previous three days with Haruka had been insightful, but this fourth day was mind-blowing. And with everything else, for the first time in his life, Nino is sincerely considering offering himself. He's dreamt about it (in color, for God's sake). He stretches his body against the mattress as the heated images flash vividly in his mind yet again.

"Should I do this?"

He closes his eyes, his heart throbbing in his ears. He wants to help his friend, but will he seem like everyone else? If he offers himself, maybe that's how Haruka will view him. Like some desperate horndog eager to please him.

Maybe... I could offer him bags?

Nino flips onto his side and exhales a deep breath. His glowing eyes finally burn out, returning to normal. He stares blankly at the wall in front of him.

It isn't any of his business.

Haruka said he would figure it out once the weekend ended, so Nino should stay out of it. His friend is an extremely capable and intelligent vampire. It isn't Nino's place to stick his nose in.

Just as he's drifting off to sleep, a loud noise startles him. He sits up straight, completely still. He listens again. The moment he decides the sound must have been his imagination, he hears another muffled crash.

The noise is coming from the room next door.

Haruka's room.

THIRTEEN

Haruka stands from the old, weathered desk and switches off the copper base of the oil lamp. The flame quietly extinguishes, casting the bedroom in shadows and moonlight.

He yawns. The third attempt to bond has failed. No dramatic flashes of light. No report of innate heaviness. No shared emotions or perceptions. No bond. He has updated the certificate stating as much, all the while trying to develop a valid excuse as to why he should leave this place tomorrow morning.

He wants to go home. Desperately. He needs a reprieve from the shallow fawning, the flowery honorifics and blatant stares. Something about England suddenly feels much worse than anywhere else he's traveled. Dublin and Quebec had been pleasant. Santorini as well, aside from Haruka's poor judgment regarding a particular male. He'd deemed Paris as the most pompous and challenging aristocracy, but England is quickly proving him wrong.

Perhaps their lack of indigenous purebreds fundamentally impacts their natures? British purebred vampires died out toward the end of the nineteenth century—disappeared from the earth as a result of civil wars, clan disputes and the Great Vanishing. The British aristocracy's hypersensitivity to Haruka's bloodline is exhausting.

He wonders if he should simply return to his own realm. It has been many, many years now, and the emotional wounds inflicted upon him have mostly scabbed over. Maybe it's time?

Just as Haruka rests one knee atop the mattress, there's a sharp knock on his bedroom door. It is late, and having politely circumvented Elsie's advances earlier in the evening, he is not expecting anyone. He focuses his mind, stretching it toward the other side of the door. He inhales to identify the scent. Damp earth and tea tree. Gael.

Haruka's body tenses, his instincts flashing bright lights of warning in his mind. The bonding ceremony had been a disaster—practically a charade. Gael was wholly unfocused on his intended mate, but Oliver seemed none the wiser. It was a perfect case of someone only seeing what they want to see, despite the obvious signs right in front of them.

Silently, Haruka moves toward the door. He'd pulled the small sliding lock after he'd entered, but the wood of the framing is warped and ancient. There is absolutely no reason for Gael to be here at this time of night. Anything he needs can wait until morning.

He stands close to the frame, but jumps when Gael knocks louder—two curt, sharp beats with his large knuckles. Haruka waits, standing still. Barely breathing. Silence. For a long moment, they both stand like this, with Haruka sensing the commanding first-generation presence on the opposite side of the door.

Losing his patience, Haruka turns to walk away.

"Asao—"

There is a loud crash, and Haruka isn't sure what's hit him

first as his body lunges forward—the broken wood of the door or Gael's massive form. Before he can even blink, his body is slammed down hard into the stone floor, an unbearable pressure heavy against his back and restraining his movement. Haruka chokes. Thick fingers are gripping and wrapping tightly against the back of his neck.

Clenching his eyes shut, he tries to push himself up, but Gael is too heavy, too imposing over his leaner frame. Haruka's ear is pressed against the cold stone as Gael grips his neck even tighter, making him lose his breath from the intense burn of it.

"Meu lindo, me mostre o livro," he whispers, his deep voice threatening but teasing. Evocative. His breath is damp and hot against his ear. Haruka thrashes as Gael drags his rough, wet tongue up the side of his face—like an animal tasting its prey. Staking its claim.

Beautiful, show me the book.

Haruka's eyes shift, burning fierce against the darkness as he concentrates. He unravels the heavy knot of his aura in his core, willing it to flourish and come alive.

Defensively pushing his energy outward like this, in a castle full of hungry, shameless vampires, isn't wise. If the scent of his unique nature attracts the others, there is no way Haruka can defend himself from multiple vampires in his current state. He hasn't fed from another purebred in years, and it's been six days since his last bag from Elsie.

But what other choice does he have?

Haruka focuses and manipulates his energy deep within him, allowing it to rush from his core and tightly wrap itself around Gael's body. The enormous male tenses from the subjugation, but digs his fingernails deep into Haruka's neck. Haruka winces, the pain searing hot as Gael scratches his flesh. Haruka pushes his energy even further, strictly holding Gael and shifting him up so that he can move from underneath his weight.

He quickly crawls away from the large vampire's frozen, elevated frame and moves toward the wall. Gael is physically powerful—the mass of him substantial in Haruka's mind. This isn't like quickly shifting his energy outward to stop the young Amelia in Oxford. That had been like holding and restraining a fawn with his psyche. This... this is restraining an angry bull.

Gael's eyes are frantic. Haruka can't subdue him completely and already his throat feels raw, his chest aching from breathing heavily. He's too weak. He reaches up, touching the wetness of blood trailing down into his shirt. His body's healing capabilities are also failing. *What the hell am I going to do?*

And where is Asao? His essence has been exposed for at least a minute now, he needs to do something before—

Haruka's glowing eyes widen. He draws further into the wall as Gael independently moves his fingers, breaking through the defense. Haruka narrows his eyes, trying to wrap his essence even tighter around him. But soon, Gael jerks his neck, eerily craning it toward him.

"*Asao!*" Haruka calls out, louder this time.

There's a sound by the door. Haruka looks up, hoping to see his manservant. But Nino is standing there, a look of unfiltered shock on his face. His expression shifts into something indiscernible as he breathes in Haruka's flooded essence and scent. Nino's irises flash and burn with rich golden light—like honey lit with fire. A new sense of panic fills Haruka's entire being. He can barely subdue Gael, so there is no way in hell he can subjugate a purebred.

Like an ominous flash of lightning in a dark sky, a singular thought cuts through the dense fog of his terrified mind.

I will die here.

FOURTEEN

Nino can't believe his eyes as he stands in the doorway. It's like a scene from an intense action movie.

Gael is frozen and hovering in mid-air at least a foot from the ground. His body is outlined in a bright, extraordinary red haze that seems to be the cause of his levitation and motionless state. Nino looks at Haruka. He's huddled with his back pressed into a far wall, his eyes blazing crimson in the dimly lit room.

Haruka looks outright horrified. Nino takes a step forward and something hits him. Not physically, but emotionally. A strong scent stirs him fundamentally and deep within his core, making his eyes alight from the sheer pleasure of the sensation. It's Haruka. This rosy, cool and earthy scent that's always subtly wafting from his body is exposed in full force. It is truly divine, swirling into Nino's nose, down his throat and through his veins to arouse and warm his entire body.

Gael suddenly drops hard to the floor, free from the magical levitation. His face is twisted in anger. Nino hesitates only for a second—the danger of the moment and innate fear flashing in his mind. But he firmly shakes his head. He takes a deep breath.

Frantically, Nino glances around. When he sees a massive, antique-looking ceramic vase atop a nearby pillar, he makes a quick decision. Just as Gael is shifting to his knees, Nino swiftly grabs the vase, rushes toward Gael and slams it down over the large vampire's head. He thrusts it hard. Full force. Gael flops back down to the floor in a heap. Nino waits for him to move. He doesn't.

Straightening his back, Nino blinks. He's honestly amazed that this worked. He's seen this done in action movies too, but he wasn't sure if it would truly be effective. He looks up and takes a step forward, but when Haruka holds his hand up, Nino halts.

"*Do not—don't come closer.*" Haruka's deep voice is ragged but stern in the frigid silence.

They both remain still, their glowing eyes warily examining each other. Nino's stomach is tense as he gasps. Haruka is bleeding from his neck. He mechanically takes another step forward. "Jesus, you're—"

"I said *stop.*" Haruka's voice rises. He haphazardly scoots along the wall, trying to put more distance between them. He looks ashen and ravaged, his night clothes disheveled and stained with blood.

Nino stands completely still but raises his palms. He keeps his voice low. "Haru... I am *not* going to hurt you."

"Then why are your eyes alighted?"

Nino frowns, thinking quickly. "Because it smells nice in here?"

There's a sound behind him and Nino turns. Asao walks into the room and stops dead at Nino's side, taking in the scene. He exhales a heavy sigh. "Oh hell."

"What took you so long?" Haruka fumes, his voice bitter as

he scowls at his manservant. Asao walks past Nino and leans down to touch the side of Gael's neck.

"How many times did you call me?" Asao asks absently, standing upright.

"*Twice.*"

"I didn't hear you the first time, Haruka. I'm sorry, but I actually sleep sometimes too. Are you okay? What would you like me to do?"

"I—I am fine. Please wake Emory," says Haruka, leaning his head against the wall and closing his eyes. His chest is quietly heaving from stress. "Tell him Gael attacked me, and please request that Elsie come here to provide sustenance for me as soon as possible."

Nino's throat tightens. Oddly, he and Asao exchange a pointed moment of eye contact. Asao looks back at Haruka, his voice serious. "Are you sure this is what you want?"

"Please do as I have asked."

Asao exhales yet another audible sigh, then focuses on Nino again as he turns to leave the room. "Am I okay to leave you with him? You're in your right mind?"

"I'm alright," Nino promises. "It just smells nice... in here."

Asao firmly pats his shoulder before leaving the room. Nino takes a deep breath. The wonderful scent flooding his nostrils is slowly dissipating, as if Haruka is drawing his energy back into himself. Nino focuses his thoughts and rolls his shoulders. It takes a few seconds of jumping and wiggling his body, but soon, his eyes have burned out.

When he's finished and glances down at Haruka on the floor, his friend is looking up at Nino as if he's insane. "No more glowing eyes." Nino smiles, his palms up in submission. "May I sit with you?"

Haruka presses his long fingers into his forehead and closes his eyes. "Yes."

Stepping over Gael's bulky, unmoving body, Nino rests on his knees directly in front of Haruka. "Rough night?"

"To say the least," Haruka grumbles, his eyes still closed with his fingers massaging his forehead.

"You have real power." Nino stares, awestruck at the memory of what he's just seen his friend do. "I've heard of vampires in the past having supernatural abilities, but I've never seen anyone physically manipulate their aura like that. It's incredible."

With his eyes still closed, the corner of Haruka's mouth twists up in a bitter smirk. "Do not be so impressed by my sheer desperation to survive. I am a disgrace to my bloodline."

Old blood. Nino stifles the urge to roll his eyes at the dramatic statement. But he firmly comes to a decision. "Don't feed from Elsie. You don't even want to and you can't trust her."

Haruka opens his eyes. Instead of their usual deep brown, they're milky and washed out. He looks so tired, gray and miserable that Nino's heart breaks.

"I cannot survive like this," Haruka breathes, his voice brittle. "I have no choice."

"Would you... feel comfortable feeding from me?" Nino asks.

Haruka stares with his translucent eyes, unblinking for a long moment before he answers. "What do you want in return?"

Nino shakes his head. "Nothing. I don't want anything from you. Well, maybe I would want you to be healthy and not sitting here looking miserable."

Haruka's gaze is searching. Disbelieving. Like if he looks hard enough, he'll find the answer to his question. "And you *truly* require nothing of me as recompence?"

"Nothing," Nino repeats.

Haruka shifts his eyes away, considering something. It feels like several seconds before he meets Nino's gaze again. "May I have your hand?"

"My hand?" Nino tilts his head.

"Yes... please," Haruka says, his gaunt expression finally softening. Nino holds his open palm in between them and Haruka gently takes hold of his wrist. His fingertips are cool as he pulls Nino's palm toward his mouth. The innocent contact sends warm tingles up Nino's arm.

Haruka hesitates briefly. He keeps his eyes on Nino as he softly licks then bites into the base of his palm near his thumb. He feels Haruka's incisors elongate to pierce his skin. Slowly, Haruka's eyes alight, burning bright crimson as he feeds.

He doesn't feed long. Nor does he pull deeply. When he finishes, he lifts his head from Nino's palm, neatly licking the quickly healing puncture marks before sitting up straight. He intentionally breathes in, then out. Nino can physically feel the subtle shift in Haruka's innate energy, as if something hidden is gradually swelling. Cool and strong.

When Haruka looks at him, the apprehension in his eyes is obvious. "Thank you, Nino," he says, his irises slowly burning out.

"You're welcome. How do you feel? Much less miserable?"

It's quiet—barely perceptible—but Haruka breathes a soft laugh through his nose. "Yes... much less."

LATE THE NEXT MORNING, Nino paces the room with his smartphone, desperately searching for service. The dramatic, old stone castle set in the sweeping English countryside isn't exactly cellular friendly.

When he finds a promising spot in his bedroom beside a

full-sized medieval suit of armor, he quickly hits speed dial for his best friend. After three rings she picks up.

"Ciao ciao," she says warmly, making Nino smile.

"She answers," he teases. "It's a miracle."

"You always call me when I'm in the museum working. Don't be a brat. How's Sussex? I hear it's pretty shitty this time of year?"

"English weather." Nino shrugs, relaxing back against the faded red-gold tapestry hanging from the wall. "Things are okay. The ceremony was as awkward as I thought it would be."

"No kidding. Yuck. Well, actually... I guess it could be hot, depending on the couple?"

"It wasn't. And one of the grooms-to-be attacked Haruka in the middle of the night."

Nino pauses for reaction and Cellina delivers. Her typically sultry voice is practically a shriek.

"*What?* What are you talking about?"

"It's been crazy here, Lina. You know I get the occasional weirdo in my bar, but the stuff Haruka goes through is next level."

"No wonder he hides in his house all the time," Cellina says. "Poor guy."

Nino rubs the back of his neck, a small grin forming on his lips. "I... offered myself to him. Last night."

He pauses again, but instead of the anticipated reaction, the silence goes on a little too long. "Lina?"

"Nino, are you being serious?"

She can't see him, but he nods anyway. The seriousness in her voice serves as a mirror for the reality and weight of his bold decision. "Yeah," he says. "I am. His bloodline is so damn old... He can't really function on first-gen blood like most purebreds can."

"That's amazing," she says, her voice sincere. "Goodness...

I'm just so surprised. I mean, you were practically gushing over him a couple days ago—"

"I was not *gushing*."

"Okay," she says, amusement behind her voice. "But you're obviously comfortable with him and think highly of him. Did he accept? Are you his source now?"

Nino lays his head back against the wall. "We haven't talked through the details yet. He was in a bad situation when I fed him, so I let him get some rest afterward. Hopefully we can talk about it today... I don't want things to be awkward."

"Do you want to be his source?" Cellina asks.

Nino only pauses a beat, registering the question. "I do. He definitely needs a higher-level source than what he's been getting. I told you his skin is a weird color?"

"Yeah, I remember."

"I realized it's probably because he's underfed all the time. I know what severely underfed looks like because of Father, but I've never seen anyone walk around in a mild state like that. Haruka has helped me learn a lot the past few days. If I can, I want to help him too."

"You're so sweet, Nino. You've never been this trusting with another ranked vampire. You really like him, huh?"

"Well..." Nino massages his scalp, the heat of embarrassment flashing in his cheeks. "I've always trusted *you*—and he's my friend. Of course I like him."

"Right," Cellina says. "So he fed from you, but how did it feel? Were you able to relax? Did he pour nice feelings into you?"

"It didn't feel like anything because he fed from my hand."

"Your *hand*?" Cellina says, the frown in her voice obvious. "Did you initiate that? Nino, you know that's not normally how—"

"I *know*, and I didn't. *He* initiated it." Nino exhales a heavy sigh. It's the same way he feeds from Cellina. By hand. His relationship with her is more like a big sister, so feeding from her neck has always been off the table—a mutual decision.

But with Haruka... Nino vaguely worries he's destined to be some kind of perpetual hand feeder. Like a forty-year-old virgin or a grown man still riding a bike with training wheels.

Nino continues to massage his scalp, clearing the pitiful image. "It was a weird moment. And Haru always tries to be polite."

"Interesting. Oh, by the way, I'm going home for two weeks in February because I have interviews. So unless *you* have another source by then, you better buy your plane tickets."

"Text me the dates?" He loves this female. She is truly family. He suddenly wishes they were holed up together in his bedroom and eating junk food, marathoning some human sci-fi TV series like they'd done fairly often during the 1990s.

There's a light knock on the bedroom door and Nino lifts his head from the phone. "Come in."

The door slowly opens. Haruka peeks his head around the corner. When he spots Nino, he smiles sweetly.

Nino's breath catches in his throat. Haruka looks... radiant. His skin is like smooth, satin almond milk contrasted against the very dark luster of his hair. Even his eyes are vibrant now—rich and shining like a vintage red wine. And his scent...

Cellina calls out Nino's name on the phone and he realizes his mouth is hanging open. "Lina, can I call you later? Haru just walked in."

"Sure. Give me an update later. Go have fun with your new friend that you like."

FIFTEEN

On the outside, Haruka smiles as Nino finishes his phone call. Inside, he is trying very hard to ignore the immense amount of disgrace currently weighted on his shoulders.

Gael physically overpowering him and wounding him had been horrible enough, but having Nino there to witness the aftermath only adds another layer of humiliation. He can't imagine how weak and pathetic he looked, so much so that Nino had taken pity on him and offered to feed him.

What's more shameful is how much Haruka enjoyed Nino's blood. He tasted heavenly, as if his blood were an intricate concoction of cinnamon, heat and smoke. Haruka has never tasted anything so singularly satisfying to his nature. Not even Yuna's blood had stirred him this strongly.

Smoothly pouring into his mouth, down his throat and weaving throughout the canals of his body, the sensation was euphoric. Heavenly. In truth, Haruka wants another taste—to indulge in Nino more deeply and with intention.

But it's improper to directly request that another vampire becomes your source. Cultural etiquette aside, Haruka still wouldn't dare. Nino has experienced trauma with feeding, and he would never want his friend to feel obligated or pressured to do something that might cause him distress.

Nino hangs up the phone and beams in his warm, open way. "Good morning."

"Good morning," Haruka says. "A friend of yours?"

Nino wears a look of confusion, then glances to his right at a medieval suit of armor. "This thing?"

"No." Haruka holds back a laugh. "On the phone, Nino."

"Oh." Nino laughs. "Yeah. It was my best friend, Cellina. How are you feeling? Better?"

Haruka hesitates, deciding to be honest with him. "Yes. Much better than I have in a long time, truthfully."

"You look so healthy now." Nino blinks, walking forward to meet him in the center of the room. He stops when there are only a couple feet between them. "You've been underfed all this time, haven't you?"

"Well..." Haruka says, his knotted aura pulsing from the nearness of Nino's body, the intense focus of his gaze. "I was not very uncomfortable. I simply became accustomed to that state of being."

"You shouldn't have to settle for that, Haru..." Nino's haunting eyes are searching. Distraught. Looking into his eyes... Haruka likens it to staring into the depths of the ocean, if the waves and currents were the color of honeycomb. Golden and confounding.

As casually as he can, Haruka turns and moves to sit in an armchair near the edge of the bed to create some distance between them.

"I have some unfortunate news." He switches subjects, because he doesn't know how else to respond. "After Emory's servants collected Gael from my room last night, they locked him in a bedchamber on the southern end of the castle.

However, this morning when they went to check on him, he was gone."

"Oh shit," Nino says.

"Indeed."

Nino pauses, tilting his chin upward ever so slightly and briefly closing his eyes. "I can't even smell him. Can you?"

"I cannot. He must be too far outside the scope of our awareness. Perhaps he is several miles from the castle by now." Thinking about what Gael had said the previous evening, Haruka is stunned. Yes, the research of *Lore and Lust* is valuable, but he never would have anticipated such a maniacal reaction to his family's humble endeavor. He immediately decides he should be more careful in bringing it up going forward—if he does at all. "The root of last night's scuffle appears to be the *Lore and Lust* manuscript. Gael demanded that I show it to him."

Frowning, Nino moves to sit on the edge of his bed, a short distance across from Haruka. "Really? I thought it had something to do with his openly flirting with you."

"His language toward me during dinner was certainly suggestive," says Haruka. He doesn't mention Gael's licking him. He'd like to erase that from his memory altogether, if possible. "But he made it clear that he desired the book. Could this research be so desperately coveted?"

"It *is* an impressive resource. Like you said before, everyone thinks that bonding is this big, mysterious gamble that we can't control—that you just feed from each other, have sex and eventually bond if you're *lucky*. But your family's research paints a more detailed picture and talks about specific bloodlines and compatibility. It suggests that we have some control over it. It's a big deal."

"I suppose. Is it worth attacking someone over? Gael's objective in coming here was to formally mate with Oliver.

Why would he suddenly change the course of his life over this?"

"You heard him at dinner," Nino says. "He wanted out of Brazil. Maybe Oliver was just his path to escaping the Almeida Clan and Ladislao? Like a ticket for the express train going anywhere."

Haruka's stomach turns. He doesn't consider himself a romantic, but if Gael had intended to use Oliver in such a callous way, then he is truly despicable.

"How's Oliver taking the news about Gael's attack and disappearance?" Nino asks. "Poor guy seemed so excited."

He remembers seeing Oliver just before visiting with Nino. The young vampire had been sitting in a small, elaborately designed drawing room with Elsie and his mother. After Haruka had finished talking to Emory, he'd walked past the door. The sound of Oliver's quiet sobs echoed in the antique space.

"Not well," Haruka admits. "If he truly loved Gael, it will take him much time to recover from this betrayal. The ceremony is henceforth cancelled. We are free to leave the castle immediately following lunch."

"So..." Nino clasps his hands between his gaped thighs, briefly diverting his eyes from Haruka's gaze. "We're done? It's over?"

"Yes," Haruka says. "You can return to London." Nino drove separately from the estate. Since Sussex is much closer to the capital than Sidmouth, there was no use in him riding all the way back to Devonshire and then driving three hours back to London.

"What will you do?" Nino asks.

"I will return to Sidmouth."

"No, I mean what will you do about feeding?"

"I..." Haruka places his hands against his thighs. The knot

of his nature inside him is pulsing warm again. He wants Nino as his source, but he can't say it. He won't. It is improper and selfish and—

"Can I be your source, Haru? Would you accept me?"

Haruka blinks, meeting Nino's bright, honeyed eyes and feeling a flood of warmth wash over him. "I would be honored to have you as my source..." Haruka hesitates, wanting to clarify a point but not wanting to seem cold. "But... as far as recompense, I should be honest in telling you I do not wish to form a bond under any circumstances. However, if there is something else you desire—"

"Haruka, I already told you I don't want anything from you."

"The arrangement is unbalanced," Haruka explains, nervously rubbing the back of his neck. "I would not be comfortable with selfishly consuming your blood."

"Alright, how about this—when I come feed you each week, can we spend the day together? Just you and me, like before."

"Okay..." Haruka says, sensing there is more.

"I don't open the bar on Sundays, so I could drive down in the mornings, then spend the day with you in the library and reading your resources. I like long drives, so I don't mind the trip... I was also thinking, maybe we could add a new section to *Lore and Lust*?"

"A new section? On what?"

"Intent," Nino says. "We could create a new article focusing on the correlation between a couple's intent and the number of attempts before a successful bond is activated. I think it would be fairly simple, top-level research on our part. Nothing too invasive. Just asking couples questions and collecting data. How does that sound to you?"

Haruka pauses, genuinely considering. It sounds like a lot of time-consuming work, but intriguing. They could start with vampire couples within the UK, then branch outward to other European countries to acquire a scientifically sound research sample. Eventually, Haruka might even return home to Japan and take a sample there.

"I think it sounds exciting," he says. He's never done any of the groundwork related to *Lore and Lust*, only the compilation and arrangement. It would be nice to have his own contribution within his family's legacy.

"So you accept?" Nino asks. "I'm your new source?"

"Yes, I accept," Haruka says, a quiet joy spreading in his spirit. He can't remember the last time he's felt genuinely happy or excited about anything. "Do you wish to start this weekend? Since our time here has been unexpectedly cut short, we could return to my estate, but only if you are comfortable. Please do not feel any pressure to accompany me. If you wish to begin next weekend that is fine as well, whatever you prefer—"

"*Haruka*," Nino interrupts, laughing. "Why are you bumbling?"

"I don't know," he says, rubbing his palms against his face. Happiness feels so foreign to him. Awkward—as if he's suddenly wearing his shoes on the wrong feet. He doesn't know how to settle into this feeling.

"I'll follow you back to Sidmouth," Nino says. "Let's start this weekend."

Haruka drops his hands and breathes a sigh of relief. "Okay."

MID-JANUARY

SIXTEEN

A month has passed. Nino sits staring out the clear bay window. He loves days like this—when the sky is blue and bright, painted with fluffy, textured clouds. They're massive. Floating across the sky like celestial islands drifting in the wintery breeze.

Inside, Nino is surrounded by warmth and literature, perfectly comfortable in Haruka's expansive library. He sits with his legs folded on the cushion and his back straight, resting against the wall enclosing the cozy sill. He turns his head to look down at Haruka sitting on the ornate rug in the middle of the floor. A disarray of books and notes spirals outward from his position—he is the eye of an academic hurricane. Haruka holds a black mug of steaming coffee in one hand while with the other he casually flips through a reference book on qualitative data analysis.

Nino keeps his voice low, not wanting to disturb the peaceful atmosphere but wanting to engage with his friend. "Did you talk to Emory last week?"

"Yes," Haruka says, still focusing on his book.

Nino breathes a clipped laugh through his nose. "Did he spend the first ten minutes of your conversation apologizing profusely and insisting that he didn't intentionally forget the blood bags last month?"

This time, Haruka rolls his eyes, bringing his cup to his mouth. "Yes."

"When will he have a list for us?" Nino asks. Haruka lifts his head. The afternoon sunlight does that tricky thing where it catches the rich burgundy glint of his eyes. He looks handsome and Historian-like sitting on the floor with his coffee, but sometimes the outer shell cracks, revealing something tender beneath Haruka's façade of purebred vampire refinement and prestige.

When their eyes meet, Nino's stomach clenches. He casually glances down at the book in his lap to avoid Haruka's lovely gaze. *Stop, Nino. Don't turn into a crazy pervert like everyone else.*

"He says he should have the list of contacts for us next week." Haruka sighs. "We still don't have a concise way to collect this information. Obtaining quantitative data should be simple enough, but the qualitative piece is challenging. There is so much gray area with intent, Nino. How can we measure something so subjective?"

"With basic questions," Nino says, refusing to look over at him until the butterflies in his stomach take a rest. "Was your bond initiated as a business transaction—yes or no? Did you love your intended mate at the initiation of your bond—yes or no?"

"How are we defining love?" Haruka asks. "It means different things for different people—are we talking about agape love? Eros? Pragma?"

"I feel like you're overthinking this," Nino says, finally meeting his focused gaze.

"I feel that perhaps you are oversimplifying," Haruka counters. "Some individuals think that they love or are in love, but their actions cause pain. Their harsh expectations and corrupt behaviors are justified in their minds, sometimes under the guise and misrepresentation of love. It does not always mean the same thing to all beings."

There's something significant in Haruka's eyes as he reasons. Nino can't pinpoint what it is. Like maybe his words aren't solely conjecture. Maybe they come from a place of experience?

"Okay, I hear you," Nino says. "What if we keep it simple? Free will versus an arranged bonding. Even if we take love out of the equation, we can still gain a strong understanding of the intent behind the bond if they willingly chose each other versus not."

"That should produce less ambiguous results," Haruka agrees. "Has your brother sent another list of contacts?"

"Yes. We have fifty altogether... only nine thousand, nine hundred and fifty more contacts to go before we have a scientifically sound sample," Nino says brightly, a weak attempt to make the task in front of them seem less insurmountable.

Haruka groans and drops his shoulders. "Will it even be scientifically sound? We cannot be sure of the total population of bonded vampires. This is merely a guess."

"I think if we hit ten thousand, it'll be plenty." Nino pauses, then smiles as he glances up at his friend once more. "The only downside is that you'll be stuck with me for a while."

Haruka sets his coffee cup down and stands from the floor, stretching his long arms up as he moves toward him. "On the contrary," he says. "That is the primary benefit of this research." He folds one leg against the cushion as he sits in front of Nino in the sunlit window. Thankfully, the intense heat Nino feels in his chest isn't outwardly visible.

Nino smirks, teasing. "Because you'll have a guaranteed purebred source for a while?"

"Because I take much pleasure in your company," Haruka says matter-of-factly. "Nino, why should we rely on your brother to obtain contacts for us in Italy? I can understand relying on him for other areas of Europe, since his business dealings are wide-ranging. But do you not have correspondence with the vampire aristocracy of Milan?"

Nino rests his back against the wall. Confession time. Again. He should start referring to Haruka as Father Hirano. "When I lived at home, I didn't engage with the members of our aristocracy. After everything with my uncle, and then my mother dying... I just kept to myself in our estate."

Haruka's eyes are patient as he listens. He shows none of the awkward stiffness that had been there the first time Nino talked about his childhood.

"Have you not cultivated a specific role within the aristocracy?" Haruka asks.

"I haven't. But I'm learning that I'm pretty good at running the bar. I earned a twenty-five percent gain of profit from capital within the first year and a half of opening."

Haruka grins. "While I am not an expert in business economics, that does sound impressive."

"I have proper skills. I just haven't established them in any official capacity in the aristocracy."

"I think you could easily adopt the role of Business Consultant. You are thoughtful and easy to talk with as well, so perhaps even Social Liaison?"

Nino hesitates, meeting Haruka's gaze. "I'm not always like this, Haru... just with you, or if I'm around other vampires I trust."

Haruka's hand is resting near Nino's in between them against the cushion. He subtly shifts his hand forward, brushing his fingers against Nino's. Understanding the gesture, Nino reciprocates his touch, gently entwining their digits together. Haruka wants to feed. Nino has learned over the past month that this is his quiet way of communicating his needs.

"Why do you trust me?" Haruka asks, his eyes searching. "This is not the first time you have expressed as much."

"Well... when I first moved here two years ago, all everyone talked about was the mysterious purebred vampire who never left his house." Nino remembers both humans and low-level vampires alike coming into his bar and speculating.

Was he old and creepy? Was he like Dracula? Some kind of horrific, self-loathing monster that they should all leave alone? People had these wild theories, but having been someone who'd hidden himself away practically all of his life, Nino wondered if Haruka might simply be like him: fearful or deeply wounded in some way.

"When I met you, you were so polite and nice," Nino says, decidedly leaving out the part where the energy of his aura had reached out and pulled him toward Haruka like a magnet. "You'd always stayed isolated, but then you offered to help me. I just had a good feeling about you."

Haruka nods in understanding, softly caressing his thumb against Nino's with their fingers still entwined. His gaze flickers down to their hands, then back to Nino's eyes.

"May I feed?"

Nino swallows hard, conflicted yet again. Caught between speaking his mind or keeping his mouth shut. "Yes..."

Haruka shifts Nino's hand upward, but Nino instinctively grips his fingers tighter, keeping them linked against the cushion. Confused by the subtle resistance, Haruka looks up, his voice quiet in the intimate space. "Is something wrong?"

Nino rakes his free hand through his hair and takes a breath, steeling himself. "Why do you keep feeding from my hand?" The first time he'd done it, Nino had understood. Haruka had been attacked, he was wounded, shaken. It was a tense moment and a spontaneous offer. His reluctance to feed more intimately was natural. Expected.

But for the past month, he's continued the practice. It feels odd. They're both adults and Nino has given his consent—even initiated. There's no reason for Haruka to keep doing this.

Haruka blinks, the sudden unease like a veil over his dark head. "I... Well—"

"Are you feeding from me this way because it's comfortable for you?" Nino interrupts. "Or because you're worried about hurting me?"

Haruka rubs the back of his neck. "It is always my intention to make you feel comfortable in my presence and home. I take your confiding in me very seriously and I wish to be sensitive to what you've experienced."

"I appreciate all that, it's exactly why I trust you. But, here—"

Nino lets go of Haruka's hand, then moves his fingers to unfasten the first few buttons on his shirt collar. Haruka's burgundy eyes widen at his actions and Nino stifles the urge to laugh. He opens up his collar, takes hold of Haruka's hand and slowly brings it up to his right shoulder, snaking it underneath the fabric of his shirt. He presses Haruka's fingertips against his skin, guiding him to caress his upper back.

"Do you feel that?" Nino asks quietly, ignoring the warmth in his belly from Haruka's fingers on his flesh.

"Mm," is all Haruka says, his face full of trepidation.

"That's where he bit me." Nino sighs. "It was always in the same area, so there's a cluster of bite marks in that spot. My skin never properly hardened there."

Nino stops guiding Haruka's hand and allows him to feel

for himself. He softly strokes his long fingers across the old wounds.

"Is it sensitive to touch?" Haruka asks, finally breaking the silence.

"Yeah," Nino says, staring into his eyes. "But it doesn't hurt. I think as long as you don't feed from me in that exact spot, we're okay. You won't break me. You can feed from me normally. And you don't need to ask me every time, either. Remember? We're friends. You don't have to be so polite all the time."

Haruka slides his hand from inside Nino's shirt, then offers a weak smile. "I—This is the first time that I have had a relationship like this."

"Like what?"

"A true friendship," Haruka says. "Aside from Asao, everyone I have met across the span of my life has explicitly wanted something from me, or expected something of me. Not unusually something of a sexual nature. I have never been in this situation before, so please have patience with me."

The vulnerability of Haruka's confession surprises Nino. He smiles. "Of course."

Haruka sits back a moment, blinking his bright eyes. He lifts up from the cushion, simultaneously running his fingers into the back of Nino's hair and against his scalp. Cradling his head, Haruka leans into the left side of his neck. Nino's heart rate skyrockets as he instinctively lifts his chin, stretching his neck to allow Haruka full access to his flesh. Trusting him.

When Nino feels him delicately drag his tongue up the length of his skin, his heart practically stops altogether. He clenches his eyes shut as something like fire engulfs his groin and abdomen, then shoots up the length of his spine. Haruka bites down. Nino swallows, stifling a groan of pleasure from the sensation of his incisors elongating and sinking deeper into his skin.

Haruka gently pulls to feed from him, and in exchange, Nino clearly senses his mind. Warm, quiet thoughts of gratitude and affection are being poured into him. The tenderness of it floods his body, making his breath short. It's wonderful and singularly the most intimate thing Nino has ever experienced.

Haruka pulls again and something deeper within Nino shifts. Something primal, as if his nature is breathing and pulsing, desperately wishing to be released.

Pull harder... Nino's eyes suddenly flash and burn golden. He needs Haruka to free it, to release it and claim it. The pressure and want of it are unbearable. Unexpected. Nino clenches the cushion in his fists as his shaft hardens in his pants. *God...*

Haruka lifts his mouth from his flesh. Nino sucks in a silent gasp as Haruka licks the space where he fed. Nino's hands are shaking as he places them in his lap, a weak attempt to hide his arousal. When Haruka brings his face up from his neck, his beautiful eyes are glowing the color of red roses. Breathtaking.

He presses his forehead into him and Nino shuts his eyes tightly, his heart skipping from the closeness and cool scent of him. Haruka's deep voice is soothing, like a spellbinding song to his ears. "Are you well? I intentionally did not feed too deeply."

"Mmhm," is all Nino can manage, his eyes still closed as he tries to calm his body and breathing. Haruka sits up. Nino casually grabs the large book he's been reading and places it back in his lap. He avoids Haruka's gaze by running his palms against his face, needing to do something to stop his hands from shaking.

"Are you alright?" Haruka asks. When Nino drops his hands and looks up, Haruka's eyes have returned to their normal vintage wine color. Nino's eyes are still burning, but there isn't anything he can do about it except breathe until the rush of arousal passes.

"I'm fine," Nino says as brightly as he can, looking down at the book and opening it to avoid Haruka's eyes and the sexy little mole upside his nose. "Don't worry about me... I can handle you."

Haruka laughs in his deep, bubbly way. The way he always does when he's unexpectedly amused by something. His smile is painfully sincere. "Thank you for always being so honest with me. If you are ever uncomfortable with our arrangement, please tell me. I—I would rather maintain our friendship over anything else."

Feeling his eyes finally burn out, Nino takes a deep breath. "Okay, Haru. I will."

Haruka moves back toward his spot on the floor within the cluster of books. As he sits and makes himself comfortable, Nino feels a genuine sense of panic in his chest. He closes his eyes and runs his palm down the length of his face again.

Can I handle him?

SEVENTEEN

"Your grace, I must emphasize that I would *never* attempt to entrap nor coerce you." Emory bows for the third time, his wrinkled hand reverently placed against his chest. "The very idea goes against the honor of my bloodline—"

"Emory, we do not need to do this on every occasion that we meet," Haruka implores. "Sit down, please."

Haruka sits across from a blundering, apologetic Emory. It is their monthly social visit. They are nearing the end of what has become their atonement ritual—initiated by Emory at the start of every meeting they've had since the weekend at Hertsmonceux a little over a month ago.

Emory bows a fourth time before he sits. Haruka is beginning to feel like a feudal lord. Which he hates. "Do you have any news on Gael?"

Emory runs his hand over his smooth gray head, his pale blue eyes distressed. "Unfortunately no, your grace. My son is still extremely troubled over the embarrassment, but I have made Gael's realm leader aware of the circumstances. Have you ever met Ladislao Almeida?"

An image of the exotic, long-haired and chiseled male flashes in Haruka's mind. Ladislao is prominent in both vampire and human society. Haruka has seen his face on the news often. "No, I have not. But I know of him."

"Interesting male, he is," Emory says, raising a silver eyebrow. "I flew to Rio de Janeiro prior to the ceremony to pay my respects to him as Gael's realm leader. He detests the frigidity of our traditional aristocracy and strongly wishes to immerse vampire culture with human culture, whether it be business, economy, arts..."

Emory leans forward, his face serious as he whispers, "And *procreation*, your grace. He openly has sex with humans. Can you believe it? A *purebred* doing this. He has low-level, half-vampire children scattered across his realm!"

His life, his business. Haruka assumes many vampires have intercourse with humans, but the practice is still largely taboo within their culture—especially for higher-ranked vampires. Human blood lacks the proper nourishment necessary for pure-bred, first-, second- and third-generation vampires to function at their optimum capacity.

Aversion to sunlight, lifeless blood cells, decaying skin, stunted reproduction capabilities and lack of emotional control all stem from feeding on humans. Consequently, most ranked vampires choose lovers and mates of their own kind. If Ladislao desires to live his life otherwise, it is his prerogative.

"The vampires under his realm feel that he is mucking up our race." Emory sits up straight, his voice returning to normal now that the apparently shameful part of their conversation has finished. "They feel that as a purebred, he should hold more honor and be more concerned with the decline in the pure-blood population since the Vanishing, not frivolously consorting with humans."

"One man cannot be held responsible for repopulating our

race," Haruka says. "Nor should he be held accountable for the inexplicable circumstances of our past."

"I agree, your grace. But one man can have great *influence*. His decision to blatantly ignore the concerns of his kin is causing quite the commotion."

Reaching down to grab his cup of coffee, Haruka nods in agreement. "Perhaps *some* diplomacy would help to ease the tension." From what he's read in the news, Ladislao seems arrogant in his views, often shocking reporters with colorful, vulgar statements. The situation in Brazil serves as a poignant example of what happens when disapproval of a vampiric leader malevolently spreads throughout a realm.

"My lord, are you still satisfied with your new source?"

Only pausing a beat, Haruka brings his cup to his lips. "I am."

When he thinks of Nino, "satisfied" is a gross understatement. He looks forward to Sundays when he can spend time with his charming source.

Haruka often watches him, wondering how a vampire like this can exist, and also how he could be so fortunate in crossing paths with him. Sometimes Haruka is distracted by the golden light in his amber eyes, or the beautiful glow of his honeyed skin and bright smile. He breathes Nino's scent and his nature twists and shifts from want of him.

Consuming his spiced, delicious blood is heavenly. He always wants to pull deeper—to release Nino's aura and give him intense emotional pleasure. To formally mark him as his own, making it clear to any other vampire that Nino is *his* source.

But he resists. Strictly suppressing the urge each time. Haruka prides himself on his ability to control his nature, and he and Nino are friends. He deeply values their relationship and would never jeopardize it. Haruka has never known anything like it.

To talk and interact so freely with someone, without the burden of strict societal roles, great personal sacrifice or rigid expectations... Haruka never could have imagined this circumstance. Not even in his wildest dreams.

———

"YOU GOT ANOTHER LETTER TODAY," Asao says, just before sipping a spoonful of soup. When he finishes, he picks up his glass of water. "This makes eleven."

It's evening. Asao and Haruka are having dinner together in the kitchen. Haruka sits back and sighs. "What could she possibly want? And why does she know where I am?"

Asao stands from the table and gathers their bowls. "If someone is determined enough, you're not that hard to find. She obviously wants something from you. Selfish harpy."

Haruka closes his eyes. Despite not having seen her in almost seventy years, the delicate features of her face emerge behind his closed lids: warm brown eyes speckled with flecks of blue and set in a delicate, oval-shaped face. With the image comes a wave of bitterness and regret. Shame and self-loathing. He'd made a vow to her. Sincerely chosen to dedicate the span of his life, blood and body to her. But where is Haruka now? He tries not to think about it too deeply. When he does, he feels wayward and lost—like a kite without a string.

With his eyes still closed, Haruka lifts his chin and silently sniffs the air. Like a sensitive alarm system programmed within his body, the familiar vibration of his vampiric senses dispatches a wave of warning up his spine and directly to his brain. Someone unfamiliar is drawing closer to his home. He furrows his brow, narrowing his perception as he breathes. Not just someone, a group of unknown creatures.

Asao is at the sink washing dishes when Haruka opens his eyes. "We have guests approaching."

"Do we know these guests?" Asao says over his shoulder.

"I'm not certain..." Haruka says. He doesn't recognize the scents but... He focuses and breathes again. Tea tree. Maybe he knows one.

"How far out?" Asao asks.

"Perhaps an hour." Sensing the presence of another ranked vampire isn't an exact science. He can only approximate the distance, but it is a fairly reliable and archaic trait within every purebred vampire's biology. Other ranked vampires have the ability as well, but their homing skills are much less compelling.

Asao turns off the water and grabs a dish towel to dry his hands. "Well, we should give them a proper welcome."

AN HOUR PASSES and their guests are being oddly shy. Haruka sits with Asao in the study. The dark bramble of woods on the other side of the glass wall is ominously illuminated by the soft glow of the full moon. The study is silent save for the warm, crackling fireplace behind their armchairs. Asao abruptly yawns, making Haruka flicker his eyes over to his manservant sitting across from him.

"Can we end this?" Asao says, standing. "I'm ready to go to bed."

Haruka stands as well. Enough is enough. He walks out of the study and down the hall to the main entrance. He grabs his long wool coat and swings it onto his body. When he opens the front door and steps outside into the moonlight, his manservant is at his side.

The night air is frigid and crisp. Haruka exhales to untie the knot of his aura deep within him, his breath fanning out in a puff of wispy smoke. The pressure within him expands, making his eyes alight and burn bright red against the darkness. Looking out and scanning the woods, he concentrates. It's been a while and he doesn't want to make any careless mistakes.

Two... one... two.

He presses the heavy weight of his vampiric aura out and over the wide expanse of the skeletal woods. It stretches before him like a wide, infinite fan of light, rushing forward against the ground in search of its targets.

Loud cries echo through the air, one after another, as Haruka successfully grasps each of his victims. When all five are secure under his subjugation, he slowly lifts his head, simultaneously raising each vampire high above the cover of dark trees. They come into view, their bodies completely stiff and floating against the night sky like a group of red, hazy asteroids drifting through space.

Willing them forward and directly into his line of sight, Haruka holds them a short distance from the porch where he stands. He places his hands in his pockets and walks forward. When Haruka is standing in front of the one he holds in the center—the largest of the five—he looks up and into his dark, strained face.

"You have an affinity for these late-night, unannounced visits," Haruka says, watching Gael's eyes flicker wildly in panic.

Asao yawns, stepping up beside Haruka. "He brought friends this time."

"I suppose I should be honored by this? I was weak before, but he still sought assistance."

"Yeah, but did he not realize you'd know they were hiding

right outside the damn door?" Asao says, frowning. "Give me a break."

"Asao, please call the police and Emory. He is realm leader so he should deal with this. I am sure Oliver would appreciate some time with Gael as well."

"Sure," Asao says, turning. He smirks. "The police won't be able to hold a bunch of bulky first- and second-gen vampires. You should help them out."

Haruka tilts his head, considering. "I will make certain the police have an advantage."

Asao moves toward the house, his boisterous laughter echoing in the night. "Remind me to kiss Nino next time he comes over."

Haruka's concentration falters, just long enough for the five males to drop a foot in the air from where he holds them. He quickly catches them again and shakes his head, decidedly pushing the phrase "Kiss Nino" from his mind. He looks up at Gael. Haruka has left all of their conscious minds untouched, so although they cannot move or speak, they can hear and comprehend.

"Is this book so significant to you?" he asks. "That you would attempt to attack me *twice*?"

Haruka removes one hand from his pocket and raises his arm. He spreads his fingers toward Gael's chest, specifically lifting his hold on the first-gen's lungs, diaphragm, vocal chords and mouth so that he can speak.

Gael's smile is sinister—eerie as he stares down at Haruka. "Me dê isto, old blood. *Agora*."

"Não dou. O que você faria com isso?" Haruka frowns. *No. What would you do with the book?* Gael only snarls in frustration. Aggravated, Haruka flicks his fingers. Gael screams a bloodcurdling sound and both of his legs are now limp and dangling—cleanly broken in five places.

"*Answer* me," Haruka says. The large first-gen whimpers pathetically, like a wounded animal. Haruka rolls his eyes. "Ridiculous." Depending on the quality of blood he receives, Gael will be completely healed within a month or two.

Without warning, a powerful flash of cool energy registers in Haruka's consciousness, his nature telling him that another, unfamiliar purebred vampire is now present. The scent of something heavy and earthy like sage floods his senses. His eyes wide, Haruka turns, hastily scanning the dark woods. The moment he catches a glimpse of a black figure standing between the trees, it's gone. Disintegrated, as if he'd only seen a shadow. Gael's voice is suddenly loud, panicked and crying out in the silence.

"*Não! Por favor—*"

Haruka draws back, watching as Gael slowly evaporates before his eyes. His body rolls like a dense fog within his subjugation, gradually vanishing into thin air. Then there's nothing. As if he never existed.

The purebred presence has also disappeared, and Haruka is left standing with his four hostages. He is still, his mind spinning wildly, trying to discern what's just happened. Who was that? Where the hell did they come from? There are no other purebreds besides himself and Nino in all of England. But suddenly, there is. And the vampire had manipulative control over their energy—in the same way that Haruka can wield his essence, but fundamentally different.

He blinks, his concentration broken by the sound of sirens cutting through the cold night.

Focusing on the remaining four vampires in front of him, he quickly moves and flicks his fingers through the air, precisely manipulating his energy to break bones and snap ligaments and tendons. The vampires' screams are muffled, and since they are lower ranked than their evaporated leader, their legs will inevitably take much longer to heal.

Haruka breathes in, willing the heavy outpour of his aura back into his body. He twists it deep within himself and back into a knot, letting the four males fall and hit the cement driveway. Hard. Now their whines echo loudly through the trees.

He frowns at the sight of them, but he is deeply unsettled. It had only been a blip in time—the moment not even lasting ten seconds. He's never crossed paths with another vampire who could wield their energy so powerfully and precisely.

Gael has vanished again, but this time against his will.

The distant flash of police headlights coming up the long drive brings Haruka's attention to the present. He turns, sticking his cold hands into his pockets as he heads toward the house. Without speaking, Asao brushes past him, confidently moving forward to direct and manage the clean-up contingent.

EIGHTEEN

Nino looks at his watch. 2:28 p.m. He moves from behind the bar and to the opposite side, then sits atop one of the oak stools. His employees did an amazing job cleaning the previous night, so he doesn't need to do much before opening the bar.

He pulls his phone from his pocket and unlocks the home screen. "Let's see if she picks up."

Scotch & Amaretto opens at 3:00 p.m. on Fridays. It's not busy until about 5:00 p.m., and by then one of his two employees will have arrived for their shift. Shalini is human and typically starts the earlier shifts. Mariana is vampiric in nature but low level. Because of her sun aversions, she always closes, but she's exceptionally smart about the business. She's been with Nino from the beginning, and the bar is successful in part because of her shrewd insight on the local market. Nino is seriously considering asking Mariana if she wants to become part owner.

He hits speed dial and brings the phone to his ear. After three rings, the line is picked up.

"Hello dear," Cellina says warmly.

"Ciao bella. Do you have a minute to talk?"

"Only a few minutes," Cellina says. "I have to finish writing this damn acquisition proposal before I leave in two weeks."

"Oh, for that artist you don't like, right?" says Nino. She complained about it a few weeks earlier. Nino knows business and economics like the back of his hand, and he considers himself to be pretty well read. But art is *not* his forte.

"Right," she sighs. "For one, this artist was my director's choice. I don't even think the artist's style matches the feel of our other exhibits. And two, his shit paintings are borderline cultural appropriation of African Masquerade. Why would you ask your Black intern to write a proposal to acquire this *garbage?*"

"Because people are ignorant?" Nino says flatly, sympathizing. "Lina, you have less than two months before your internship is done, and you already have interviews for those jobs in Milan and Greece. You got this."

"I know, I know," she breathes. "But I'm a fucking century-old vampire. I *know* my modern art history. I was there, for God's sake. Why do I have to jump through these ridiculous bureaucratic hoops? Whatever—thanks for letting me vent. What's up?"

Nino rolls his shoulders. "When I feed from you... I know since it's from your hand the impact isn't very strong, but I pour good feelings into you, yeah?"

"Yeah..."

"Okay... You've always made it clear that you don't want anything from me, but have you *ever* wanted more? Have you ever wanted me to please you more intentionally when I feed—"

"*No,*" she says plainly. "Where is this coming from?"

His body tenses. He leans against the bar with his elbows,

dropping his head. "Haruka finally fed from my neck last weekend."

"That's good," Cellina says brightly. "You've graduated."

"Yeah, but..." Nino exhales. Just thinking about what he'd felt when Haruka fed sends a rush of heat down his navel and to his groin. "It felt *intense*—like my insides were on fire. My eyes even alighted, Lina. It was insane."

"Ah. So you're trying to figure out if that's normal, since he's the first person you've ever offered yourself to?" She can't see him, but Nino nods, running his palm down his face from the stress. She goes on in his silence. "Did you want him to pull your aura?"

"Yes. Very much."

"Having someone feed to emotionally please you is a very intimate thing. For you purebreds it's basically a form of sex. If someone pulls your aura, it leaves you vulnerable and exposed. If you trust him enough to do that to you and instinctively crave that from him... maybe deep down, you see him as much more than a friend, Nino."

Nino groans, rubbing his hand down his face again. "I can't. This is *not* what I wanted to hear."

"Why?" she says, concern in her voice. "I think this is wonderful. You actually attended your first formal aristocratic event as an adult, and you've grown so much in the past month just spending time with him."

"But Haruka isn't... He does *not* want this from me." Nino's hand is like a permanent fixture against his face. He massages his forehead now, his eyes closed. "He was hiding *because* vampires are always lusting after him and wanting something from him—and he has strong opinions about bonding. We've only grown close like this because we're friends, so I can't..."

What is he supposed to do? How can he stop this feeling from consuming him? He knew it was there from the moment he first met Haruka—like the tiniest ember glowing deep within him. Now, the ember is a full-grown flame and he doesn't know how to snuff it out.

"But you're nothing like those other vampires, are you?" Cellina reasons. "Don't stress over it, Nino. Just take it slow. Did he agree to come visit you in Milan next month?"

"Yeah." Nino sighs, sitting upright. He's invited Haruka to his home estate, reasoning that they can start distributing surveys for the new section of *Lore and Lust*. Also, Haruka won't have to go two full weeks without feeding or finding a new source (neither of which is ideal).

"I'm looking forward to meeting him. *Oh*, I heard about a vampire attack in Sidmouth earlier this week. Was Haruka involved in that?"

Nino smirks. He'd heard about it as well, and had promptly called the house phone at Sidmouth since Haruka doesn't own a cell phone (which is both shocking and not shocking).

Asao had answered. He'd confirmed that the report had been about them, but the manservant had sounded downright bored when Nino asked questions, as if Haruka had only been bitten by a mosquito rather than attacked by five ranked vampires in the middle of the night. The report said that four of the trespassers had been easily taken into custody by the local police, largely due to the mysterious mutilation of their lower extremities. The fifth attacker, who Asao had privately identified as Gael, had escaped.

Although no motive, Haruka's name nor any other details were released in the news report, Nino knows that Gael likely wanted to steal Haruka's manuscript. Does he want it for personal use? Or does he think he can sell it? *Lore and Lust* is valuable, but is it worth all this? This barbaric behavior that ranked vampires rarely exhibit in the modern age?

"Yeah, the attack happened at Haruka's house, but he's fine." Nino smiles, thinking fondly of his handsome friend.

Stop that.

"So insane," Cellina says. "What the hell is happening with our people lately? Are you keeping up with all this bullshit about Brazil and Ladislao? He's basically being ostracized by other ranked vampires. Everyone is being so snooty and classist. It's painful to watch."

"I know," Nino says, standing and moving toward the front doors of his bar. There are already humans waiting outside for happy hour. "Life in our culture has been peaceful for the past century—even with those terrible human wars. Hopefully things will settle down again, somehow."

"Ugh. Can we meet for dinner tomorrow? I need comfort food."

"Sure." Nino grins. "Let me know what time works for you."

NINETEEN

The snowfall is heavy outside the following Sunday. Steadily it descends like large, wet tufts of cotton from the sky, practically obscuring the view of the moor from the library window.

Haruka swivels forward in his seat, his gaze naturally landing on Nino. The news has reported severe winter storms for today, so he'd wondered if his friend would even bother visiting him. But he arrived punctually at ten in the morning, like he always does.

"Don't... take this the wrong way," Nino says, his amber gaze still focused on his laptop as he sits on the floor typing.

"Mm?" Haruka acknowledges.

"Sometimes you remind me of a panther." Nino grins, looking up and meeting Haruka's eyes.

Haruka puffs out a laugh. "Excuse me?"

"You *watch* me, with those deep burgundy eyes, and it makes me think of a panther getting ready to pounce on his prey."

Haruka laughs again, but this time from embarrassment.

He caresses his fingers into the back of his hair, lowering his head. "I assure you I am not getting ready to do that."

"I know." Nino laughs. "It's just the vibe you give off sometimes."

God. Shaking his head, Haruka picks up his pen. He hadn't realized he was watching Nino so much. He needs to pay closer attention to his *own* actions.

"Did you buy your plane ticket for next month?" Nino asks. Haruka keeps his gaze down and on his journal.

"I did."

"Good. I'm excited for you to come home with me. I think we'll be able to get a good preliminary sample for our research."

"About that..." Haruka looks at him again, dismissing the earlier shame. "Do you think five questions is enough? Should we not strive for something more in-depth?"

"I think simple is better to start with, then we can build as necessary from there. So how did you stop those vampires?"

"Your transition is abrupt."

Nino laughs. "Because I want to *know*. I've been here for an hour and you haven't even brought it up. I was waiting!"

"I restrained and manipulated them with my aura," Haruka says, sitting back in his chair and folding his arms. "There is no dramatic tale behind the encounter." Except toward the end, there was. Haruka had asked Asao if he'd felt anything strange that night—the presence of another purebred, something unfamiliar. With all the chaos his manservant hadn't noticed anything.

He knows he didn't imagine it. The heavy scent of sage still lingers within his mind like an ominous haze. Aside from disclosing the truth to Asao, he has firmly decided to avoid discussing the aberrant occurrence. He informed Emory that Gael had escaped, intentionally keeping the exact details of the circumstance vague.

"You being able to push your aura outward *and* manipulate it to the point of restraining other ranked vampires is plenty dramatic in my mind," Nino says, shaking his head. "So you just wrap them in your energy and... squeeze?"

"Squeeze?" Haruka frowns. "*No.* While I am indeed capable of wrapping them in my energy, I am able to subjugate them based on my knowledge of anthropoid anatomy. The more I learn about a creature's physical body and the biological framework therein, the more specifically I can manipulate them."

Nino folds his arms as he sits with his legs crossed, thinking. "So you could hold someone still, then break their baby toe?"

"Yes... although I do not know why I would do that."

"Rupture a spleen?" Nino asks.

"Yes. Again, so oddly specific."

Nino straightens, his eyes playful. "Can you show me?"

"I primarily only use this as a defense mechanism."

"That means... you can't do it without force? You'd hurt me if you did it now?"

"No, I would *never—*" Haruka sighs, then rolls his shoulders. He unravels the knot of his aura in his belly. His eyes immediately burn bright. He gently presses his energy outward, carefully wrapping it around Nino as he sits against the floor. Nino gasps, surprised as his body floats upward. Haruka has only subjugated him from the neck down, so Nino's eyes are wide with wonder as he rises higher.

"Holy shit..." He blinks, smiling. Haruka stands and walks around the desk so that he's directly in front of him. He lifts his hand and rotates his wrist as if he is turning a doorknob, and Nino quickly flips upside down. The warmth of Nino's laughter fills the space of the library.

"This is *wild.*" He beams, his amber eyes scanning the room from his new perspective. Haruka smiles. His friend's innocent joy is infectious.

"Why can't I smell your aura like this?" Nino scrunches his handsome face in confusion. "It's all around me, but your scent is missing... It's not like from before, when you fought Gael."

Haruka nods, appreciating the way Nino has worded the embarrassing encounter. "You obviously have the same energy source inside of you," he explains. "But imagine having two different filters. One filter represents the natural allure of your resting aura. The other is much more focused. Purified and streamlined. Now that I am properly nourished, I can distinctly control the two. During the first altercation with Gael, I could not, so they discordantly released from me."

He slowly turns Nino upright, then straightens his legs and lowers his feet to the floor. When Haruka releases his hold and withdraws his aura, Nino stretches his arms up, still grinning with delight. "Amazing," he says.

"I doubt the other vampires were as amused by this as you are."

"Yeah. I guess I'm lucky you actually like me." Nino stiffens, his face dropping. "I—I don't mean anything specific by that. I just mean I'm glad I'm on your side."

Confused, Haruka steps into the space of Nino's body. He lifts his hands and gently slides them into his hair at the back of his head. "Should I not like you?" Haruka asks quietly, cradling and massaging his head with his fingertips.

Nino's eyes search his face as he stands perfectly still. "No... you can like me."

Haruka moves one hand from his hair to wrap his palm around Nino's bicep, then smoothly leans into the concave of his neck. He runs the tip of his nose up the stretch of skin there, then along his jawline, indulging in Nino's woodsy, cinnamon essence before truly partaking of him. His eyes burn when he drags his tongue up his warm, salty flesh. He bites into him softly, not wanting to startle him.

His blood is so rich and spicy to Haruka's senses, innately satisfying like nothing he's ever experienced. He feels the initial tension in Nino's body melt underneath his grasp, and soon, he registers the weight of Nino's hands resting against his hips. They slide to wrap around the small of his back, sweetly urging Haruka to satisfy his needs.

He wants to pull harder, drink deeper. His nature twists within him, urging him to do so. But he pulls his head up, strictly ignoring the sensation. He licks Nino's neck to clean him, then looks into his face. His eyes are closed tightly and his breathing short. Haruka brings his palms to his cheeks. "Why do you seem distressed lately when I feed this way? Is this uncomfortable for you?"

"*No*," Nino says, breathless. He moves his hands from Haruka's back and steps away from his grasp. His voice is muffled as he rubs his palms against his face. "I told you before you're not hurting me. I'm fine, I just—" He shakes his head, taking a deep breath.

"You just what, Nino?" Haruka asks. "Please tell me."

When Nino opens his eyes, they're glowing in their beautiful golden hue. Haruka's heart warms, looking into his handsome face. He is thinking that he doesn't simply "like" Nino. He likes him a lot.

"Nothing," Nino says. "Everything is perfect, don't worry. So what exactly happened with Gael? How did he manage to escape? Do you think he'll come after the book again?"

Haruka scratches the back of his head. It seems he'll be talking about this after all. "It... is not simply that he escaped of his own volition. He disintegrated during the altercation."

Nino frowns. "What do you mean, 'disintegrated'?"

"I unexpectedly felt the heavy weight of another purebred

as I confronted Gael, and immediately, he disintegrated into a mist before my eyes. The purebred essence disappeared as well."

Nino's mouth hangs open. "Holy shit—"

"Nino, please calm down."

"Is 'disintegrated' your euphemism for 'vanished'?"

"I admit it is unsettling, but the moment was extremely brief. Nothing has happened since. I cannot explain how, who or why, but we are safe. The purebred did not threaten me in any way."

Nino shakes his head, his eyes wide. "You're telling me that Gael *vanished*, Haru—and a random purebred appeared out of nowhere. This is a big deal."

"But there seems to be direct cause for Gael's disappearance. This is not necessarily associated with the cultural phenomenon of one hundred and fifty years ago. For now, can we please keep this between us? I do not wish to provide fuel for additional societal distress, which is inevitable if your reaction is any indication."

Nino takes a deep breath, relaxing his shoulders. "Sorry. Alright, I understand."

LATE FEBRUARY

TWENTY

Milan. Home. A stylish city and bustling metropolis with a healthy vampire population. Nino walks through the halls of his family's private estate just outside the city. He can feel the energy of his kin buzzing through the air. Thousands of them, contentedly living within his clan's realm and under the peaceful leadership of his older brother.

In popular magazines year after year, Milan is considered one of the "Best Places to Live" for vampires. It's a stark contrast to England. Here, vampires and humans coexist seamlessly—respectfully sharing space and opportunities, jobs and higher education. Things are improving in England, and vampires are far from being chased in the streets with pitchforks and torches. But largely, they're still seen as "others" among the British: a darker race, a genetic mutation or flaw of nature. In Italy, the existence of vampires is more widely accepted. Normalized.

The hallway is quiet as Nino walks. Large picture windows line the walls on either side, allowing the winter sunlight to brighten the narrow space. When he reaches the arched door to his brother's office, it's already cracked open. Nino inhales, then exhales. Steeling himself. He knocks lightly before poking his head inside.

Giovanni's office is a perfect blend of classic and modern Italian design. The back wall is painted with a lavish mezzo fresco mural from the Renaissance era. The other walls are pristine beige, offset by intricate taupe molding. The wide archway leading to the inner room creates an added bit of refinement to the stunning space.

When he passes through the archway leading into the inner office, Giovanni is sitting at his hard maple desk. Broad-shouldered, tall and very male as usual. His white dress shirt is perfectly pressed and he isn't wearing a tie. His beard has been recently trimmed and his warm brown hair is pulled back in a low ponytail at the nape of his neck.

Giovanni flickers his hazel-green eyes up at Nino for only a moment, then focuses back down on whatever he's reading. "The baby duck is home."

Nino sighs. "Please stop calling me that."

"Where's mama duck? Is she coming by today?"

"No." Nino rolls his eyes. "Cellina has interviews today, but she'll come to lunch tomorrow after Haruka arrives."

"You smell like him," Giovanni says without looking up.

Nino draws back. "Really?" He lifts his arm and sniffs his pit.

"Faintly." Giovanni sits straight and rests his back against the chair, finally giving Nino his full attention. "You're carrying another purebred's scent, but he must not be feeding deeply from you to mark you as his. He hasn't pulled your aura."

A statement of fact. Not even a question. "No, he hasn't." Every time Haruka feeds from him lately, the longing for him to drink deeper practically cripples Nino—like blazing heat sparking in his abdomen and shooting wildly up and down the length of his body.

He accepts the nature of their relationship. Completely. But Nino is also reaching a point where he would give just about anything to have Haruka release his aura from his body. Never having experienced it before, he doesn't know exactly how it would feel. Whatever the result, his body wants it. *He* wants it. His nature craves more from Haruka with each intimate feeding.

Nino likens it to having an intense itch deep within his body that he can't scratch on his own. Only Haruka can reach it.

"We're just friends." Nino firmly stamps down on his unruly instincts. "We don't have any intention to bond. Haru has pretty strong opinions about it."

Giovanni leans forward, picking up his papers again. "How boring. And you say he's around your age?"

"Yes."

"The two of you get along? You enjoy each other's company?"

"Of course."

"Is he physically appealing to you?" Giovanni asks.

"Y-yes..."

"So what the hell is the problem? Why would two young, attractive purebreds be dancing around each other in this day and age? Give me a fucking break. Does he know that he's the first vampire you've ever offered yourself to?"

"That doesn't matter, G. Like I said, we're just friends."

"It *matters*." Giovanni picks up a pen from his desk and writes on his paper. "It's taken you almost a hundred years since you came of age to offer yourself to someone, Nino—it's a big deal. I'll be here to greet your boyfriend, but then I'm flying to Paris tomorrow evening. I hate Paris. I'll be back in two days unless I can get away sooner."

"Alright," Nino says, not even bothering to correct his brother. He turns to walk through the archway, but Giovanni's boisterous voice makes him pause and look back.

"Go sit with Father," he says plainly. "I already told him his golden child was arriving today, so he's expecting you."

Nino nods obediently, sensing his brother's palpable bitterness and knowing better than to challenge it.

TWENTY-ONE

Haruka travels across land and sea to reach Italy. He marvels—not because of the geography (although it is indeed impressive). If someone had told him three months ago that he would acquire a genuine friend and purebred source, and that he'd willingly leave the comfort of his home to travel and see that person... he would have rather made a sizable investment in goggles for flying pigs—which would have been the more believable option.

Life has surprised him. Just when he thought he understood the cruelties of the world—the greed, injustices and hopelessness therein—the universe has thrown him a curve ball and he's taken it directly in the gut. In the best possible way, of course.

When he arrives in Milan and to Nino's family estate, the morning weather is cold and breezy, but bright under a perfectly clear sky. The grounds of the Bianchi compound are a sight to behold—cypress tree–lined paths lightly dusted with snow, neatly squared hedges and brownstone villas standing in perfect harmony with their natural surroundings.

Haruka is greeted by Nino and his brother when he arrives at the main house of the estate. Giovanni is older but still young. He's at least three inches taller, his build muscular with broad shoulders. He wears a sharply tailored heather-gray suit and a black shirt underneath. No tie. The raindrop shape of his eyes is similar to his younger brother's, but Giovanni's irises are more hazel and with flecks of green instead of Nino's pure, golden amber. He has a clean but rugged, very masculine essence to his countenance—a designer warrior.

The two brothers guide Haruka down a vaulted hallway beautifully lined with sand-colored brick and shiny terracotta flooring. They step inside a warm botanical sun-room off the back of the main house. The room is cylindrical with a domed ceiling. Glass walls offer an almost three-hundred-and-sixty-degree view of the wintery garden and surrounding brush outside.

Giovanni settles in a chair directly across from Haruka at the intimate table centered in the room. "It's an honor to have you visiting with us. Do you speak Italian? Or should we continue in English? Unfortunately, my Japanese is severely out of practice."

"Thank you for the kind welcome," Haruka says politely. "Italian is fine."

Giovanni gives a short nod of approval. "Gradite uno spritz o un bicchiere di vino mentre aspettiamo?"

Would you like some appetizers or a glass of wine while we're waiting? Haruka nods. "Sì, certo, per me uno Spritz va bene. Dividiamo un tagliere di salumi e formaggi?"

Giovanni smiles, impressed as a maidservant appears in the doorway and moves toward them. "Maria Laura, cocktails and appetizers, please."

"Haruka can speak and read a ton of languages." Nino beams, looking at Haruka fondly with his warm eyes. "He has

Gilgamesh in its original Akkadian form, and a whole section of books in his library written in Hebrew and Latin. He also has an Armenian version of the Bible."

"The Bible, huh?" Giovanni smirks. Haruka rubs his palms against his thighs. He is accustomed to perpetual remarks about his appearance—he's even developed canned responses for efficiently deflecting the comments. Being praised on his actual skill and effort is something new.

"I enjoy languages, philosophies and cultures," Haruka says, returning Nino's smile. "It aids me with my research and cultural record-keeping."

"Nino told me that your realm is in western Japan," Giovanni says. "Considering you live in England, who is currently overseeing your community?"

"Presently... another local purebred is assisting the members of my aristocracy," Haruka admits. Although Asao tells him the situation is far from ideal and Haruka's presence is greatly missed.

The maidservant reappears and places a colorful board of grapes, meat and cheese on the table—mortadella, prosciutto and sliced salami. Taleggio and parmesan along with a simple bruschetta topped with diced peppers and a sampling of olives. A second servant appears with their cocktails.

Giovanni picks up his glass and brings it to his lips. "Interesting. And how long have you left your realm with this substitute purebred?"

"It has been nearly seventy years," Haruka says, feeling shamed. Yes, he has experienced something unimaginably painful, and yes, the stress and humiliation of it nearly broke him. Nearly killed him. But there is no true reason for him to have stayed away from his home this long. If he must identify a reason, maybe it's apathy?

Life handed him lemons. Instead of making lemonade, he packed his suitcase and left the fruit rotting on the counter.

"What have you been doing in the meantime?" Giovanni asks.

"I have traveled to many places, visiting various aristocracies across Japan, North America and Europe. I spent a large portion of the sixties and seventies traveling to America... a personal indulgence in jazz music..."

Giovanni raises his thick eyebrow. "Do you feel that's wise? To leave your realm unoccupied for so long? What if the vampires there resent you? Especially in this increasingly tumultuous environment?"

"The things happening in Brazil have nothing to do with the rest of us," Nino chimes in. "Not really, anyway."

"Wrong," Giovanni says flatly. "The things happening in Brazil have a ripple effect across our entire culture. Tensions are rising and it's shifting everyone's focus to the alleged purebred population crisis."

"Alleged..." Haruka pipes up. "Do you not feel the population is truly at risk? That we have been misled somehow?"

Giovanni sits back in his seat, folding his arms across his broad chest. "I don't question that the Vanishing was a real thing that happened, and it definitely reduced our population. But it's impossible to take a true census of purebred vampires, because a lot of us are still unregistered. Not everyone in our population subscribes to human policies and government, especially purebreds of old blood or age. So yes, I think this widespread panic is premature. Why should we give so much attention to a human-released census? There could be other factors we're not considering."

"I share your sentiments," Haruka says, appreciating Giovanni's pragmatic point of view. Now that Haruka has privately experienced a vampire vanishing before his eyes in conjunction with an unexplained purebred, he thinks there might be even more to consider.

When there's a light knock against the door to the sunroom, Haruka turns. A maidservant is standing in the doorway, another female vampire beside her. A beautiful, young female vampire.

The maidservant gives a polite bow as she speaks. "My lords, Cellina De Luca has arrived." The new guest moves toward the table. Nino and Giovanni stand. Haruka follows their lead. He intentionally breathes in to discern her scent.

She is first-generation, but the purebred half of her bloodline registers as clean and old in nature. She smells of magnolias and has smooth, warm brown skin that reminds Haruka of hot cocoa. Her dark auburn hair sits in heavy curls against her shoulders. Her eyes are the most haunting shade of gray.

Nino walks forward and when he reaches her, he picks her up by her waist in a tight embrace. She wraps her arms around his shoulders. When they finish their very warm greeting, Nino holds her hand as he turns toward Haruka.

"Haruka, this is Cellina, my source. Cellina, this is Haruka Hirano." Nino beams as if this moment is long-awaited. The excitement radiating from him is palpable. Cellina smiles sweetly and offers a polite bow.

"Your grace—"

"Just Haruka—please."

"Hi, Haruka. It's so nice to finally meet you."

"It is nice to meet you, too." He returns her bow, slightly taken aback but hiding it. Her shape is that of an hourglass, and she is stylish and stunning. Nino has casually mentioned Cellina in passing, and Haruka knows that she is his source. But they seem... extremely close. "Cellina, may I ask, what is your age?"

She smooths her hair away from her shoulder as she considers. "Oh God. I think I'll be one hundred and twenty-one in June? And you're one hundred and one, right? Nino told me."

"I am," Haruka verifies. "One hundred and two in April." She has the upper hand in this meeting. Clearly, she's been told more about Haruka than he has been informed about her.

"How was your trip to Milan?" Cellina asks brightly. "You just got in today, right?"

"I did. It was an uneventful trip, thank you," Haruka says, his eyes flickering down. Nino keeps a firm grasp on Cellina's hand while she speaks, and a small shift occurs in his mind.

It's a distinct feeling. A hollow discontent. As if he has quietly been considering himself the knight on a chess board, but in reality, he is just a rook.

Again.

"You're not going to greet me?" Giovanni's heavy voice carries across the table. They all look at him, but Cellina's smiling face falls flat. The air in the room is suddenly stiff.

"My apologies, your grace." She nods, but with unmistakable contention.

Giovanni narrows his hazel eyes. "Don't do that. I don't like that."

"Is that an official order?" She frowns. "How am *I* supposed to know what you like? I'm just doing what you want—"

"I *never* wanted this with you—whatever the hell this is."

There is an uncomfortable pause as Giovanni stares hard at Cellina, like time itself is standing still and Haruka is caught in a deep chasm he cannot even begin to understand.

Nino runs the fingers of his free hand through his hair. "Jesus... can we all just sit down and have lunch, please?"

TWENTY-TWO

The first course (il primo) consisted of a delicious, hearty canederli soup. Haruka has learned that Nino's family owns a property in northeast Italy. Growing up, they spent much time there and this soup is a specialty from that region. The second course was roasted chicken seasoned with white wine, sage and rosemary. Considering blood is their primary source of nourishment, not all purebred vampires eat table food habitually. However, Haruka is always more contented when he's in the company of those who also embrace life's little pleasures.

Conversation throughout dinner has been surprisingly comfortable. Aside from the sporadic, facetious and therefore prickly banter between Cellina and Giovanni, their discussions of news, business trends and their respective professions have been enthralling.

Haruka relaxes in his chair, bringing his post-dinner coffee to his lips. Giovanni sets his own cup down, watching him. "Nino mentioned that you had some trouble during the bonding ceremony. Your attacker was first-gen—from Brazil, correct?"

"He was."

"Do you think it was in relation to the uprising?" Giovanni asks.

"No. He made it very clear that he wished to possess my family's research on bonding. We reported him to the police and informed his realm leader."

"Nino told me about the book—*Lore and Lust*?" Giovanni asks. "It goes back five centuries?"

"It does."

"The research sounds invaluable. If you had someone properly format and run analytics on the information you've collected, there's no telling what kind of trends and patterns you'd find. You could potentially reveal the mysteries behind establishing vampiric bonds, which would create stronger, more powerful pairings *and* easier child-bearing processes. Maybe your attacker wanted it for himself to peddle for an astronomical price—or to take back to his realm leader."

"That would be Ladislao, wouldn't it?" Cellina asks. "Have you actually met him, Haruka?"

"I have not."

Nino relaxes with his elbows on the table, his arms folded. "Giovanni met him once, a few years ago. Right, G? You said he was obscenely flirty with you."

His elder brother frowns and shakes his head. "They were priming that freak to take over for his ailing father. He was trying so hard to get in my damn pants that I couldn't even establish any serious business conversations. He'll sleep with anything that moves."

Cellina smiles brightly, her voice warm as she looks at Giovanni. "You two should have gotten along well then? Two peas in a pod." She blinks, her expression innocent as Giovanni turns his nose up in a clear snarl. He doesn't say a word.

"*Anyway*," Nino says, a little louder than necessary.

"Hopefully we've seen the last of Gael. The poor guy he was supposed to bond with is still pretty devastated."

Giovanni shifts his intense gaze from Cellina to Haruka. "Speaking of, Nino also tells me that you have strong opinions about bonding."

Haruka stops short, the black liquid in his cup sloshing in its journey toward his mouth. He clears his throat, setting the coffee down on the table.

"Why?" Giovanni presses.

"*God.*" Cellina frowns. "Straight for the jugular."

Nino's face is also disapproving. "I didn't tell you that for you to harass him about it."

"It's a valid question." Giovanni returns their frowns, righteous. "We've been sitting here for an hour and a half. It's not like it was the first question I asked—even though I fucking wanted it to be."

Nino turns, his eyes apologetic. "Haru, you don't have to answer that if you don't want to."

"Yes, he does," Giovanni asserts, sitting back and folding his arms. "We're not children, and he wrote the damn book." At one hundred and twenty-two, Giovanni is the eldest vampire within their intimate group. It is a very nuanced thing that Haruka has yet to truly define, but in general, age precedes blood quality—particularly if two vampires are equally ranked. His own bloodline is cleaner and more ancient than Giovanni's, but the gladiator-esque vampire is openly postulating his seniority over Haruka.

Haruka's throat tightens. This isn't like past situations where he's been asked this question—where he could offer his canned response and swiftly change the subject. This circumstance is much more intimate. He shouldn't lie to Nino and his family. He cannot.

He takes a deep breath, ignoring the heavy weight in his

chest. "I... do not wish to bond because I have been bonded before."

Silence. The three vampires stare at him utterly perplexed. Haruka can feel the confusion among them, like a dense fog has settled and no one knows which way to turn. No one can see their hand in front of their face.

Slowly, their gazes morph into a curious (slightly disturbed?) understanding. Now, he is no longer one of them. He is like an alien life form beamed down and sitting among them. As if his face is suddenly covered in purple spots.

"What?" Giovanni shrewdly offers.

"You've been bonded before?" Cellina asks. "What does that mean? Are you still bonded now?"

"No," Haruka says, casting his gaze toward his friend sitting completely still beside him. "I *was* bonded, but not any longer. The bond was broken."

Silence again. A long series of ellipses.

"*What?*" Giovanni draws back in his seat. The hypothetical purple spots are moving.

"How... how can you have broken a bond?" Cellina asks. "Bonds can't be broken once established. It's not possible —*everyone* knows that."

"And yet..." Haruka smirks. It is unheard of. It is supposed to be impossible. Once two vampires entwine their natures and enter into the secure, mythical vow of a bond, it can never be broken. They are mates and partners for life, creating a deep biological connection, shared responsibilities, emotional support and profound intimacy. Uniquely and monogamously dedicated to one another until death.

Or so the lore has traditionally stated.

Betrayal of the bond by directly feeding from an outsider or engaging in sexual intimacy means death to the bonded indi-viduals. Except it doesn't. Not in Haruka's case. He is still alive (by definition, anyway), and so is Yuna. After much trauma, his body has endured. But what of his spirit? His hope? The innate yearning for a fulfilling, contented life?

"You broke a bond..." Cellina continues, seemingly the only one at the table capable of forming full sentences besides Haruka. "But you're alive. I don't—I can't understand."

"To be clear, I am not the instigator of the dissolution," Haruka says, glancing sideways at the cinnamon-mahogany vampire seated next to him. His amber eyes are blinking. Staring. Haruka picks up his coffee. "Am I so grotesque to you now?"

"*Never*," Nino says, his brows suddenly drawn together. "Of course not. I just, are you... in pain? Does it hurt?"

Haruka pauses just before taking a sip, considering. "Not anymore." He is numb now. There's no more pain, but there isn't much of anything.

Shaking his head, Giovanni folds his arms. "Not grotesque. Just fucking unbelievable—"

"*Giovanni.*" Cellina's perfectly shaped brow is raised in obvious displeasure. The room falls silent yet again in a poignant moment before Giovanni speaks.

"I apologize, Haruka," he says, sitting up a little straighter in his seat.

GIOVANNI DIDN'T ASK Haruka any more personal questions. Having received more than he'd likely bargained for, the broad male intentionally transitioned the conversation to more impartial topics.

The plan is to introduce Haruka to members of the Milan aristocracy during his week-long visit. The practice is customary for a visiting purebred from another realm unless special exceptions are requested, as had been the case when Haruka first moved to Sidmouth.

Cellina had enthusiastically suggested that they attend a dinner party with her the following evening. With the additional need to conduct their own research for the new section of *Lore and Lust*, Haruka's schedule in Milan is quickly filling up.

"I know Lina means well, but I would rather not go to this party." Nino sighs heavily as they walk out the front door of the main house and into the bright, wintery afternoon. Nino's bedroom is in the western structure of the main cluster of buildings. It serves as a small home unto itself. Luciano, Nino's manservant assigned to his quarters, has taken Haruka's luggage to the guest bedroom within his building so that they can stay together.

"You are adamantly reluctant to attend aristocratic events," Haruka observes, walking just behind him. "Even more so than myself."

"It's obnoxious—pontifical, stiff old vampire rhetoric," Nino says. He mocks, "My lord, your grace, dear me—oh my!" They enter the two-story home. It's similar to the main house where his brother lives, but more intimate. Less opulent. They move toward the stairs, passing a small living room with white walls, earth-toned furniture and a speckled-brick fireplace. There are two rectangular windows offering a flood of bright light into the rustic space.

When they're on the second floor, Haruka follows Nino into his bedroom. His friend holds the door, and once Haruka is inside, Nino closes it behind him. "Plus, G is already trying to monopolize your time by dragging you on his social visits. I told him we have things we need to do," Nino complains. He kicks his shoes off before climbing onto his bed.

There's a snug-looking armchair near the window, so

Haruka takes a seat there. "We will accomplish our goals. There is no need to worry. We have much time," he says.

Nino folds his legs atop the thick comforter and leans back against his palms. "I'm sorry if my brother made you uncomfortable during lunch. He's pretty... forthright. If I'm being nice. It's a good trait to have in business but it can be irritating on a personal level."

"You do not need to apologize." Haruka sits back, relaxing. Nino's room is saturated with his natural scent. Something about it settles Haruka. It soothes him, like a warm, healing mineral bath in the cold winter night that is his life.

"You're not mad?" Nino asks.

"No. The questions your brother asked were indeed direct, but not unusual." He closes his eyes, reveling in the soft glow of sunlight pouring in through the glass and the heady smell of the room.

"Haru..." Nino's voice is low. Haruka slowly opens his eyes, and when their gazes meet, Nino continues. "If it's alright, will you tell me more? About how you were bonded before?"

Talk about my bond... He has never spoken of it. Not aloud. Not with anyone. It is a significant thing that has happened in his life—that in many ways has permanently altered its trajectory.

He inhales deeply, his chest rising and falling. Nino has been open with him on many occasions about his own life and experiences. Haruka supposes that it's finally his turn. "What exactly would you like to know?"

TWENTY-THREE

What do I want to know?

Everything. Nino wants to know everything, but he isn't sure he can process it all, because there are already too many things to digest. The thoughts are zipping around in his mind like shiny metallic dragonflies.

Haruka was bonded.

How long ago? Why? What happened?

Bonds can be broken?

Haruka is sitting in his bedroom... He smells nice.

Haruka was *bonded*.

Nino sits straighter in his bed, rubbing his palms against his thighs. He looks up. Haruka is sitting in an armchair beside the window. The lighting there gives his milky, almond skin an incandescent quality.

"Who were you bonded to?" Nino asks, thinking it better to start simple.

Haruka leans with his elbow against the arm of the chair, lazily cradling the side of his face with his palm. "Yuna Sasaki.

We were betrothed to each other as children through an arrangement between our parents."

"When were you officially bonded? And for how long?"

"As customary, we mated when we came of age at twenty-one. Our bond lasted ten years."

Nino nods in understanding. The general practice of formally arranged bonds had died out by the 1970s.

"Only ten years?" Nino asks. *Why so short? Did you love her? Did she hurt you?* The questions are still frenzied in his mind, all of them desperate to push through to the funnel of his mouth.

"Yes," Haruka says. "She..." He pauses, his wine eyes focusing on Nino. "How much of this would you like me to explain?"

"As much as you're comfortable with."

"I do not wish to bore you with the mundane details of my life."

"Haru, you never bore me. I would *never* be bored with you."

A little half-smile pulls at the corner of Haruka's mouth. The subtle gesture makes Nino smile as well in the fleeting moment.

"Yuna had a close friend growing up. Kenta Miyoshi," Haruka explains. "He was first-generation. Despite their obvious affections for each other, our parents arranged that Yuna would bond with me when we both came of age."

"Because you were both purebred?" Nino guesses.

"Correct. Yuna's bloodline is also old like mine, so the pairing was ideal. But as we grew, Yuna and I developed... what I believed was genuine affection for each other. As you know, my parents died when I was twelve. When Yuna and I reached twenty-one, I asked if she truly preferred to form a bond with me over Kenta. Although her parents were still alive, if we wished to sever the arrangement, it was my prerogative to do so."

"She chose you, even though you gave her an out?"

"Yes," Haruka breathes. "She expressed her... love... for me, and insisted that I was her choice. So I trusted in that. In her."

Haruka sits up straighter in the chair, rubbing his palm down his face. His eyes seem far off somewhere as he recalls this situation. Nino gives him another moment before he speaks.

"So what happened?" he asks quietly.

The dark vampire laughs from his throat but the sound is bitter. It isn't warm and bubbly like usual—the way Nino is accustomed to hearing it.

Dropping his hand into his lap, Haruka smiles weakly. "This is the rather... humiliating part. Later, I realized that Yuna and Kenta had orchestrated many clandestine meetings after she and I had formed our bond. One such meeting resulted in Kenta's feeding intimately from Yuna. I felt the bond between us break almost instantly—like profound cracks in a foundation."

"Did you know that something like that could happen? Had you ever heard of it within your research?"

"No." Haruka rests back against the armchair. "It was the first time I had ever heard of such a situation and I have yet to find anything like it."

Nino remembers the empty section at the end of the *Lore and Lust* manuscript. *Broken Bonds.* When he'd read the words, they hadn't made sense to him. It was like reading "sober drunk" or "angry peace." How could these two words exist side by side? It emphasizes how profoundly ingrained the lore of bonding is within the vampire psyche. Within their culture.

"The result of the infidelity," Haruka says, his deep voice quiet, "was immense pain. A profound shooting, almost stabbing sensation in the depths of my nature within me. We decided to formally absolve our relationship, and for the following six months, my body... very harshly rejected Yuna's nature from within me. Even with the passing of my parents, perhaps *that* was the most horrific experience of my life. I—I did not think I would survive it. I did not want to... To this day, I truly do not understand why I did." Haruka brings his fingers to the top of his dark head, twisting his hair as he slumps. He clenches his eyes shut as if he's still in pain.

Nino quietly crawls off the bed and takes the few steps necessary to reach him. Once there, his friend blinks his lovely eyes open. Nino bends down, placing his palms against the armrests. He leans into Haruka, softly pressing their foreheads together. He closes his eyes. Haruka briefly tenses from his nearness, but as Nino extends the warmth and peace of his aura further outward, Haruka relaxes.

Soon, the dark purebred's breathing is slow, in perfect rhythm with his own. Nino opens his burning eyes and lifts his head. Haruka's eyes are still closed, his face calm.

"Are you okay?" Nino asks.

When Haruka opens his eyes they're glowing scarlet. Beautiful. "I am... My apologies..."

Nino steps back and extends his hands, offering to pull him up. "My father has an old library on the southern side of our compound. Would you like to spend some time there today?"

His friend's eyes widen as they slowly shift back to their healthy burgundy color. "I would." He places his hands within Nino's, allowing himself to be firmly pulled upright. Once they're both standing, Nino steps into him and fully wraps his arms around his shoulders. He isn't sure if this is okay—if he's overstepping a boundary. But as he holds Haruka close, he turns his face into the dark silkiness of his hair at his temple.

"I'm very grateful you survived," Nino says quietly. "Thank you for sharing that with me. I know it wasn't easy."

Haruka slides his hands around Nino's waist, embracing him against the length of his body. Nino's eyes widen in the hug, but he quickly closes them and holds his friend a little tighter.

"Thank you for listening," Haruka says. "I have never... spoken of it aloud. Not once."

How long can they stand together like this—embracing each other in the soundless, golden sunlight? The solidity of Haruka in his arms, and the gentle rise and fall of his breathing swelling against his chest. Nino has no clue. But he could do it all day. Even then, it wouldn't feel long enough.

TWENTY-FOUR

The following night, and as per Cellina's insistence, Haruka accompanies Nino in meeting one of Milan's most esteemed aristocracy members. Francesco Moretti is curator for the Galleria d'Arte Moderna. Based on Haruka's admittedly shallow research, Moretti has held the prestigious title for the past two centuries and is best known for his personal relationship with Pompeo Marchesi.

Upon their arrival, Haruka and Nino are escorted down a long marbled corridor washed in dim, romantic lighting. Classic European artwork set in golden antique frames adorns the walls—*Trivulzio Madonna* by Mantegna, *Portrait of a Warrior* by Dossi. Moretti has a blatant affinity for priceless Renaissance-era artwork.

The hallway ends at a set of oak doors. The maidservant escorting them pulls one open and steps aside. To his amazement, there is a large atrium set behind Signor Moretti's home.

The space is a rectangle lined with lush, deep green landscaping. Everything is drenched in the beautiful color: twisting cypress trees along the inside perimeter and thick, manicured grass running throughout the garden like a luscious emerald carpet. Strings of clear light bulbs are beautifully hung above a long table on the brick patio set in the center of the glass house. The modern lighting casts a soft, almost dreamlike haze.

During the ride to Moretti's estate, Nino was uncharacteristically quiet. Haruka knows that his friend loathes these types of formal events, but he isn't exactly sure why. It is only a dinner party and Nino isn't in any danger. The only true threats are boredom and the uncomfortable barrage of flowery compliments.

They walk toward the table and all the vampires there pause to stare. When an older male at the head of the table stands, the remaining vampires follow his lead. From his Internet search on Nino's laptop, Haruka recognizes the leader as Francesco Moretti. The older vampire's thick silver curls glisten under the soft light of the atrium. His face is chiseled and attractive with a strong jawline. Clearly, he is a dignified and well-groomed vampire.

"Younger Bianchi, it is a pleasure to have you join us for dinner in Lord Bianchi's absence."

Signor Moretti opens his arms wide and Nino awkwardly steps into his embrace. The older vampire neatly kisses him on the cheeks before drawing back and looking him in the face. "Such a stunning young male you've grown into. Perhaps I haven't seen you since before you came of age? Pity."

"Maybe." Nino smiles, but the gesture doesn't reach his eyes. "Signor Moretti, this is my friend Haruka Hirano of Kurashiki, Japan. He's visiting with us for the week."

"I have heard." Moretti beams as if Haruka is a large bag of rare gemstones. He offers a slight bow from his waist. "Impressive creature you are. Welcome to Milan, Master Hirano."

"Thank you, signore," Haruka replies, nodding politely. "Please simply call me Haruka. It is a pleasure to meet you."

"Your Italian is beautiful, Haruka. Please have a seat and make yourselves comfortable."

Moretti goes around the table to introduce each of his guests—their rank, age, profession and any noteworthy distinctions they have achieved. It is tedious. And pointless. Based on his experiences across European aristocracies, none of these other creatures will talk at any length tonight. The host always dominates, rarely letting the other guests get a word in edgewise.

Nino pulls his smartphone from his pants pocket and discreetly checks it underneath the table. Haruka doesn't need to ask why. Cellina is not here yet.

Signor Moretti calls for Haruka's attention and he straightens his back, preparing for the inevitable onslaught of questions.

WINE IS POURED. Warm appetizers are served. Just as Haruka had anticipated, much of Signor Moretti's focus has been on him. His background, his opinions, his breeding, his interests. The conversation is engaging if not slightly wearisome.

Nino has barely said a word since they arrived.

Signor Moretti takes a long sip of wine, then diverts his attention toward Haruka yet again. "We are all *well* aware of the younger Bianchi's... troubles. But may I ask—what with your intellect, alluring aura and poise, why have you chosen to remain unbonded?"

Haruka blinks. *Troubles?* He casts his disbelieving gaze over to Nino, but his friend avoids his eyes and casually picks up his glass of water—as if nothing untoward has been stated. Haruka takes a deep breath and focuses on Signor Moretti. He quickly reverts to his canned answer. "I have not yet found a vampire that I am compatible with."

"Perhaps that will change whilst you are in Italy?" He grins, mischievous. The elder vampire already has someone in mind for Haruka. Perhaps a few someones. They always do. Simultaneously, Nino exhales a quiet groan.

"The younger Bianchi is... inexperienced and ignorant of our social hierarchy." Moretti lifts his chin. "It is the *elder* Bianchi, Giovanni, on whom you should focus your precious attention. He is an exceptionally shrewd male and well known all across Europe—truly the pride of our region. There is also a ranked female in Rome—"

"Amore, you are being discourteous." Lilliana, Moretti's mate, gently smacks his shoulder. She offers an apologetic smile to Nino.

"Are my words untrue?" Signor Moretti says proudly, lifting his large hands in a yielding gesture. "This male has not acknowledged nor properly engaged with *any* of us in his life-time. How can he know? And do you still privately consort with that *leech* Cosimo De Luca?"

Nino's jaw drops in naked shock. "*No.* How do you—"

"Oh, everyone knows about that." Moretti flippantly waves his hand. "Don't be a child. There are no secrets in this community. He is a disgrace, but his sister, on the other hand... exquisite creature. I am looking forward to her arrival tonight."

Nino runs his fingers through his coppery hair—a clear sign to Haruka that his friend's stress level is climbing higher.

"Before tonight," Moretti says, focusing on Nino, "had you even *heard* of any of the vampires at this table—aside from me, of course?"

Nino glances down the length of the table before offering a polite smile. "No, signore, but—"

"What knowledge do you have of the art world? Did you

research prior to this dinner? You have contributed nothing to our conversation—"

"Amore, *please*." Lilliana speaks up once more. "He is a very delicate male. Remember the trauma he has experienced."

"Delicacies aside, *why* does he not know our art history?" Moretti asks, lifting his wine glass toward Nino. "It's our culture, for God's sake, and it isn't as if you haven't had plenty of time alone to research."

Moretti starts to sip his wine, but abruptly stops, the liquid sloshing in the glass as he leans forward. "Have you heard of *da Vinci*? How about listing three works of his? Can—"

Haruka quickly releases the knot of his aura from the center of his body, extending the strength of his essence outward to cover the occupants of the dinner party.

He's had enough.

TWENTY-FIVE

It takes much focus on Haruka's part, but everyone at the dinner table is suspended in time except for Nino. He has successfully circumvented his energy around his friend beside him so that he remains unaffected.

Nino cautiously turns to look at him with his bright amber gaze. Haruka frowns, unable to mask his discontent. "Nino..."

"Yeah?" Nino's voice registers much higher than usual as he discreetly scans the table.

"*Why* is he treating you like this?"

Nino nervously glances around again. "Can they hear us? You froze me before, but I could still hear you."

"That is because I left your consciousness intact, but I have not done that now. I try to avoid impeding creatures in totality because it disrupts their awareness of the passage of time. Why is Signor Moretti speaking so discourteously to you?"

Nino closes his eyes. "I haven't... You know I don't have an official societal role. Along with that, I haven't formally engaged with our aristocracy at all since I was little. So on the rare occasion that I go to these things, vampires are either resentful of me for not engaging in society or they pity me. It's just how it is. I think Lina wants me to do these things more so it'll get better. But I don't know if it can at this point."

"Where is she?" Haruka asks. She'd been invited to this dinner because of her passion for the art world. The two of them are technically here to support *her*.

"She had another interview today and it turned into a dinner thing. She's been apologizing to me all night via text."

"I understand," Haruka says patiently. "But he cannot disrespect you. I *will not* sit here and allow this to continue. What shall we do about it?"

"I'll—I can say something..." Nino frowns. "*Shit*, he's older though—and he's a bigwig in our society."

Haruka reaches over to gently grasp Nino's hand against his thigh beneath the table. Nino immediately flips his palm up, lacing their fingers together. Haruka gives his hand a firm squeeze.

"There are ways to assert yourself without being disrespect-ful," says Haruka. "You expressed yourself well toward Gael when you spoke on my behalf at the bonding ceremony. The same action is appropriate here. You can voice your general discomfort with Moretti's candor, for starters?"

Nodding in agreement, Nino sighs. "Alright, I'll tell him."

Haruka is about to pull the heavy weight of his aura back inside his body, but he hesitates. "Can you answer his question? Do you know three works by da Vinci? If possible, please list *more* than three."

Nino scrunches his nose in playful consideration. "Hm... how about that one statue? The thinking guy?"

An affectionate warmth pulses in Haruka's heart, making him smile. Something about the moody white lighting of the atrium makes Nino's honeyed features glow. He looks hand-some and bright in a layered mustard sweater over a subtly patterned navy blue dress shirt. "That is *The Thinker* by Auguste Rodin," Haruka says. "And he is French."

Nino considers. "Okay, how about the other naked guy? *David?*"

"That is Michelangelo."

"The Sistine Chapel?"

"Also Michelangelo."

"*Dammit.* Wait. One more. What about the one where the fingers are touching?"

Haruka laughs. The sound of it echoes through the silent space. "That is *The Creation of Adam* and also by Michelan-gelo. It is unfortunate that Signor Moretti is not quizzing you on *him.*"

Nino shakes his head, exasperated. "Alright, just tell me."

"*Mona Lisa, The Last Supper, Vitruvian Man, Head of a Woman, The Baptism of Christ.*"

"I've heard of some of those. You want me to name all five?"

"I do," Haruka says, sneering at the motionless older vampire. "Confidently."

Nino holds on to his hand tightly as he rolls his shoulders. "Alright, unfreeze them—*Wait.*" Haruka pauses, feeling the burn behind his irises as he waits. Nino grins. "Should you break his baby toe?"

"He deserves a ruptured spleen."

They laugh openly, reveling in the ironically private moment before Nino turns back toward Signor Moretti. He waits with their hands warmly clasped. Haruka withdraws his energy and the older vampire is moving and speaking again— like a movie that had been paused but suddenly resumes playing.

"—you manage *that* much? Three works?" Signor Moretti says, his chiseled face frowning in incredulity.

Nino stares, his gaze unwavering. "Sure. *Mona Lisa, The Last Supper, Vitruvian Man, Head of a Woman, The Baptism of Christ*... Do I need to go on? Are you familiar with those?"

Signor Moretti sits back with his eyebrow raised as he takes hold of his wine glass. "Of *course* I am, child. How could you think—"

"Another thing," Nino says. "*Please* don't call me that. I've been alive for a hundred and thirteen years. I'm obviously not a child. It's demeaning."

Signor Moretti draws back and puts his hands up in mock offense. "Heavens, well I do apologize, young master. First my *mate* chastises me all night, and now the younger Bianchi as well. In the words of the great King Julius Caesar, 'Et tu, Brute?'"

"Julius Caesar did not say those words," Haruka says flatly.

The guests at the table pause. The gentle song of nocturnal creatures hidden in the surrounding brush outside the glass walls is now more apparent.

"What?" Signor Moretti smiles arrogantly. "I apologize, Haruka, but it is a well-known fact that he *did*."

"You are mistaken, signore," Haruka says. "That is a fictitious line from the Shakespeare play *Julius Caesar*. Just as some believe that Caesar was deaf in one ear, but there is no documented historical evidence of it. It is *also* a common misconception derived from the Shakespearean play."

Signor Moretti scratches the back of his head. "That is... an interesting fact—"

"In addition," Haruka goes on, "Julius Caesar was not a 'king.' He intentionally held the title of 'dictator' in ancient Rome and was never formally recognized as emperor."

Nino squeezes and tugs his hand underneath the table.

Haruka blinks, swiftly pressing his energy outward again to halt all movement. He shifts his glowing eyes toward Nino.

"I acknowledge," Haruka says, "that I am being petty."

Nino sits back against his chair in a warm laugh, his face bright with amusement.

"Normally I would not draw attention to something so trivial, but his behavior *grates* me," Haruka continues. "You should sincerely consider declaring a societal role for yourself. You are unquestionably talented."

Historians in the aristocracy are expected to know specific, ancient aspects of their culture spanning a self-chosen subject: music and arts, religion, politics, genetics, biology or a particular time period. Sometimes a combination of topics, as in Haruka's case (he is heavily inclined toward both arts and genealogy). Nino may not have an official societal role, but it is unfair for Signor Moretti to hold him strictly accountable on this particularly narrow topic.

"I should, you're right," Nino says. "I will soon."

"Good." Haruka sighs. "I should release my hold on these contemptuous vampires." A moment later, he pulls his energy back into himself once more and movement at the table resumes.

"I have never professed to be an expert on the historical details of the Roman Empire," Signor Moretti says curtly. "So *please* forgive my offense, your grace."

"No offense has been committed." Haruka picks up his wine glass. "We all have our strengths and weaknesses. I believe it is better to *educate* and share our knowledge instead of patronizing each other. Nothing productive can be accomplished that way, and *none* of us is perfect. Do you not agree, signore?"

Haruka calmly takes a sip of his wine to allow Signor Moretti time to respond. Simultaneously, Nino affectionately squeezes his hand underneath the table. Moretti's flat eyes flicker to Nino before focusing back on Haruka. The older vampire raises his eyebrow in arrogance.

"I *agree*, your grace," Signor Moretti says. "Point well taken."

TWENTY-SIX

Nino climbs the stairs toward his bedroom a couple hours later, still aggravated by Signor Moretti's behavior. He'd anticipated some adverse response to his suddenly attending a social event within his realm, but the older male had seriously gone overboard.

Nino flips his coat from his shoulders a little harder than necessary. "I can't get over how much of an asshole he was. *Why* would Lina tell me to go to his house?"

"Perhaps she was unaware of his arrogant demeanor?" Haruka says, trailing Nino up the stairs. "Although... how this fundamental truth could be kept hidden is beyond me."

Walking into his room, Nino throws his wool coat over the ottoman at the end of his bed. His manservant has already lit the small hearth, so the room is warm and filled with orange firelight. Nino kicks his shoes off before throwing his body onto the bed. He lies flat on his stomach, his voice muffled as he presses his face into the down comforter. "I'm not going to another social, aristocratic damn vampire event for a *long* time. Jesus."

The bed shifts as he hears Haruka's deep, calm voice. "Practice makes perfect?"

Flipping himself onto his back, Nino sees that Haruka is sitting on the edge of the mattress beside him. Nino scoots up higher so that he can rest his head against the pillow.

He smiles. "Do I need to be perfect? You once told me that I was lovely just the way that I am. Remember that?"

"I do." Haruka grins, his outline glowing from the fireplace burning brightly behind him. "And I stand by my statement. But *because* you are an exceptionally intelligent, bright and engaging male, it would be a shame to deprive our society of your talents and thoughtful nature."

Nino's smile broadens, his heart light and feathery. He pulls one leg up and relaxes with his hands cradling his head. "Thanks, Haru... I'll keep trying. Why did you tell Moretti that you haven't found a vampire you're compatible with when he asked you about mating? You said you never wanted to bond again."

"I do not. That was my socially couth response to an invasive question. To declare that I do not wish to bond creates a spectacle that I am unwilling to endure."

"Makes sense..." The room falls silent as Nino thinks back to Haruka pressing his energy outward, coolly stunning everyone at Moretti's party. "Thank you for helping me tonight. When you're with me at these events, it's always much better."

"I feel the same way about you," Haruka says. He briefly looks away, like he's considering something. "Nino, who is Cosimo De Luca? Is this person related to Cellina?"

Nino groans and drops his leg flat onto the bed.

"You do not have to answer me," Haruka reassures him. "I don't mean to pry—"

"No, you're not prying." Nino turns onto his side to face

Haruka. He leans against the pillow with his elbow, resting his face in his palm. "Cosimo is Cellina's younger brother. I grew up with Lina and Cosimo because our fathers were best friends. Maybe around the time I came of age, Cosimo started being flirty with me."

Haruka nods in understanding. "He was a romantic interest."

"Not really. Not for long. He—he's not a bad vampire. He was just adamant about wanting to feed from me eventually. He always told me, 'You know, when you're ready.' But he asked me if I was ready every day."

His friend laughs at this, deep and throaty the way Nino adores. His laugh is like the rumble of thunder, but if the oncoming storm were a thing of great joy. Nino grins as he continues. "He was like, 'Whenever you're ready,' and then literally five minutes goes by and he looks at me, dead serious. 'So are you ready?'"

Laughing openly this time, Haruka brings his palm to his forehead. Nino loves making him laugh. It feels as if he needs it, and every time Nino succeeds, the sensation is akin to sunlight breaking through a dark, overcast sky. Haruka breathes, gathering himself. "That does not sound ideal."

"It wasn't. I... had a female lover for a little while in England. Human."

"Really?" Haruka's eyes widen as he whips his head toward him.

"Yeah. But I never fed from her. Humans don't even smell appetizing, you know? I thought she was nice, but she... I don't know. Maybe I was fulfilling some kind of fantasy for her? She always begged me to feed from her. She used to call me 'my purebred vampire,' which was awkward. Like I was some kind of pet... Showing me off to her friends."

"Nino, these situations sound terrible." Haruka shakes his

head, his palm still covering his face. "And her moniker for you was... painfully unimaginative."

Nino laughs. He agrees wholeheartedly. They *were* terrible. Being cautious and primarily keeping to himself across the span of his life, Nino has only had a handful of sexual experiences with other vampires. None of them worth discussing in any detail.

Biting his lip, Nino shifts his foot, playfully digging into the comforter and underneath Haruka's body. The dark vampire jumps, startled when Nino's toes touch his ass. "What about you? Did you have experiences with other vampires after your bond broke with Yuna?"

Haruka freezes as if he's used his own unique ability on himself. A nervous smile spreads across his face. "Do I... have to answer this question?"

"You don't have to do anything, Haru. I just thought maybe we were sharing?"

He shakes his head. "I would rather not."

That's an obvious yes. Nino puffs out a laugh through his nose as he comfortably rolls onto his back again. He is suddenly imagining his eloquent, young, professor-like friend having sexual escapades across Europe.

Nino frowns and quickly squashes that image. He dislikes it very much.

Haruka rubs his hand against the back of his head. "Now our sharing feels unbalanced—am I obstructing some rite of passage within our camaraderie?"

"You're not. We're fine."

"Nino, you never offered yourself to this Cosimo creature?"

"No."

"But... surely another vampire made you feel comfortable enough to do so?"

Nino's heart rate quickens in his chest, his breathing shallow. Haruka is funneling down to the obvious conclusion and the room feels a little too warm. Nino keeps his eyes up, focusing on the ceiling. "Well... no."

"Wait," Haruka says, leaning forward against the bed with his palms. "Do you mean to tell me that you have never had your aura intimately released from your body? You have never experienced this in your entire life?"

He's really driving this home. Nino closes his eyes. "I haven't, but it's fine. Don't feel sorry for me, I just—"

"I do not pity you," Haruka says firmly. "Your life, your choices. However..."

Nino opens his eyes, waiting. He stares up at the thick, exposed wooden beams in his friend's silence. "Yes?" Nino prompts.

"What is your true relationship with Cellina?" Haruka asks. "Why has she not pulled your aura for you?"

"Cellina is like a big sister to me. That's not our relationship." Nino flickers his eyes over to Haruka. He's looking down at his hands in his lap, his typically perfect posture gently rounded.

"I see," he says. "But... perhaps you secretly wish that she would—"

"*No*," Nino says, a little louder than he should. Haruka whips his head in Nino's direction in surprise. Thankful for his full attention, Nino speaks more softly, but firmly. "No, Haru. I trust Cellina, but there is *nothing* romantic between us. Nor has there ever been. I wouldn't want her to do that to me."

Haruka's head bobs in understanding, but his handsome brow is furrowed. "Would you—" He stops, shaking his head. He stands without preamble, which makes Nino sit up straight from the bed—instantly vertical like a rake someone has stepped on. Urgency is radiating in the depth of Nino's spine.

"It has been a long night," says Haruka, rubbing his hand against the back of his neck. "I should go—"

"What were you about to say? Would I *what?*" Nino's adrenaline has gone from zero to sixty. From relaxed to utterly desperate. They are on the cusp of something important. Something they've been delicately, politely avoiding. He can feel it trickling and sparking in his nature—warmly rushing over his skin in a flood of goosebumps.

"No," Haruka says, his eyes downcast. "I am presumptuous. And I do not know my place—"

"Just say it. *Please.*"

They watch each other in a still moment before Haruka relaxes his shoulders. His melodic voice is quiet. "If... you are comfortable with me doing so, perhaps I could do this for you? Pull your aura."

The heat Nino feels in his spine intensifies. Blooms. It is an emotional cocktail of relief and excitement swirling within him. He swallows hard and nods, maybe a little too hard as he stares at his friend. "Yes please. I would like that *very* much."

TWENTY-SEVEN

Nino's pulse is still racing when Haruka sits back down on the bed—which is much better than leaving, so the urgency Nino feels dissipates slightly.

"Having your aura pulled by someone is a very intimate act," Haruka says, his voice low against the gentle crackle of the fireplace.

Mesmerized, Nino stares into his side profile. The hairs on his arms are standing on end, as if his body is charged with electricity. "I know…"

Looking down into his lap, Haruka rubs his palms against his thighs. "If we are choosing to alter the nature of our relationship, I want to be certain that I am not foolishly interfering in someone else's love story again."

Nino swallows, his throat tight from the image of his friend sitting there in the firelight, waiting for his answer. "You're not. I promise."

Haruka finally looks up at him and Nino takes a breath. He'd genuinely forgotten to.

"Nino, I deeply value our relationship. I have never experienced anything like this with another vampire."

"Me neither," says Nino, unmoving. Waiting.

Dropping his shoulders, Haruka lifts his head to the ceiling. "I am worried that if we are intimate, our relationship will change and we will lose this... our friendship. I sincerely do not want that to happen."

Slowly, Nino scoots a few inches down the bed and toward him. "Things will change. But... what if the changes are good? What if our relationship gets even better?"

Haruka shifts his burgundy eyes to slyly meet his gaze. One corner of his mouth quirks up. "You are a romantic."

"Maybe?" Nino hunches his shoulders. He smoothly moves down the bed until one leg is folded and lightly touching Haruka's hip, the other hanging off the side of the mattress. "We won't know unless we try? And we can go slowly."

Haruka exhales a heavy sigh and folds his arms. Nino sits quietly. Breathing for a long moment and steeling himself as a simple question pushes to the forefront of his psyche. "Haru, do you find me attractive? I mean physically or within your nature... Are you drawn to me?"

He turns, his wine-colored eyes unblinking. "You are exquisite to my nature. In *every* way." Haruka looks forward again, as if he's simply uttered a statement of fact and not something that has knocked the wind out of Nino.

He wants to tell Haruka he feels the same way—that being with him... talking, laughing and researching with him feels like getting a gift on some special occasion. A birthday or a favorite holiday where plans have been made and anticipation bubbles warmly in your heart.

But there are no plans. There are no gifts. It's just Haruka. He is all there is and nothing more is needed.

He can't say any of it. He won't. Haruka hears these things all the time from desperate vampires who want to bond with him. Saying these things will make Nino seem as shallow and needy as the rest of them.

"Nino."

"Yes?" Nino sits straighter, his eyes focusing on the dark male in front of him. The longer they sit here, the more Nino realizes how much he wants him. Not just as a friend, but as more. To be closer to him, freely touch him and hold him. To comfort Haruka and give of himself. Even more, Nino wants to feed from him and feel his true aura. To fully experience the lovely thing inside of him that he constantly keeps restrained and locked up so tightly.

"I think..." Haruka begins, taking a deep breath. "If you feel that I am acceptable, I would like to try. But you should not feel pressured in any way—"

"Stop." Nino reaches out, placing his hands on either side of Haruka's slim face and meeting his eyes. Pure bliss swells in his chest. "You are so much more than 'acceptable' to me. And yes, I want to try, too. Let's just do what feels natural?"

"Natural..." Haruka shifts his eyes to the side, mulling it over. "I like this. Agreed." He rests his fingertips against Nino's chest, gently urging him to lie back against the bed. Nino complies, biting his lip in a weak attempt to stifle his overwhelming excitement.

It's happening. The pounce.

He watches in awe as his friend moves like a shadowy, wild animal gorgeously lit by firelight. He slowly crawls onto the bed, settling himself at Nino's side. Nino instinctively relaxes back, fully trusting in whatever is about to happen to him. He needs it. He desperately wants it with this beautiful male.

Haruka never takes his alluring burgundy gaze off of him as he sweetly rests his palm against his cheek. Nino closes his eyes from the simple contact, feeling his nature twist and writhe in his belly and lower back.

"It will not hurt," Haruka says, his voice low and calm. "You know this?"

Nino grins, opening his eyes. "If it's you, I know it won't hurt."

"You should relax. I will feed from you as usual, but gradually, I will pull harder at your skin." With his fingertip, he draws a line down Nino's jaw toward the base of his neck. Nino stretches the bottom of his spine against the soft bed, trying to ease the warm shiver there.

"When I feed deeper," Haruka continues, "you'll feel a distinct pressure in your abdomen to submit to me, but try not to do so. You should resist me for as long as you can. The release will be more satisfying for you this way."

Nino laughs, already thinking this might not last very long. "I apologize in advance if I give in too early."

"It's okay," Haruka assures him. "If you do, perhaps we could simply try again another time. Are we ready?"

Stretching his overheated body against the downy comforter, Nino wishes Haruka would shift over and lie on top of him. His groin aches from the thought of his weight and long body pressed against him as he feeds... but he probably shouldn't look a gift horse in the mouth.

"I'm ready."

Haruka leans across his chest, then licks the concave of Nino's neck—just as he does whenever he feeds. This time, the feeling behind it is different somehow. Intentional. Seductive. Nino closes his eyes, taking in every moment, every second of this experience that he's been waiting for.

Nino gasps when Haruka softly bites into his neck. His sleek fangs press deeper into his skin and Nino exhales, instinctively sliding his fingers into the back of his friend's dark, silky hair. Haruka pulls. Just as it had before, something innate stirs deeply within Nino's being. It moves, sending flashes of heat throughout his entire body. It's telling him to trust and let go—to set his nature free and submit.

Haruka sucks harder at his flesh. The sensation feels so warm and good that a deep groan escapes Nino's parted lips. He slides one hand from Haruka's hair, down past his shoulders to rest against his spine.

This thing that Haruka is doing feels primal—sensual. He can't see it, but Nino can inherently feel him using his mind to pull and gently urge, twist and coax his nature from him. It's as if Haruka is sweetly enticing a timid thing out of its deep hiding place. The very thing that defines Nino's vampiric essence.

When Haruka pulls again, the thing inside Nino pulses hot—threatening to release. Nino arches his lower back in another gasp, gripping Haruka's crisp shirt in his fist. With his eyes burning brightly and his breathing labored, he decides to trust in the sensation overwhelming him. He relaxes his body and allows Haruka to take it from him.

Like wildfire, the warmth and energy of his aura rush from his abdomen and up the length of his spine. It releases from every pore and fiber of Nino's being. It feels as if his aura and everything within him is being flipped inside out, and he moans from the sublime pleasure and liberation of it. The sensation grips him like an intense, emotional orgasm. Nino has never experienced anything so all consuming—so completely gratifying—in his long life.

He stares in awe as the glow of his golden aura encircles them, tenderly wrapping itself around Haruka. He pulls his mouth from Nino and breathes in sharply, then closes his eyes. The room is filled with dazzling light. Nino's heart is still racing as he takes in the abundance of sensations.

The light of his aura slowly dissipates, fading like the soft glimmer of a firefly as it burns out. Nino's irises are still glowing, his body hot and trembling as he watches Haruka. His friend's eyes are closed, but Nino feels overwhelmed with affection for him. For who he is and for the incredible feeling he's given him. Smelling his milky-almond, rosy skin and sensing his tightly knotted aura... If Haruka were a lake, Nino would swim in him and submerge himself. Happily drowning in him.

He has given of himself. Nino has wrapped Haruka in all that he is—his very composition as a vampiric entity. Now, Nino's body yearns for something in return. Anything from this enigmatic creature lying beside him.

Closing his burning eyes, Nino lifts his chin. He drags his tongue up the edge of Haruka's jawline. Just to taste him. To have *something*. His skin is cool and sweet—raindrops on fresh cherries or clean earth and roses. Perfect. Delicious. Haruka opens his scarlet eyes, quietly staring down at him.

Still mindless with pleasure and need, Nino lifts his chin again, this time pressing his mouth into him.

Soft. Haruka's mouth... It puckers. Naturally. Nino has privately taken note of this across their interactions. His lips aren't pouty, not thick or full... but the way he holds his mouth and the supple curve of his lips feels like a subtle invitation. Maybe a dare. One that Nino has always adamantly ignored but doesn't now.

The feel of his mouth on Haruka's is dizzying, but he opens his eyes and pulls back when he senses him smiling against the kiss. The dark purebred is watching him, his glowing irises seductive in the firelit room. Slowly, Haruka dips and tilts his head, tenderly catching his mouth once more.

Nino parts his lips and caresses Haruka's bottom lip with the tip of his tongue. He feels Haruka open wider to him, inviting Nino inside to deepen the intimacy and explore in this unchartered territory. He does. Angling his head and slowly dipping into the cool, earthy sweetness of him. His tongue finally slides and twists with Haruka's. Wet, smooth and satiating. Nino breathes a sigh against the kiss, gripping his fingers in his thick, silky hair.

This is heaven. He has never given heaven much thought. Never questioned whether or not it exists, but this is it. Here, in the warm firelight of this bedroom and kissing Haruka, is absolute paradise.

Just as Nino is beginning to feel hyper aware of the fact that he is fully clothed (and questioning the material's fundamental purpose), Haruka pulls away from the kiss.

"It is late," Haruka says quietly, his gaze affectionate. "Should I return to my own room?"

With his fingers still tangled in his hair, Nino smiles, rubbing his fingertips against Haruka's scalp. "I think you should go get comfortable and then sleep in here with me? If you're okay with that."

Haruka nods. "I would like that."

TWENTY-EIGHT

Haruka wakes up disoriented the following morning. Where is he? What time is it and whose life is he suddenly living?

His face is halfway swallowed by a large pillow as he opens his eyes. He doesn't move. Instead, he breathes in. The delectable, smoky and cinnamon-laced scent of Nino pours into him, drowning his senses in the most satisfying way. He rolls onto his belly under the warm comforter and shifts his face directly into the pillow.

Haruka inhales deeply, then exhales a loud, contented groan. He smiles against the puffy material.

Pulling Nino's aura from his body the previous night... He cannot easily describe it. Simple words are inadequate—useless in painting the exquisite masterpiece that is Nino's essence. Maybe if he tried in Latin, or arranged a new language entirely? He has pulled Yuna's aura in the past. Many, many times. But the experience of releasing her aura versus Nino's? The two events are incomparable.

It was like magic. Fizzy, bright and golden. Champagne inexplicably laced with fire. The energy had rushed from

Nino's body like a spell. It was so pure and filled with deep affection, it was almost cleansing as it warmly caressed and wrapped itself around Haruka's frame. It had intentionally enclosed him, as if it were seeking his own aura within him—a beautiful entity desperately searching for its long-lost friend.

Haruka's nature had unexpectedly responded, pounding fiercely within him. He'd needed to stop feeding from Nino to concentrate, otherwise his nature would have unwrapped itself from its imposed knot and rushed from his body.

The bedroom door creaks open and Haruka lifts his head from the pillow. Sensing Nino there, he sits upright. The overcast sun washes the room in cool, filtered lighting. Nino is fully dressed, his coppery waves neatly swept back and his sides freshly tapered. To Haruka, his handsome friend always appears effortlessly stylish and casual. Unassuming, as if he'd innocently stepped off the pages of a men's lifestyle magazine.

"Good morning," Haruka says, rubbing his palms down his face.

"Good *afternoon.*" Nino frowns, pouting.

"What time is it?"

"Twelve forty-five."

Confused, Haruka scratches the back of his head. His hair is standing straight out instead of lying flat. He can't imagine how ridiculous he looks. "Why did you not wake me?"

"I *tried.*" Nino's eyes widen as he walks into the room and toward his corner desk. "You scared the hell out of me this morning. Your body was ice cold and you wouldn't budge no matter what I did."

Haruka laughs as he drops his hands from his meager attempt to quell his hair. "If I expend much energy, sometimes I need to sleep deeply to compensate for the loss of it."

"I know that now," Nino says, bending and unplugging his laptop from the wall. "I called Asao because I was worried and he told me. I thought I was going to wake up and have a nice, cozy morning with you—but instead I woke up next to a corpse."

After feeding deeply from Nino the night before, Haruka thought he might not have needed the recuperation time. Perhaps withholding his aura during the feeding had expended an additional amount of his energy?

"I apologize, Nino. Is it too late for us to establish a more appropriate morning greeting?"

Nino pauses with his laptop and plug wrapped in his arms. He grins, then walks toward him. When he's at the side of the bed, Haruka lifts his face. Nino bends down and places two swift kisses on his mouth. "Hi."

"Good afternoon," Haruka says, feeling the warmth of his affection for Nino glowing all throughout his body. Somehow, and even though they established the intimacy only a few hours earlier, kissing Nino feels completely natural. Like doing something one way when a different way may have been better all along.

Nino stands straight, contented. "I'm grateful you're not dead."

"It would take a considerable amount of starvation and trauma for me to truly die. You need not worry."

"Right." Nino smirks, walking backward toward the door. "We need to get these intent surveys stuffed and mailed out today. G will be back tomorrow, and he'll definitely want to drag you all around Milan to introduce you to everyone. Let's work in his office in the main house, since the formal seal and supplies are down there. Can you meet me after you're dressed?"

"Of course," Haruka says, obedient.

"Let Luciano know if you need coffee or anything. I'll see you downstairs?"

"I will be there shortly."

Nino closes the door. Haruka stretches his arms up in a yawn. He cannot remember the last time he's felt so healthy, rested and generally alive.

WHEN HARUKA eventually walks into Giovanni's elegant office in the main house, Nino has organized and laid everything out to accomplish their work for the day: surveys printed on parchment paper, a stack of corresponding envelopes, a wax seal and calligraphy tools to stamp the documents with the Bianchi Clan's crest.

Nino has been busy this morning—drafting professional letters to introduce themselves and their research objectives. He's also composed a second page with the agreed-upon survey questions. Fifty letters are already personally addressed to vampire couples across Florence, Milan and Venice. At present, Giovanni has acquired a list of three hundred contacts, and according to Nino, his brother will soon communicate with the purebred leaders of Rome and Sicily.

Throughout the afternoon, they type and address more letters, then stuff and seal envelopes while discussing potential next steps should the surveys yield the desired information. Nino also suggests that they rearrange the older articles of *Lore and Lust* so that the sections are further classified by each vampire couple's rank. Haruka isn't sure if he is willing to commit to this. It sounds like a lot of work. As such, he will inevitably procrastinate.

"I think it'd be much easier to find specific entries if we reorganized it," Nino proposes. He is sitting at his brother's desk and typing on his laptop. "Then, maybe you could consider having it reprinted? Maybe even distributed? What if Gael told other vampires and they come after you, too?"

Leaning back against the soft leather sofa, Haruka folds his arms. The low coffee table in front of him is cluttered with papers, stacks of envelopes and the wax seal. "My hope is that Gael's reaction to the research is the exception and not the rule. Mass distribution is tricky since the information in the manuscript is sensitive. It is a matter of privacy."

Nino shrugs. "We can change the names to numbers? Or only use first names? I just think valuable research should be shared. Why keep all this insight a secret? And you don't even oversee a realm right now to help other vampires if they have questions."

Haruka raises his eyebrow. In the silence, Nino glances up from his laptop. He smiles, sheepish. "Obviously this is not a criticism. I've never overseen anything other than my bar and right now I'm not even doing that." He laughs, scratching his head before he goes on.

"What I'm saying is, maybe other realm leaders—*good* ones, vampires that are reputable and trustworthy—would benefit from receiving a copy of this? G told me he'd love to see it, and my father's eyes practically bulged out of his head when I told him about it. I think the book has the potential to benefit the population. Like a roadmap to bonding. Maybe it'll help put everyone's fears at ease?"

Everyone's fears. The decline in purebreds. A lack of successfully mated couples, and therefore, a deficit in thriving purebred families. Much hysteria, all rooted in bonding. It amazes Haruka. From his perspective, bonding was the biggest mistake of his life. "I understand your argument." He sighs. "Let me have some time to consider it."

"Sure, no pressure." Nino looks down at his laptop and continues typing. "Just offering an alternative perspective.

Speaking of my father, I think he wants to talk to you again sometime before you leave. He really enjoyed meeting you the other night."

"It would be my pleasure."

Domenico Bianchi is gray and weak in his vampiric aura. Still, an undeniable air of dignity radiates strongly from the sophisticated male. To survive the loss of a mate is extremely rare considering your primary, practically bespoke source of nourishment is cut off when they perish. To be so dependent upon someone then have them disappear can create great trauma for a bonded vampire's complex biology.

"Nino, I hope that I do not come across as callous, but how has your father survived this long without his mate?"

"Well. It's... kind of complicated."

Silence. Haruka blinks. Nino is always exceptionally transparent, so this rare instance of confidentiality feels odd. "Alright, understood."

"I'm sorry, Haru. But I can tell you that he misses Mom a lot. I guess I favor her in some subtle ways, so he talks about her whenever I sit with him... which isn't as much as I should, but..." Nino shrugs.

Haruka isn't certain, but when he had sat with Nino and Domenico, he noticed that the dynamic of their relationship felt odd. Nino's father had seemed very grateful to have them both sitting there, as if he didn't usually receive guests.

"Do you not visit your father often?" Haruka asks. If his own father were alive, Haruka feels certain that he'd still be living in Japan. Perhaps he never would have left. His father had been an incredibly loving and doting vampire.

"I don't." Nino sits back in his chair. "Our relationship is a little strained. G would be mad if he heard me say this out loud, but remember I told you that my uncle attacked me?"

"Of course."

"He and my father were identical twins, so the dynamic of the entire situation was uncomfortable. I didn't tell you this, but the reason my uncle stopped feeding from me was because my mother walked into my room one day and saw him doing it. No questions asked, she went primal. She literally ripped his throat out right in front of me. I'd never seen that side of her before. It was terrifying."

Haruka keeps his breathing even as he digests the horrific details of Nino's childhood.

Nino stands from the desk, then moves toward the couch to sit beside him. "After Mom died, Father just... I don't know. He's hands-off with me. I think it's guilt? He's never pressured me to do anything or encouraged me to learn the aristocracy or socially engage. I ended up keeping to myself—*lots* of time with private tutors or on my own, indulging in human pop culture. But Father pressures and restricts *the hell* out of Giovanni, which of course creates tension between G and me... and there's some more weird tension because G *really* likes Cellina, but she feeds me. Soooo that's the story of my messy family!"

"The situation is indeed multifaceted," says Haruka. "But perhaps any complex, emotional relationship is guaranteed to have some element of... messiness?"

Nino breathes a laugh. He gently bumps his thigh against Haruka's as they sit close on the couch. "Do you think we'll be messy?"

Haruka shakes his head. "I don't know."

Nino points to the table and frowns. "You're already messy so it's probably inevitable. *Look* at this. What are you doing? How is this organized?"

"It is a controlled chaos."

"It is not." Nino chuckles as he straightens the table. "We need to keep the piles straight, not 'spontaneous'... Are there ink smudges on these envelopes—"

Haruka leans into him, stealthily sliding his fingers onto his leg until they follow the curve inside Nino's thigh. He hasn't used his energy at all, but Nino is suddenly motionless, his eyes blinking. Haruka caresses the tip of his nose along Nino's smooth jawline, then leans down to lick the concave of his neck. His honeyed skin pulses warm and salty. Haruka wishes he could feed from him again, but it's too soon since he fed deeply the night before.

"I express spontaneity in many ways." Haruka kisses the spot he licked. Then again, firmly pressing his lips into the elegant curve just beneath his jaw. Nino softly inhales as he slides his fingers higher up his thigh. "Is this also unacceptable?" Haruka asks between kisses.

Nino still doesn't speak, but his eyes shift, glowing with bright golden light. Haruka grins, pleased. He knowingly allows himself to indulge. Just a little. He slides his fingertips closer toward the firm bulge between Nino's thighs. "You were so garrulous just a moment ago, but now nothing?"

There's a knock at the door to the outer room. Haruka casually removes his hand from inside Nino's thigh. He sits back and folds his arms just as a maidservant appears beneath the archway. She bows.

"Apologies, my lords. Master Giovanni has returned early from his trip. He wishes that the three of you would go to Porta Romana for dinner tonight. The attire is semi-formal."

The maidservant looks to them both. Nino is leaning forward, his elbows against his thighs and his palms massaging his face. The maidservant raises her eyebrow. "Your grace?"

"Yeah, *okay*," Nino says, his voice muffled. "Tell him we said okay."

TWENTY-NINE

A couple days later, Nino is sitting at a tall, sleek black table in a fashionable restaurant. He glances toward the bar area. A beautiful floating shelf filled and lined with leafy green palms hangs above the bartenders as they work. Tall potted plants have also been tastefully placed along the glass walls, giving the delicate impression that he is eating lunch outside in a tropical garden rather than within an enclosed space.

It's impressive, but his business mind wonders how much time and money it costs to maintain all these plants.

When he senses Cellina nearing the restaurant, he looks up toward the door. A moment later, she enters. Nino beams. Cellina never just walks. She saunters—confident, like a creature that knows its beauty and worth. Her tightly coiled auburn hair is swept up in a bun to emphasize her dramatic earrings. She is wearing light jeans that perfectly hug her fit curves, a deep teal sweater and a fashionable, oversized beige coat. As always, she looks impeccable.

Nino stands when she reaches him and wraps her up in a tight hug. She's carrying a pink bakery box that he recognizes.

"Ciao bella—is this for me?" he asks, releasing her.

She sits on the other side of the table. When she's comfortable, Cellina slides the box across the smooth surface and looks up at him from beneath her dark lashes. "A peace offering."

"For telling me to go to that miserable party and then ditching me?"

She pouts. "Nino."

"I'm not mad," he says. "But I'll take the cannoli anyway. Chocolate cherry?"

"Of course." Cellina winks.

When Nino thinks about that night at Moretti's estate, it turns out it was a blessing in disguise. The tumultuous evening had somehow brought him and Haruka even closer.

Cellina leans onto the table with her elbows, cradling her chin in her palms. "You smell like you've made some significant progress with your handsome friend."

Nino turns his head and lifts his arm to sniff his coat. "G said that as soon as he saw me the other day. I can't smell anything."

"Well, the purpose is to let *other* vampires know that you are off the market as a feeding source. That you're being taken care of."

Nino smirks. "Is that why you never let me feed deeply from you? So you were always free to shop around?"

"Don't be stupid." She waves her hand. "What's going on? Give me the *scoop*. He finally pulled your aura, yeah?"

"He did. It was better than any sex I've ever had."

Cellina laughs and claps her hands, bubbling with delight as a waiter approaches to take their drink orders. When he walks away, Cellina coolly runs her hand up her hair, patting her large bun. "I'm so happy for you, Nino—you *need* this. The actual sex will be phenomenal."

Nino's entire lower half stiffens. He takes a breath to calm the arousal. "Lina... Jesus."

"It *will*." She smiles warmly. "You two are gorgeous together, like perfect bookends. Sunlight and moonlight. Jupiter and Mars... Mercutio and Romeo."

"Cheesy." Nino frowns. "They weren't a couple."

"Maybe they should have been? So talk. I'm listening."

He considers for a moment, allowing the charming image of Haruka to flood his mind. "We're just... taking it slow and doing whatever feels natural. It's unbelievable, Lina, I never—I don't know. I never imagined that I would meet someone like him. It sounds cliché but being with Haru is so easy and comfortable, and now..."

Nino stops to think again, the warmth in his heart overwhelming him.

"And now?" Cellina gently prompts.

"He's opening up. In a new way. It's slow, but I'm seeing more of this... seductive and frisky side of him that I didn't expect. He's still being careful, but a lot less formal and rigid than he was when we first met. Maybe... this is the real him? When he's comfortable..."

Cellina sits straight and smooths her hair again. "Ugh, I am eating this shit *up*. This is amazing."

Nino laughs. "I'm glad you're entertained. You know what I told him? He's like a black panther. He's watching me and taking his time thinking, prowling around me in a circle with those wine-colored eyes."

"Mm, if he's a panther then you're a tiger."

"Can you please stop?"

"When is the panther going to start feeding you?" Cellina leans against the table, folding her arms as she rests. "Am I off the hook today?"

Nino frowns. "Have you been *on* the hook? Am I troubling you?" The waiter returns to the table with their drinks and appetizers. He lingers a little longer than necessary, smiling and chatting in Cellina's direction. When he walks away, he winks at her.

"Of course you're not," says Cellina. "But if he's seducing you, pulling your aura, and you enjoy these things, he should feed you. You feed *him*. Don't you want his blood?"

He sighs. Nino wants his blood like a hungry wolf wants meat. His body is aching for it. He ignores the feeling as best he can, but the longing burns hot from the inside out. He leans forward with his elbows on the table, running his hands into his hair as he drops his head. "I want *everything* from him. I want all of him."

For the first time, he admits it aloud and to himself. The quiet truth has been acknowledged. He can't keep pretending otherwise.

"So..." Cellina says. "You want to bond with him?"

"I just want to be with him. I love having him close like this and always talking to him. I want to touch him and I don't want any more boundaries between us. If all that means forming a bond then *yes*."

Cellina pouts in a sigh. "But he doesn't want to bond."

"Right," Nino says, his head still low and pounding.

"You can only go so far."

Nino nods in his hunched position. He doesn't know exactly how far because they haven't discussed it. But there is absolutely, unequivocally a limit.

"He's been traumatized by having a bond break," Cellina muses. "I mean, it's *unheard* of. The fact that he even survived something like that. Wow... Did he talk to you any more about it?"

Nino lazily sits upright. "He did. He told me what happened."

"I think that's a positive sign, Nino. Don't be so down-hearted. You two are making beautiful progress, so just keep being patient and let him heal. He used to hide in his house all the time, but now he's here in Milan, *with you*. And I think he's damn lucky to have you. Most vampires are horny jerks these days. With that rosy aura he keeps wrapped up, he's like a magnet."

"You're right. Thanks, Lina."

"Has he ever let it rest for you?" she asks. "His aura?"

"Not intentionally, no."

Cellina picks up her cocktail and takes a quick sip. She makes a face that tells Nino she is pleasantly surprised by its contents. "I think he will. He trusts you. It's inevitable. Whether he wants it to or not it'll probably just slip out. His blood feels even older than mine, so it's probably potent. You better be ready for that shit." She takes a bigger sip of her cocktail.

Nino smiles. "You mean your *mother's* blood—that 'two-thousand-year-old Tanzanian royalty' blood?"

Cellina pulls her glass from her lips and lifts her chin in a proud smirk. "Damn straight."

Nino laughs. "G keeps asking me when you're coming by the house again."

"Tell your brother to mind his own fucking business."

"He has a lot of business already." Nino scrunches his nose, teasing. "He's busy but he's always asking me about you."

"Well he needs a hobby. He made it very clear a long time ago that he wants nothing to do with me."

"Lina..." Nino shakes his head, sighing. "Everything that happened... Honestly, I think G feels—"

"Nino, are we here to enjoy lunch together or talk about

your brother? Because if it's the latter, there are about twenty other things I could be doing."

Understanding loud and clear, Nino picks up his own drink. He knows when to quit. "Got it. How was your interview the other night? Have you heard back?"

THIRTY

By the time Haruka returns to the Milan estate, takes a shower and changes into his night clothes, it is well past one o'clock in the morning. Giovanni had taken him to see the symphony at Teatro alla Scala, followed by a late dinner and drinks with the orchestra's second-generation vampire conductor. The evening had been truly lovely, and much unlike his experience at Hertsmonceux, Haruka is genuinely enjoying the vampires of the Milan aristocracy.

He knocks quietly against Nino's bedroom door. No answer. He cracks it open and steps inside. The room is dark. Even moonlight is scarce tonight as Haruka moves toward the bed. Nino is resting comfortably on his side underneath the heavy comforter. Haruka slides into the bed behind him. "I'm back," he whispers.

Nino inhales deeply, his eyes still closed. He exhales his sleepy response. "Bentornato, amore mio."

Haruka pauses, his smile broadening and his heart beating warm in his chest. *Welcome back, my love.* Nino has never addressed him so affectionately before. He likes it. "Sono il tuo amore?" *Am I your love?*

"Mm." Nino's eyes are still closed, his breathing even. He's silent.

Haruka slips his arm underneath Nino's and cradles his chest. As he envelopes him, Nino naturally shifts back into the warmth of his body. When they're settled, Haruka softly kisses his neck, drawing a line down his spine to the curve of his shoulder.

With the passing of each day, Haruka feels starved for him. As if feeding deeply from Nino is only teasing a profound desire within him. He needs more, and he is gradually losing sight of himself and his strict control over his nature.

Has he ever truly allowed himself to let go? To acknowledge his innate desires, release his aura and embrace the vampire that he is designed to be? To submit to the thing inside him that is fueled by his ancient bloodline—explicitly made to lure and entice, to give and receive much pleasure.

To love deeply and be loved.

Being with Nino progressively stirs that entity. Haruka has never fully accepted this part of himself. Not even when he was bonded. Then, he had tried, but was told that he was at times "overwhelming." As such, he has always focused on the aspects of himself that are outwardly tangible. His talents and expertise. His dignity and civility. What would happen if he indulged for once? If he finally gave in to the deep passion within himself and trusted someone?

THE SUN RISES and Nino finally stirs. Haruka is lying beside him, waiting. He is lazily running his fingers through the soft coppery waves atop his head. Nino slowly opens his eyes as he rests on his back, the morning light making his amber irises even more captivating. He grins. "Hey."

"Good morning."

Nino's handsome brow furrows. "You're not usually up this early. Did you sleep?"

"Some. My mind was preoccupied. Are you going for a run this morning?"

"Preoccupied?" He yawns and stretches his spine. "I don't think so. I usually run five days in a row before I take a break, but yesterday was six. I should probably let my body rest."

Leaning down, Haruka softly presses their mouths together. He only lingers for a moment before pulling away and gazing into Nino's peaceful face. "I will help with this."

He sits upright, shifting the heavy covers off of them as he straddles Nino's thighs. His friend is wide-eyed as Haruka presses his hands to Nino's waist, then urges his nightshirt up to expose his taut, honey abdomen. His skin is perfectly clear and gorgeous. The delicately sculpted muscles and dusty, golden-coppery hairs there make Haruka's mouth water.

Understanding, Nino grabs the hem of his shirt, lifts and swiftly yanks it over his head. When his upper body is fully exposed, Haruka breathes his cinnamon essence, simply taking him in. Nino's voice is almost a whisper. "Haru, what are we doing?"

Haruka's eyes glow to life, his nature twisting with want in his core. "May I feed?"

"Of course," Nino breathes.

Haruka moves again, this time encouraging Nino to spread his thighs. Nino lifts his knees, his chest rapidly rising and falling. Haruka settles between his gaped legs, resting himself low so that his face hovers just above his belly. He can feel the hardness of Nino's arousal against his chest as he leans down to lick his stomach. He hungrily drags his tongue up Nino's salty flesh, following the deep definition of tight muscle to the right of his navel.

He bites down into Nino's abdomen, feeling it clench underneath his mouth as he pulls. Nino's blood is woodsy and spicy as he swallows and breathes. In exchange, Haruka pours his gratefulness and desire into Nino's body. He drinks deeper, sensing the metaphysical border of his intrinsic nature. Nino moans loudly as he exhales, shifting his firm body underneath him in his pleasure. The movement only encourages Haruka, and he sucks hard again, willing the handsome male to let go and submit to him.

Nino trembles and breathes Haruka's name in ecstasy as his aura releases. Yet again, the rush and heat of it is effervescent and full of life—pure and golden. It encloses Haruka's body like a warm cocoon, making him pull his mouth from Nino's stomach in a gasp. Haruka's knotted aura is pulsing and threatening to break free. Nino's bright energy embraces him tightly, urging him to release what is inside of him—to allow the two entities to meet and entwine together.

Pressing his forehead down to Nino's belly, he clenches his eyes shut. Out of habit, he forces the knot within him to tighten. He can't let go. He isn't ready.

"Haru?"

The bubbly pressure of Nino's aura subsides. Haruka lifts his head, blinking. He takes a deep breath, registering the rush of Nino's blood swirling throughout and nourishing his body. When Haruka looks up at him, his beautiful chest is still rising and falling from shortened breaths. His face looks unsettled.

"Did I hurt you?" Haruka asks, troubled by his expression.

"No—I..." He runs his palm down his face. "That was amazing but... I—You should probably get up. I need to—I should clean up."

Haruka frowns, not following. He shifts against Nino's

body to sit up, then pauses. He understands. Haruka looks at him, his eyes patient. "Nino, you do not need to be ashamed of your body's reaction. This is natural."

"Right, okay. But if you get up, I can go take care of it really quick."

They only watch each other for a moment before Haruka swiftly wraps his fingers inside the waist of Nino's pajama pants, then smoothly urges them down around the curve of his ass and to his thighs. Nino protests in shock as Haruka quickly sits up and pulls the cotton pants down and off his body, tossing them onto the floor.

Haruka immediately settles back down between Nino's long, tanned legs. Without hesitation, he eagerly licks up the inside of his firm thigh. Nino writhes and swears while Haruka diligently cleans his body, lazily dragging his tongue across Nino's skin where his raw release has settled. Every aspect of this purebred tastes divine—his woodsy, spicy essence resonating strongly all throughout his body.

When he grips Nino's shaft, he considers briefly, but only licks and cleans the tip. His nature within him is already twisting and threatening to voluntarily release. It is taking considerable effort to keep it constrained. Plus, they need to be careful. Haruka sighs. *This will not be easy.*

When he's finished, he slowly crawls and kisses up the center of Nino's tight stomach and chest—fully indulging in his sumptuous body. He presses his lips to the nape of his neck before finally hovering over Nino's handsome face. Haruka smirks. "In truth, it was *my* mess to clean up."

"*Jesus.*"

"I felt strongly that I should take responsibility for my actions."

Nino's eyes are filled with something. Stress? Trepidation? He reaches up and twists his fingers into his coppery waves.

Looking down at his naked body in the morning light and against the soft white sheets, Haruka blinks, suddenly afraid that he has gone too far. He has lost his composure and acted without thinking. Has he read this situation incorrectly? Is this something Nino wanted?

He sits up slightly, his face very serious. "Nino, have I overwhelmed you? If—if I have overstepped my boundaries I sincerely—"

"*Don't.*"

Nino reaches out and threads his fingers into Haruka's hair, pulling him back down toward his face. "No—I... *Don't* be polite right now. I'm fine, Haru, I just..." He takes a breath before lifting his chin and pulling Haruka down into a firm kiss. He immediately parts his lips, urging Haruka inside. Haruka accepts the invitation and Nino promptly meets his tongue, licking and stroking into him with want. With urgency.

Their previous kisses were cautious, sweet. They were carefully learning each other and politely walking this new line between friends and lovers.

This kiss is different. Passionate—ravenous and seeped in unspoken need. It's as if Nino desperately wishes to convey something to Haruka that he cannot say with words.

Haruka rests his body down against his him, exhaling a muffled moan from the satisfaction of his own arousal being pressed into Nino's naked warmth. They slow the rhythm of the kiss, the affection turning more playful as they lie together against the cool sheets.

Nino slides his hands underneath Haruka's shirt and up the center of his back. When his palms rest firmly at his spine, Nino softly breaks the kiss. "Should we... Can I take care of you?" He slowly lifts and rolls his hips up and into Haruka, acknowledging his hardness between them.

Haruka shakes his head. "You take care of me by feeding

me, and I simply enjoy being with you like this. But I would like for us to talk about something. Are you free today?"

"You're the busy one... running around town and going on dates with my brother."

"*Not* dates." Haruka frowns, sitting upright. "However, in spending time with him, perhaps I have come to a conclusion. Separately, why is Giovanni unbonded?"

Nino pauses briefly, then pushes himself upright as well. He is suddenly anxious as he looks around the room. "My brother's situation is complicated. Sorry, Haru. What's your conclusion? And where did you throw my pants?"

THIRTY-ONE

Haruka shamelessly watches Nino's long, naked frame as he scoots from the bed, swiftly grabs the discarded pajama pants from the floor and disappears into his closet. He hadn't intended to completely undress Nino when he instigated things, but he is not ungrateful that it has happened. His beautiful, golden-honey body is lean but perfectly sculpted, like an exquisite work of art that he would like to devour.

He shakes his head, focusing and ignoring the hot pulse in his groin. "The situation in Brazil is causing much restlessness among our race—across many aristocracies."

"I don't understand," Nino says from inside his closet. "What's happening in Brazil feels isolated to me. Whatever the argument is over there, it's *over there*. Nothing is being reported in any other geographical aristocracy, so why is everyone focusing on this?"

Haruka shifts to the top of the bed, relaxing his back against the headboard and folding his legs. "The concern is that the discontent will spread to other communities. Much of the conflict comes from Ladislao's lack of diplomacy—his lack of balance and leadership. He ignores his kin and their concerns, and left to their own devices, this uprising has formed. I know that you dislike hearing it, but on an admittedly smaller scale, this environment is similar to the events preceding the Vanishing. As I have met with many members of the Milan aristocracy, they share my opinion of the situation."

Nino walks out of the closet wearing soft-looking sweatpants and a long-sleeved shirt that drapes his square shoulders. He sits on the bed beside Haruka.

"That being said," Haruka continues, sighing, "I feel that I should consider returning home."

Nino's eyes widen. "Really?"

"I believe it is irresponsible of me to leave my family's realm unattended given this increasingly tumultuous environment."

"When would you go back?"

"I'm not sure... I wanted to discuss this decision with you." Haruka reaches over. He entwines their fingers together as their hands comfortably rest against Nino's thigh. "You are my true friend and source, and now my lover. Your opinion is weighted heavily in this situation. You are also my research partner."

Haruka smiles and waits, but Nino doesn't speak. The amber vampire sighs heavily as he runs the fingers of his free hand through his hair. Sensing his distress, Haruka holds his hand a little tighter. "To be clear, it is *not* my intention for us to end our relationship. This is not a farewell conversation."

"How can we continue as we are if you move back to Japan?" Nino's beautiful eyes are naked in their anguish. "I can't feed you if we're in different countries."

"Correct. Which means that I would need to secure another resource. But this is not so uncommon, Nino.

Unbonded vampires feed from multiple sources in a lifetime, sometimes simultaneously."

"But you can't just feed from any random vampire, Haru." Nino frowns, shaking his head. "You need consistency and high quality because of your bloodline. If you get another Elsie, your body chemistry and nature will be all messed up again."

"Feeding *aside*..." Haruka grins. "How should we maintain our working and personal relationship? Would you be willing to visit me? Once I am settled and if your schedule allows? Please do not feel pressured to—"

"Of *course* I'll visit you. I think... If you wanted me to, maybe I could..."

Haruka waits, but no words follow. "Yes?"

"I... I don't know." Nino drops his shoulders. He rests back against the headboard. "Maybe as we collect more surveys from couples across international communities, we could meet in different places? Like research vacations together."

"The phrase 'research vacation' feels oxymoronic, but I understand your intent. I would like this very much."

A peaceful silence settles between them, their hands firmly clasped. The clouds shift, allowing the sun to shine a little brighter through the skylights.

"So..." Nino breaks the silence. "We'll just be apart then."

Haruka takes a breath, nodding. The sadness of the statement weighs heavily in his chest. He doesn't want to be apart from Nino, but he should return to his realm. He has been running away from his responsibilities for seventy years.

The irony is that Nino has been the primary catalyst in strengthening and healing Haruka. But in doing so, they will now be separated.

"I don't want us to be apart." Nino lowers his head, staring down at his thighs. "Is there any way for us to stay together? Would you want that?"

Haruka swallows, his throat tight. "I do want that. But Nino, I would never ask you to uproot your life and established business for me, especially considering... I cannot promise you that we would form a bond."

"That's fine," Nino says, meeting his eyes. "I've never thought about living in Japan, but now that I am, it might be interesting for me. I can start a business anywhere."

Haruka's heart is light. His nature twists with joy rather than the usual angst or turmoil. But is this too much to ask of Nino? Should he discourage him? Even as the doubts float across his mind, he wants to ignore them. Maybe he is selfish, but he wants this very much.

"The only problem," Nino says, his gaze downcast once more, "is finding a new source. Once you're in charge, will you help me find someone we can trust that can nourish me?"

Nodding, Haruka quietly makes a decision. "I will take care of this. Once I am settled, you should visit. If you find that western Japan is pleasing to you during your trip, then we should decide together."

In a slow, cautious movement, Nino lets go of Haruka's hand, then shifts himself so that he's straddling Haruka's lap. He rests his weight down against his hips and in the hollow of Haruka's folded legs. Nino's eyes gleam as he bites his bottom lip. Haruka wraps his arms around his waist to hold him close.

"I love this plan." Nino cradles Haruka's head with his hands. He leans in and sweetly presses his lips to the small blemish just off the bridge of his nose. "It's much better than research vacations."

"We could do both?" Haruka smiles, closing his eyes.

Nino kisses his lips. The soft fullness of his mouth combined with the weight of him is marvelous. He lowers his face, moving down Haruka's jawline. When he reaches the curve of his neck, he breathes in deeply before kissing him there.

"You've seen me naked," Nino says, his voice low. He languidly drags his tongue against his neck—over and over as if Haruka is his most preferred flavor of lollipop. "But I haven't seen you. It feels a little unfair."

"Does it?" He smirks, opening his eyes.

Nino sits up straight, focused. "Haru, how... do we feel about sex?"

"Considering my behavior this morning, I think my feelings should be obvious—"

"Okay, but I mean... *more*." Nino lifts slightly, moving his hand down between them and tugging at the waistband of Haruka's pajama pants. He slowly crawls his hand inside until Haruka feels his warm, long fingers firmly wrapping around his naked length. "Like... *everything*," Nino says.

Haruka breathes through his nose, focusing. "How do *you* feel?"

Nino leans in again, gently pressing their foreheads together. "I want you. In every way I can have you."

"I want *you*." Haruka sighs. "However, we should be careful that we do not squander our intimacy."

Nino's hand freezes. He sits straight and inhales deeply as if steeling himself for something. "How many times are you comfortable with?"

Laying his head back, Haruka sighs. He doesn't want to seem strict, but based on everything he has read, everything he knows and all the research, the safest number is the lowest average number. "No more than four."

"*Four?*" Nino's body tenses, his voice jumping several octaves. "So *low*?"

"It is safest. Most purebred pairings in *Lore and Lust*

became bonded after making love between four to ten times. Five times might be acceptable, but it is risky."

"But exchanging blood is mandatory in establishing a bond, too," Nino reasons, his coppery brow creased over anxious eyes. "We're not, so we should be alright?"

"That... may change."

Drawing back slightly, Nino blinks. "Yeah?"

"Yes. As such, I have already limited us to only *three* times after my spontaneity this morning."

"But this morning... Does that count?"

Haruka blinks, considering. "You were physically gratified?"

Climbing off Haruka's lap, Nino sits beside him in a heap, puffing out a breath. He reminds Haruka of a child that has been told recess is over. He stares straight forward, his gaze distracted. "Okay... three times."

"Nino, I can also emotionally please you with my mind and intentional thoughts as I feed. And there is much more to our relationship than physical intimacy, is there not?"

Nino's gaze is fixed on the far wall. "Yeah. You're right."

Haruka pouts. It's as if Nino's soul has been sucked out of him. The prospect of only making love with Nino three times is uncomfortable for Haruka as well, but he doesn't want to risk being bonded. He won't. He doesn't want to be so strictly beholden and vulnerable to another vampire again. The first time had been too painful, humiliating and filled with regret. Too much self-sacrifice. He *cannot* do it again.

Anxious, Haruka raises his eyebrow. "Are you having second thoughts about our plan?" Nino breathes a laugh and rolls his shoulders, the trance broken.

"Absolutely not. Haru, I love—"

Eyes wide, he stares into the side of Nino's handsome profile. His amber eyes are wide as well as he looks straight ahead at the wall. Haruka reaches down to grasp his hand, then brings it up to his mouth to place soft kisses in his palm. Nino relaxes his shoulders, stifling a grin.

"No, I haven't changed my mind. I'm excited about my trip."

Haruka pauses in his kisses. "And I am grateful."

THIRTY-TWO

Haruka left Milan Sunday afternoon. Simultaneously, Nino feels as if there is a gaping hole in his chest.

It's Monday and Nino is sitting alone in his brother's office. As he waits, the memories of the week he and Haruka spent together run through his mind like a rosy movie reel. Everything is sepia toned with soft edges.

He can kiss Haruka now—openly. Greedily. He can also touch him. He was naked and Haruka had done... other things to him that had nearly sent his body into a state of shock. He stares blankly, recalling the moments in detail as his groin tightens.

The panther is not shy. Or squeamish.

Despite this, Haruka is still restraining himself. Nino can feel his knotted, muted aura deep within him. But if they can only have sex two more times, Nino supposes he has to hold back.

Two. Because things got out of hand again with Haruka's feeding the night before he left Milan, when Nino took him out to a jazz club in Navigli. Another surprise attack from Mr.

Spontaneous. It was great, but they still hadn't even been naked. If possible, next time, Nino is very much hoping for a lack of clothing in their final countdown of physical intimacy.

"Two more times. Jesus."

"Two more times what?" Giovanni strides into the room like a vampire on a mission. He moves toward his desk looking sharp but simply stated in tailored black slacks and a patterned button-down. "Has tall, dark and complicated offered himself to you yet?"

Nino frowns, decidedly ignoring his brother's first question. "No."

Giovanni stops before he sits down, his brow creased. "Why are you looking at me like that?"

"I'm waiting for you to yell at me or say something rude."

"Why? Because I walked in on you sucking face with your boyfriend?" He sits down, smirking as he checks his titanium wrist watch. "I'm not going to yell at you. I'll probably be rude though."

So embarrassing... Nino folds his arms tight, bracing himself. He also didn't go with Giovanni when he took Haruka to aristocracy meetings and social visits. Not once. Haruka was *his* guest, so ideally, Nino should have accompanied them. But after the terrible dinner with Signor Moretti, he had felt drained.

Giovanni lifts his chin. "What's the plan with Haruka? Talk."

He takes a deep breath. "Haru is going to return to his realm."

"He should."

"After he gets settled—maybe a couple months?" Nino guesses. "I'll go and visit him. If I like it there and we agree, I'll move and stay with him."

The room falls silent and Nino shrugs. "That's the plan."

Giovanni sits, just staring with his hazel-green eyes and his arms folded. Nino frowns. "Why aren't you saying anything?"

"Because I said I wouldn't yell at you. Let me start by saying I'm pleased that you've formed a meaningful relationship with Haruka. He's intelligent, patient and pragmatic. I think he's exactly what you need."

"Thanks," Nino says, relaxing his shoulders but not his guard. More is coming.

"I also like that you're working with him on something important that benefits our race," Giovanni continues. "Running that bar, I was terrified you'd come home with some gutter vampire or fetishy human and expect me to welcome them into our home. So I'm pleasantly surprised that you've done exactly the opposite."

Nino cuts his eyes away. *I wouldn't have brought her home. Jesus, I'm not stupid.*

"That being said..." Giovanni raises his eyebrow. "Your plan sucks. I don't like it."

"Why? It makes sense for us. And you know Haru doesn't want to bond."

Giovanni rolls his eyes. "Right. I've never heard of a bond breaking—that shit is crazy. But lover boy needs to get over himself. You're going to move there and do what, exactly?"

Nino adjusts in his seat, feeling the heat of his brother's inquisition. "I don't know yet. But I'm capable of running a successful business, G. I just need to get there and figure out where there's a need—"

"So while Haruka is dealing with busy vampire aristocracy bullshit and overseeing his entire realm alone, you're going to open a bar across town so that humans and low-level vamps can gawk at you? You're going to live in his house, eat his food and give him hand jobs when he comes home?"

Nino drops his head, laughing despite himself. "Not... necessarily."

"Nino, you *cannot* go to Japan—a new realm, a new aristocracy with this old-blooded and exquisite creature—and do the same garbage you've been doing. If you move there, you need to be his *equal partner*. You have to stand beside him and solidify your place in front of his society members in his realm. You can't go there and be his fucking house cat."

He's right. Nino sits back and runs his palms down his face. If he goes to Japan and does the same things he's always done— avoid other ranked vampires and shy away from his proper designation in their culture—he'll end up in the same situation he's in now. Disrespected. Pitied.

"You should have come out with us when I took him to greet our society members—"

"I *know*, G," Nino sighs.

"You can't let assholes like Moretti get to you. He might be older, but in the hierarchy of our culture, you outrank him, Nino. You're *purebred*. Do you really get that? You're an unflawed, rare and extraordinary creation. There are billions of humans and millions of fucking ranked vamps on this planet, but there probably aren't even a thousand purebred vampires. You need to let that sink in and think before you hopscotch over to Japan to play house with Haruka."

He understands. Spending so much time with Haruka in the past three months has shown Nino that he needs to change. That he needs to grow. In the beginning, he commiserated with Haruka over their shared reluctance to engage within the aristocracy. It is the foundation of their relationship. The irony that brought them closer.

But Haruka has slowly changed. The guarded hermit that Nino met in the beginning has transformed, shedding his heavy cloak and lifting his head to the sunlight. Now, Haruka is looking back at Nino and reaching his hand out to him, as if to say, "Come with me?"

Instead of grabbing his hand, Nino is hesitating.

"I hear what you're saying, G, but what am I supposed to do? I can't just start barging into meetings and events with my chest puffed out like some asshole."

"Practice," Giovanni says simply, letting the word sink in before he goes on. "Stay home for a while and come with me to meetings and social events. Nobody will fucking talk to you the way Moretti did if I'm with you—and I've already had a conversation with him about that."

Nino nods. He needs to make more arrangements at Scotch & Amaretto and talk to his employees. He's already spoken with Mariana about taking on the role of co-owner. With some additional staff, she can definitely handle the responsibility of running the bar long term.

"And then," Giovanni continues, "you need to go to Japan sooner. None of this 'let him get settled' shit. Within the first two weeks of Haruka being back, somebody will throw him a big soiree to welcome him home. I don't know who or when, but you need to be there."

"I shouldn't just show up uninvited," Nino says, doubtful. "Haruka hasn't told me—"

"Nino. Haruka knows that you *hate* aristocracy events. Of course he won't invite you. But it'll be an important event to be beside him and assert yourself. Based on what he's told me about the size of his realm, he's got a lot on his plate. He'll be happy you're there. Trust me. When the time comes, just go and surprise him. Show him you can handle being his partner."

Can I handle being his partner? Nino wants to be with Haruka. Whenever they're together, it feels more natural than when they're apart. Even now, Nino's skin is itchy and his nature discontented from the geographical distance between them.

"Are you accepting my offer?" Giovanni asks. "What's your decision?"

"I'll stay," Nino resolves. "I don't want to be his house cat."

Laughing, Giovanni stands from his desk. "Perfect. When is mama duck coming by to feed you? Hopefully *that* bullshit can finally stop. Who the hell is she feeding from in England? Never mind. It's best that I don't know names."

Nino shakes his head, smiling. "*So* jealous."

Giovanni stops dead, his smile dropping and his voice rising. "You *want* me to fucking yell at you now?"

"*Nope.*" Nino swiftly pushes himself up from the couch and leaves the office.

LATE MARCH

THIRTY-THREE

A month has passed since his week-long visit to Italy. Despite this, and even as he sits inside his home in Kurashiki, Japan, the warm echoes of Haruka's time spent with Nino still radiate in his body. The golden glow of him has lingered, firmly centered both in Haruka's heart and deeply within his core.

He had expected to see him in England once more before he made the preliminary move back home. But Nino had suddenly changed his plans and they hadn't been able to meet. He decided to stay in Milan longer, and he is still there. When Haruka asked why, Nino vaguely explained that he needed to take care of some things.

He doesn't let it show, but Haruka feels disappointed by this.

The crystal-clear sound of a chime rings out, breaking the silence of Haruka's small office. He perks up, his response officially an ingrained behavior as if he is one of Pavlov's dogs. He isn't salivating (yet) but his heart unquestionably beats faster.

He is sitting on a cushion on the tatami floor with one knee drawn up, his new, shiny black smartphone on the low oak table in front of him. Nino purchased it as a surprise and had it delivered to his home. Asao taught Haruka how to use it.

It isn't complicated and he likes being able to communicate regularly with Nino. But something about it feels invasive. As if it is covertly tracking his whereabouts and conversation at any given time. He greatly dislikes this feeling. When he expressed his concern to Asao, the manservant shrugged and said, "It probably is." Which wasn't helpful.

He taps and opens the device like Asao taught him. A message from Nino flashes brightly before him on the small screen.

[It's almost time, yeah?]

Haruka looks at the clock at the top of the screen, then types his response.

[Yes. Why are you awake? It is 4am there.]

[Because I'm worried about you.]

Nino's reply is quickly followed by another message.

[You're not happy about this meeting.]

It's true. He isn't. He's been receiving letters from Yuna for more than a year now. Although he hasn't read a single page, it was inevitable that they would eventually cross paths. His decision to return home has only increased the likelihood. The chime rings out again.

[I wish I was there with you.]

Haruka types his response.

[I wish you were, too. But hopefully the meeting will be brief.]

Today, a meeting with Yuna. Tomorrow, an assembly with the current business leaders of Okayama, and Friday, a welcome reception in Haruka's honor in Himeji.

Upon his return, the vampires within his realm have been much more welcoming than Haruka had anticipated. He had expected bitterness, but the overall sense within the community has been something like relief (the purebred substitute was... challenging). With Haruka's reinstitution come many social requests, meetings and responsibilities. The weight of his position is quickly bearing down on his shoulders.

It's overwhelming, but this is his true designation—the life that accompanies his lineage and bloodline. A life of self-sacrifice. Haruka's family traditionally oversees both the Chūgoku and Kansai regions. This level of accountability was much less daunting when he'd been mated, and the thought of bearing it alone had been a catalyst for his leaving home after his bond had broken.

Privately, Haruka sincerely hopes that Nino finds western Japan to his liking when he visits in two months. He fully accepts that Nino has no interest in their cultural aristocracy, but simply being in his warm and vibrant presence makes circumstances much more tolerable. Even enjoyable.

The prospect of the bonding ceremony had been a thing of great foreboding. As they spent time together, researching and relishing in candid conversation, the circumstance unexpectedly become pleasant.

His phone lights up with a new message.

[Call me after she leaves. xx]

[You should be sleeping, it can wait until later.]

[Just call. I'll be up. mmt+]

Haruka frowns, confused as he types his response.

[Nino, what does that mean?]

[Mi manchi tantissimo.]

Haruka smiles.

[I miss you, too.]

———

FORTY MINUTES LATER, Yuna appears in the doorway to the tea room of Haruka's estate... like a physical ghost from his despondent past. As ghosts do, she is silently watching him— cautious in a frozen, awkward moment.

She is wearing a sky-blue dress that gracefully flows just below her knees. There was a time when he loved this color on her. She knows this. It perfectly accentuates her slim waist and small, elegant frame as if it were tailored specifically to her pale body. Her shoulder-length dark brown hair is clean and lustrous, framing her oval face like a heavy curtain.

She gracefully steps down from the hardwood of the hallway and onto the lower tatami flooring of the tea room. Haruka stands, nodding politely as she reaches the small sofa opposite him. A modern wooden coffee table is set between them.

Yuna dips her head in a bow and Haruka notices that Asao has remained watchful of the situation in the doorframe behind her. His eyes are narrowed in distrust.

"Hello, Haruka..." she says, sitting on the couch. She breathes a laugh—a lighthearted, fluttery sound. "We seem a bit worse for wear, don't we?"

It's true. She looks pale. Gaunt. Where her eyes had once been a deep, rich brown with lovely flecks of robin's egg blue, they are now washed out, almost milky. They look as if she'd been ill and has never properly recovered from it. Haruka is also not in optimum health, having been separated from Nino for a month now and feeding from a lower-ranked source. However, Yuna's condition seems somewhat exaggerated in comparison.

Another oddity is her scent. In the past, Yuna's essence had registered as sweet but zesty to Haruka's nature—like lemon trees blossoming in the springtime. Now her scent is sour. It distinctly reminds him of the six months he'd spent violently and painfully expelling her nature from his body.

"Such is life," Haruka says. "What can I help you with?"

She pouts, a familiar hurt in her expression. "Straight to business? As if I'm some piddling member of your aristocracy? We haven't seen each other in *seventy years*. And you ignored all my letters. You sent them back."

"I could not fathom why you would write to me in such frequent intervals, or what we would need to discuss at any length."

"I've missed you." She takes a deep breath, pinching the hem of her dress with her fingertips. "Everyone has missed you. It took me *years* to track you down after you left. You kept moving around."

"It was within my right to do so."

"I know that, Haruka, but..." She furrows her brow in

obvious frustration and shakes her head. The subtle movement makes her thick hair bounce and sway. "You act as if we didn't spend our childhood together—as if we're strangers who only met in passing. Our parents were friends—my parents still love you. We were *bonded* and had a life together. I know you don't believe me, but I loved you and cared about you very much. I *still* do. Why is it impossible to you that I could simultaneously love two people?"

Haruka sighs. His chest is heavy and tight. Is this her rationale? Does this justify her choices and behavior? As if loving two people reasonably allows her to orchestrate a double life. As if she is entitled to secretly, cruelly indulge in everything her heart desires. Meanwhile, Haruka received nothing. Not even the trust, transparency and confidence of a faithful mate.

Why does he need to sit here and listen to this? He feels nauseous. The flood of embarrassment and shame he'd felt back then is quickly rising up like bile in his throat.

"Yuna, why are you here?" Haruka pleads, ignoring her question. "Is this necessary? Where is Kenta, and why are you not happily bonded with him?"

She leans forward, urgency in her voice. "That's why I tried to find you all those years and kept writing to you, because I wanted to tell you what happened. After our bond broke, Kenta and I, we—we did try to bond. But we never could. It would never take! I don't think I can bond anymore. I think I've lost the ability."

He sits with his arms folded, processing. How can you lose the ability to bond? It is an innate feature of their biology. Part of what defines them. How can something so fundamental to their species be broken?

Yuna's voice is low, her eyes sympathetic. "I heard about how sick you became after we separated... That didn't happen to me at all. I tried to come see you but Asao sent me away. When I came back a few months later, you were gone."

Rubbing his palm down his face, he sighs. He needs to treat this like a professional call—like someone in his realm who requires his help and expertise. "How long did you try to form a bond with Kenta?"

"Five years. Then we gave up. He lives in Tokyo now. He's... bonded with another female."

Five years. To go so long without a successful bond is odd. In *Lore and Lust*, the longest any documented couple went was about two and a half years.

"And there are other things," Yuna says quietly. "For one, my sense of taste and smell are damaged. No matter who I drink from, it tastes like dirt, and my body doesn't properly absorb blood anymore. I *always* look like this, Haruka. I can't seem to reach my optimum level of health again. I'm forever in this horrible, semi-dried-out state. Is it the same for you?"

"No. I am capable of properly absorbing blood. My senses of taste and smell are undamaged."

"Then why do you look like this?" Yuna blinks. "Your eyes and skin tone are wrong. And I don't know why, but I can smell *you* right now. You smell wonderful to me just like you always did. I haven't been able to sense another vampire's essence since our bond broke. Why can I still smell you?"

She never fell ill after their bond broke, but Haruka had been tragically so. Even now, Haruka's essence is aesthetically pleasing to her, while her scent makes his stomach turn.

"Perhaps in some intrinsic way, my blood still flows through you?" Haruka reasons. "Since your body never rejected my biology, it may remain within you, causing these obstructions and malformations."

It's all conjecture, since this is unchartered territory. There simply isn't any research to frame this aberrant circumstance.

Haruka's father and grandfather would have searched high and low for more instances of this had they known it possible.

"I agree with your theory," Yuna says, never taking her milky, disturbing eyes off of him. "How do I smell to you? Am I still... Am I pleasing to you?"

He casts his gaze to the side, briefly searching for a diplomatic response. In a rare moment, he comes up empty. "No."

She's silent, looking down at the hem of her dress as she rubs it between her fingers. "Is it so bad that you wouldn't want to feed from me?" she asks. "What if... what if we could fix this? What if we could sustain each other again? Help restore our bodies and natures."

Haruka turns his nose up, his face having no sense of discretion or diplomacy today either. "Yuna, what exactly are you suggesting?"

She lifts her head, her foggy eyes serious. "I'm suggesting that we become each other's sources again. I think, if we try, maybe we—"

"I am *not* interested in this arrangement." Haruka stands from the couch. The absurdity of it feels like an electric shock to his system. "I ask that you leave my home now. I don't believe I can help you."

"*Haruka*. We should at least give this a try. I can assist you with running the realm again. You'll need the support. Please at least consider—"

"That you would have the audacity to come to my home and request *anything* of me is astonishing. You only seek my help because your preferred source has abandoned you. I am *not* something to be tossed away and picked back up again at your convenience."

"No! That's *not* how I see you." Yuna shakes her head, her thick hair swaying from the dramatic gesture as she stands. "We—we made a vow to each other. If you're right and your blood still flows within me, it is your responsibility—"

"*Do not* speak to me about 'vows' and 'responsibility.' *Leave*, Yuna."

His eyes burn and glow to life from frustration, but the heat of it is low, emphasizing his malnourished state. Asao steps down into the room, his broad frame imposing as he stands beside Yuna. She bows in a short nod, but when their eyes meet again, she speaks quickly. "I'm coming to the ceremony in Himeji. Please just consider—"

Asao steps in front of her, then gestures toward the door. "Enough, Yuna."

She drops her shoulders, acquiesced as she turns to leave. When she's gone, Haruka crumbles back down to the couch. He lays his head back and closes his eyes, feeling physically hollow and emotionally drained.

In the distance, he hears the pristine chime of his new phone. He doesn't move because he is miserable. There's no use spreading discontent, so he sits in the tea room alone for a long time. Breathing.

THIRTY-FOUR

It's dusk when Nino arrives at the sprawling property tucked deep in the rolling hills of Mount Seppiko in Himeji, Japan. The sun is setting, casting watercolor hues of pink and deep orange across the partly cloudy sky.

The home set before him is sleek and modern in its design with heavy influences from traditional Japanese architecture. Open verandas, wooden siding and sliding paper doors. In some areas of the home, entire walls are fashioned in clear glass so that the majestic views of the surrounding forest and mountain peaks are displayed like landscape artwork.

Nino is being escorted around the side of the house and toward the back of the property. Following a manservant dressed in a formal kimono, Nino walks along a winding path of very tall bamboo stalks—vibrant green and reaching straight up toward the twilight sky. The ground is elegantly lined with glowing white lanterns, and the only sound is their footfalls hitting the stone path. Something about this trail feels supernatural, as if Nino is the brave protagonist in a whimsical Japanese folktale with yōkai and tengu.

He nervously pulls at the black satin bow tie around his neck. The tuxedo makes him feel stiff and uncomfortable. He hasn't told Haruka that he is coming, but with their innate ability to sense other purebreds, he knows now.

Giovanni had told Nino to simply go and surprise him. He has followed his brother's advice but still has doubts. Especially since Haruka has become somewhat unresponsive to Nino's text messages over the past twenty-four hours. He doesn't understand why Haruka suddenly feels distant, and his report on the meeting with Yuna was painfully vague.

Whatever the case, he is here now. No turning back.

The bamboo-lined path opens up to a wide garden. Rows of cherry blossom trees filled with dark pink buds line the perimeter, and there is a large koi pond reflecting yellow hanging lanterns like glitter against the dark surface. Several vampires occupy the beautiful area. The manservant escorting Nino bows and gestures for him to cross a small arched bridge to join the festivities.

He nods in thanks, then proceeds across the bridge. He can smell Haruka in the crowd and among the social clutter, his body innately drawn to him by some inexplicable force. Like a magnet or gravity. Vampires within the crowd step aside and bow politely, curiously watching him as they naturally make a path toward his target.

When the crowd parts to where he can finally see Haruka, the dark male is staring directly at him. Eyes unblinking. He looks like royalty in a midnight-blue kimono. The wool overcoat elegantly draped over his shoulders is of the same rich color, but the thick belt of his robes is dusky silver. The entire ensemble gives the impression that he is a dark celestial entity— a god of the night sky.

Nino approaches. Haruka watches him, motionless. There are two vampires flanking his sides: an older second-generation female and a younger, very tall first-gen male with smooth, brown skin the color of almond butter. The female's white hair is elaborately pinned up and she is also wearing formal robes. The male is young, but appears slightly older than Haruka. He looks stylish in a bold, deep teal suit perfectly tailored to his frame. The ensemble is rich and fashionable against his dark, curly hair and onyx irises.

They both bow when Nino stands directly in front of Haruka. Nino politely returns the gesture, but his gaze is fixed on the dark purebred.

Haruka blinks. "You... are here early." Nino can't read his face to discern whether or not he's pleased by this, but he's instantly distracted by the physical state of him. His eyes are brown instead of the brilliant wine color he's come to know and adore, and his skin is a pale shade of gray. Nino's face shifts into concern.

The older, white-haired female turns to Haruka, her face confused as she speaks in Japanese. "My lord, who is this lovely young male?"

"Sumimasen, nihongo ga hanasemasu." Nino smiles in a slight bow. "Watashi no namae wa Nino Bianchi desu. Hajimemashite."

The female draws back in surprise, her expression a little brighter. "My apologies, your grace. I am Aoi Shimamoto."

"No apology is necessary," Nino assures her before redirecting his attention. "Haruka, may I please speak with you privately?"

"If you walk around that way..." The very tall first-gen male points directly to his right. "It's woodsy but quiet. I had to make a phone call earlier. Welcome to Japan, Nino. I'm Junichi Takayama."

Nino nods, grateful. "It's nice to meet you, Junichi. Thank you." He reaches his hand out and Haruka grasps it without hesitation. He follows as Nino walks toward the area Junichi pointed out. When they're through the thick crowd and nearing a curve around the house, Nino glances at Haruka. "Why aren't you saying anything?"

"I—I did not expect you to be here. I have felt your presence for the past thirty minutes, but I thought perhaps I was hallucinating."

When they turn the corner and are out of view of everyone, Nino faces him directly. The sky is dark now. The moon high. The hum of crickets and katydids echoes through the thick forest surrounding them.

"Well," Nino says, his heart pounding in his ears, "you're not hallucinating. Are you upset that I'm here?"

Haruka steps into him, wrapping his arms around Nino's neck. "*No.* You cannot imagine how incredibly pleased I am. It feels as if I am dreaming."

Nino wraps his arms around his waist, relaxing in the embrace. Soaking him in. Haruka feels so good in his arms and being with him feels so right. They haven't been close like this since Haruka's last night in Milan several weeks earlier. His nature deep within him is purring and writhing from his nearness, making his groin stiff. Nino closes his eyes as they hold each other. He slides his hands up Haruka's back underneath his coat. "I'm just happy you're not mad at me for crashing your party."

Haruka lifts his head, looking into Nino's face with his brown eyes. He runs his fingers into the back of Nino's hair. His deep voice is quiet. "I would not be upset with you. I love you."

Nino sucks in a breath just as Haruka presses into his mouth to kiss him. His heart in his throat, Nino parts his lips, quickly giving in to him as he holds Haruka even tighter against his body.

He loves me.

They've been dancing around it. Waltzing. Nino almost said it once—has said it indirectly. But here it is. Simply. Haruka licks into him deeply, the passion of his slow movement intensified by the openness of his confession. Nino is moving his mouth and matching his rhythm, but he can barely catch his breath from the warmth flooding his chest. He feels like *he* is dreaming—afraid of being roused and snapped back to his former, uncertain reality.

This is real. Validated by Haruka's deep moan as he breathes against Nino's mouth. The rosy taste of him puffs out and overwhelms his senses like a delicious, sweet liquor. Nino is nearing a euphoric state of mindlessness when he vaguely registers Haruka's hand traveling down the length of his body and in between them.

His long fingers slide against the curve of his shaft through his tuxedo pants. Haruka gives him a firm squeeze and Nino abruptly lifts his head, breathless. Panicked.

"Haru, we—we're in *public.*"

"Not technically," Haruka says, indifferent and busily kissing his jawline. His fingers are still exploring and gripping. Digging further. Nino reaches between them and gently grabs his wrist.

"*Stop.*" He laughs, strained as he shifts his hips away. He isn't surprised though, as Haruka has exhibited similar behavior previously. Date night—their final evening in Milan together. The dark purebred is progressively unfurling and opening like a luscious rose, and similar to the flower, he is not deterred by an audience.

But this is Nino's first aristocracy event in Japan and he's been prepping for a month. The last thing he needs is for someone to come around the corner and see them making out. "Haruka, why do you *look* like this?"

Haruka's expression softens, blinking. "You... find me unattractive?"

"No." Nino shakes his head in disbelief. "That's *not*—I mean your eyes are flat and your skin is off color again. You told me you found a high-level source?"

"I did," he says. "My health is admittedly not in its optimum state, but I am not in any pain. It is fine."

Nino reaches up, swiftly unraveling his bow tie. He works the buttons at his collar. "It's not fine. You can't sufficiently protect yourself if someone challenges you. I'm uncomfortable with you walking around like this. Feed, please."

He tilts his head, encouraging Haruka to take of him. But the beautiful vampire simply stares. He reaches up and holds Nino's face with the palm of his hand, straightening his head. "I cannot understand why you show me such selfless kindness, when no one has *ever* done this for me."

Leaning in, Nino rests his forehead against him. "Because I love you too, Haru. And that's what love is... Asao shows you kindness? He cares about you."

"I pay Asao."

Nino laughs. He isn't completely sure, but even if Haruka doesn't pay him, the older vampire still holds an obvious affection for his young master. Nino lifts his chin and presses his lips to the small mole just off the bridge of Haruka's nose. In turn, Haruka scrunches his face and draws back slightly. "Why do you always kiss this blemish on my face?"

"I like it."

"It is an abnormality."

"I think it's cute." Nino grins, kissing him there again. "Will you feed?"

Haruka turns his nose up in mock displeasure before jutting his chin out to place a swift kiss on his lips. He leans into Nino's neck, grasping his tuxedo lapels as he licks his skin. He gently bites down into his flesh.

He loves me.

Haruka doesn't drink to pull Nino's aura. Instead, he pours the most wonderful thoughts into his body. Love and trust—gratitude slowly trickling over his insides like a warm, chocolate drizzle. The sensation is all consuming, stirring Nino's emotions and making them bubble and rise up his spine. With his head raised to the night sky, he closes his watering eyes. He could lift his arms and take flight from the pure high of the sensation.

When Haruka finishes, he licks his neck again, then slides his elegant fingers up to refasten his collar. Nino lowers his head, still trying to catch his breath. Haruka's eyes are glowing bright red as he works. He briefly flickers his gaze up at Nino before focusing on fixing his bow tie. "You look exquisite tonight."

"Grazie." Nino smiles.

"If you will permit me, I would like to undress you when we return home."

Nino's entire body stiffens—his quiet attempts to calm himself thwarted. He furrows his brows. "If you keep this up, I don't know how I'll manage the rest of this party." He looks down, taking in the thick, gorgeous material of Haruka's kimono. It is impeccably designed with expensive-looking fabric. It almost shines under the moonlight. "You look incredible in this, Haru. It suits you perfectly... I wouldn't even know how to take this off of you."

With his bow tie restored, Haruka takes Nino's hand. "I will show you."

It's happening. One of two. Nino takes a deep breath. No matter what he does, he can't stop his heart from pounding—his nature from twisting and writhing.

Haruka loves him. Does this mean that he might change his mind about bonding? Is he open to the two of them intentionally trying?

Shifting his hold, Nino entwines their fingers. Now isn't the time. Maybe later he'll try to talk to him about it, carefully initiate the subject somehow. As for tonight, he'll simply enjoy being reunited with this stunning male. "Should we go back?"

"Yes," Haruka agrees. "If you are comfortable, may I properly introduce you?"

"I would love that."

They turn, walking hand in hand as they head back around the curve of the large estate. As the edge of the crowded garden comes into view, a young female is walking toward them. Her frame is small and wrapped in a patterned, soft blue kimono. She's pretty, but as she draws closer, something about her eyes is disturbing.

THIRTY-FIVE

Haruka steels himself, attempting to quell the immediate anxiety weighted in his chest. He squeezes Nino's hand a little tighter as he addresses Yuna.

"Nino, this is Yuna Sasaki. Yuna, this is Nino Bianchi of Milan. He is my source."

She offers Nino a slight nod of her head. Nino returns the gesture but remains quiet. Yuna's eyes flicker down to their clasped hands, then up to Haruka's face. "You did not mention having a purebred source when I sat with you on Wednesday."

"I feel no obligation to disclose my personal circumstances to you."

"Is he *staying* here?" She frowns. "Is he just visiting? Or is he going to oversee our realm with you?"

"Again, I am disinclined to answer such forthright questions. You are being disrespectful to my guest, and you have not been a designated member of this realm in seventy years."

"Because I was *ostracized*, Haruka. But this is my home. If you formally and publicly absolve me, then others will accept me again and I—"

"Yuna, I apologize." Nino smiles warmly. "But this is my first evening with Haruka in Japan and I'm looking forward to meeting his society members. Maybe this is something you can discuss another time? Privately?"

Yuna stands straighter, then offers a slight nod. "My apologies. I didn't know you spoke Japanese."

"The world is full of surprises," Nino says.

"Agreed," she says coolly. "Did he tell you that he may not be capable of bonding? It was a jarring realization for me to accept as a result of the broken vow between us."

Haruka freezes. He registers Nino's mutual stiffness at his side.

Yuna simply bows again, smiling sweetly. "I'm sorry that I was rude, Nino. Welcome to Japan, and please enjoy your evening."

She walks away, her covert bomb successfully detonated. Nino turns to him, his coppery brows furrowed. "What the hell is she talking about?"

Haruka rolls his shoulders, stamping down his frustration. Has Yuna always been so undermining and selfish? Had he been totally blind with youthful whimsy and the inherent need to be reconnected with a family after losing his own? The more objective his view of her becomes, the more he sincerely questions the regard in which he originally held her.

"I promise to discuss it with you later," Haruka assures him, gently pulling him forward. "For now, let's enjoy our night together?"

Nino relaxes, softly bumping into his shoulder. "Alright."

THROUGHOUT THE NIGHT, Haruka marvels. He hadn't been expecting Nino to arrive early to attend his welcome ceremony. Simply having him here feels like the world has shifted and become a much brighter place.

He has surprised Haruka even further. Nino has always adamantly expressed his loath and reluctance to engage within the aristocracy. His actions in the past have strongly under-scored his feelings—his refusal to attend events with Giovanni and Haruka in Milan, his harsh silence at Signor Moretti's dinner and even his complete disregard of the bonding cere-mony invitation.

Tonight, though, Nino is different. He initiates conversa-tion and speaks up for himself. He smiles in his bright, hand-some way and asks questions. He is the same warm and cheerful purebred that Haruka knows privately, but polished somehow for these curious strangers. The response to him is a healthy mix of surprise and unquestionable delight, with vampires intrigued by Nino and asking him questions about his Japanese heritage.

As Asao drives them home, Nino relaxes with his head against the back seat. Haruka watches him in the soft moon-light—the car smoothly traversing down the dark, winding mountain roads. His body is already strong again from feeding, accustomed to Nino's unique brand of blood. He constantly gives of himself, never once asking Haruka for anything in return.

For the first time in a very long while, Haruka wants to offer himself. To somehow return the kindness that Nino has continuously shown him.

"You seemed comfortable tonight," Haruka says, keeping his voice low in the quiet environment. "Has your opinion of the aristocracy changed?"

Nino turns his head to the side and opens his eyes. "It has. I stayed in Milan longer so I could spend time with G. He took me on all of his social and business excursions. Tonight was a piece of cake in comparison to what I went through following *him* around. Jesus."

"Was it difficult?" Haruka takes hold of his hand, then slowly brings it to his mouth to place soft kisses against his fingers.

"Mm." Nino nods, watching him. "I learned two things— my brother is a machine and God help the vampire who crosses him, and not all vampires in Milan are raging assholes."

Haruka laughs. "Giovanni is an impressive male. I wonder if I will be as efficient and commanding as he is when I reach his age?"

Nino sits up and smoothly catches Haruka's face with his palm. "You won't be rude like he is, so I think you'll be even better." Nino kisses him playfully in the dark stillness of the backseat. Firm, sweet pecks, catching his mouth over and over. Haruka slowly moves down, brushing his lips against his neck and breathing him in when Asao's voice booms from the front seat.

"*Do not* pull his aura while I'm driving this car. Wait until we get home, please—"

"*Asao*," Haruka scolds, startled. Nino laughs, falling back against the seat. Haruka shakes his head, embarrassed.

THIRTY-SIX

It's late when they arrive in the small town of Kurashiki. Nino looks out the car window in awe as they pass through the charming historical quarter. There is a shallow and mossy canal streaming through the area—a sleek mirror for the stars above. The streets are cobblestoned and lined with weeping willows softly fluttering in the nighttime breeze.

Nino's sense of wonder only grows when they reach Haruka's home and he is given a tour. The house is wide and flat, but beautifully sectioned off in square and rectangular segments. Each area of the compound is connected by elegant hardwood-floor hallways and open breezeways through outdoor gardens. Directly outside of Haruka's bedroom is an impressive in-ground hot spring.

Nino walks around the perimeter. The silent steam is rolling and curling atop the placid green water. Tall bamboo stalks are pressed together to create a natural privacy fence around the large, open space. Here too, giant cherry blossom trees flank the bath area like knights watching over their king.

Nino turns to him and smiles. Haruka is standing near the

glass doors and watching him as he explores the picturesque outdoor area. "Haru, your house is beautiful. This hot spring is *incredible*."

"I am pleased that it is to your liking," he says. "Would you like to try it?"

Nino walks back toward him. "Take a bath? Right now?" Haruka simply nods. Nino grins. He can't stop grinning. "I would love to."

After reaching down to hold both his hands, Haruka steps backward toward the open patio doors leading into his bedroom. "We should shower first."

"I'm fine with that..." says Nino, his body hot and his nature within him pulsing and twisting in knots. If he isn't out of this tuxedo and intimate in some capacity with this male soon, he might explode from the strain. He needs to touch and feel him. Badly. Without restrictions or hesitations.

Haruka urges him back into the room and closes the doors. Facing Nino, he smoothly slides his hands inside his tuxedo jacket at his shoulders, encouraging him to remove it. Nino shrugs out of it, tossing it onto a nearby armchair. Haruka pulls his bow tie apart with his long fingers, then unfastens his shirt buttons.

His gorgeous, wine-colored irises have already returned. Nino is mesmerized as he quietly leans into Haruka and kisses him, taking his bottom lip between his own before dipping his tongue into him. When Haruka's hands are at his belt buckle, Nino pulls up from the kiss. "Can I undress you? Tell me how."

Haruka smiles with his eyes, seductive and focused on Nino as he lifts his hands to remove his outer coat. It slides from his square shoulders, down his long body and onto the floor. He takes Nino's hands, guiding them past his waist and around to the thick, knotted material of his belt at the small of his back. Nino holds him close as he unties it, the warmth of him pressed into his hips making Nino's breathing short and his hands shaky. Haruka quietly sprinkles kisses on his face and jawline as he works. When the belt is finally loose, it unravels from his body and falls to their feet.

Nino unties a second, thinner belt before he finally pulls the beautiful material of the kimono from his shoulders, then lets it slide and fall from Haruka's tall frame. But when Nino is met with another, lighter set of robes and belt, he laughs. "Why do I feel like I'm playing with a Russian nesting doll? How many belts and robes do we *need*?"

Haruka snickers, throaty and deep, while he continues littering Nino's neck with kisses.

"Is there another layer underneath here?" Nino frowns, untying the third belt and holding in his laughter.

"*No*," Haruka says, his voice muffled from his face being pressed into the curve of Nino's collarbone.

Nino swiftly unties the belt, then parts the light material of the second robe at Haruka's chest. He pulls it over his shoulders, urging Haruka to drop his arms and allow the fabric to fall from his body. When it does, he is completely naked. Gloriously so. His lean, sculpted body is washed in the moonlight spilling in from the glass doors behind them. Nino swallows, gratuitously taking in his beautiful almond skin, dark hair and bewitching eyes.

Haruka steps into him, pressing his bare body against Nino's suited frame as he takes his mouth. He laces his arms around Nino's shoulders and slides his fingers into his hair. Nino embraces him tightly, gliding one hand up his spine and the other down to grip the firm curve of his ass. Everything about Haruka registers as cool and refreshing. As if nature has uniquely cultivated him from its most beautiful elements— spring rain, the starry midnight skies and roses in full bloom.

As much as Nino loves the pressure of his body against him

and the feel of his nakedness underneath his hands, it isn't enough. He needs more. He wants everything.

Haruka breaks the kiss. Keeping their bodies tight and their foreheads pressed together, he whispers, "Shower?"

"*Please,*" Nino breathes. Haruka clasps his hand and guides him toward the master bathroom.

AFTER WHAT WAS UNQUESTIONABLY the most sensual shower of his life, Nino finds himself on his back in Haruka's large bed, having (somehow) failed to reach the hot spring.

His eyes are closed as he lies against the cool, plush comforter, a thick pillow tucked underneath his hips and his knees comfortably drawn up. He exhales, stretching his lower back and relaxing his body around Haruka's long, slick fingers pressed inside him. Haruka leans over, kissing a firm line down the center of his chest and toward his stomach while moving his fingers even deeper.

The heat of Nino's aura is fiercely radiating outward like a smoldering fire. His eyes are burning bright and he can't pull his nature back at all. Can't contain it. Suddenly, it has its own mind and intentions. When he feels the hardness of his shaft sliding into the warm wetness of Haruka's mouth, Nino arches his neck and groans loudly—the heat of his nature rushes down his abdomen and wills everything inside him to release.

Haruka twists his fingers, gently stretching Nino's body as he licks and sucks his length inside his mouth—tasting and caressing him with his tongue. Nino writhes against the pillow supporting his lower back, teetering on the edge of climax. He lifts his head, breathless. "*Haruka.*"

He opens his evocative eyes. Slowly, Haruka pulls his head

up. He moves to hover over Nino again, but Nino's breath catches when he smoothly presses a third slick finger into his body. Nino swallows, his chest heaving. "I want you inside me. I'm ready."

Leaning down, Haruka rests their foreheads together. Nino lifts his chin to catch his mouth, opening himself and wanting to deepen their contact. When Haruka parts his lips and meets his tongue, Nino sighs from pleasure. He tastes like his own rosy essence and sex. It makes Nino's head spin.

With their mouths joined and moving together, Haruka removes his fingers. Nino feels him settling the tip of his shaft against the soft flesh of his body. Gently, Nino lifts his hips, encouraging the intrusion—wanting it like he's never wanted anything in his long life. Haruka presses his tip inside and Nino breaks the kiss, sucking in air from the initial shock and satisfaction of the intimacy. Haruka takes his time pushing deeper, his wine eyes gradually morphing into bright crimson.

Soon, Nino's body is completely relaxed—as if a switch has been flicked on. Or off? The warm pulse and fullness of Haruka has unexpectedly settled the deep discontent and angst he's been feeling within his core for the past few months. He hadn't realized how uncomfortable it was until this moment, when the thing is finally resting. It's like a wave of loving calm is washing over him, swelling from within him.

He slides his hands down Haruka's spine, then cups his ass, bringing him even tighter and deeper into his body as he spreads his thighs wider. "You feel really good like this, Haru... It feels like you're calming something inside me."

Haruka breathes, closing his eyes as he rests on his elbows. Nino slowly sinks his hips down, then rolls them back up into Haruka as he grips his cheeks tightly with his palms. Haruka's red eyes flash open and he inhales sharply. He lowers his head so that his mouth is near Nino's ear. He whispers, "You... were incredibly provocative tonight."

Nino closes his eyes. Haruka kisses his neck as Nino repeats the movement with his hips, pulling away and then deliberately driving them back up and into him. Smooth. He swallows a groan from the slick wetness of their contact. Nino is breathless as he speaks, the pressure of arousal set firm in his belly. "Did I surprise you?"

Haruka lifts his head, lazily licking into him to press their mouths together before responding. "You did." He sighs, staring into Nino's eyes. "It was difficult... for me to focus."

Biting his lip, Nino lowers his hips into the soft pillow at his back again, then grinds himself up and into Haruka's shaft. Haruka gasps in a breath, clenching his burning eyes shut. Nino smiles, satisfied as he exhales. "Is that what turns you on, Haru? Diplomacy?"

"Perhaps?" Haruka says, his face devilish as he slowly rocks his hips against Nino's body—smoothly pumping in a steady rhythm. "In association with you, many things arouse me."

Haruka's movement has rendered Nino speechless. He shivers, feeling the warm prickling of the orgasm building and expanding low in his groin. Nino lays his head back, opening himself and willing the sensation to overtake him. He needs relief from the heavy tension building between them.

Nino breathes in and the atmosphere unexpectedly shifts. His eyes flicker open as a beautiful crimson haze slowly caresses and moves up his body. It makes the dusty golden hairs on his arms stand straight.

This is Haruka's aura. Usually it's strictly stifled, and his aroma is subtle like the distant recollection of a scent rather than something active within the present.

Nino can discern it clearly now. It's perfectly crisp, sweet and clean. A cool breeze on a vibrant spring morning. This is different from when he heavily presses his nature outward defensively. In this moment, it's light and airy, like an enchanting, passionate fog slowly engulfing everything it touches.

With his senses flooded by Haruka's essence, the need for him that lies deep inside Nino spikes. He wraps his arms around Haruka as he carefully shifts and rolls their bodies. When the dark purebred is on his back, Nino sits upright against his knees. He smoothly repositions himself back down, slowly taking Haruka's shaft back into his body.

Haruka opens his mouth to speak but Nino rocks hard against him, making him exhale a rough grunt of pleasure. Nino repeats the movement again and again, needing Haruka to release—to let go and give in to this beautiful nature of his that's somehow calling out to Nino.

With his body writhing underneath Nino and his fingers digging into his hips to encourage his movement, Haruka arches his lower back and cries out. He clenches his eyes shut, his entire frame trembling. Slowing, Nino closes his eyes. He gasps, surprised by the sensation of Haruka's warm release making their contact even more slick inside him. Nino wraps his fingers around his own shaft and lifts his head, finally allowing his body to succumb to the abundance of sensations.

When his body unwinds from the height of pleasure, he looks down at Haruka underneath him. His breathing is ragged and his glowing red eyes are filled with the haze of sexual gratification. His dark hair is mussed as he lies against the pillow. For the first time since Nino has known him, he looks completely relaxed and open. Perfect.

Nino bends down toward his chest, gratuitously inhaling his intoxicating, rosy aura as it still envelopes them. Haruka lifts his chin and parts his lips expectantly. Nino meets the gesture, lovingly entwining their tongues in a sensual kiss. When Nino raises his head, Haruka's fingers are tangled in the back of his hair. His voice is low and ragged as he stares into Nino's eyes. "Would you like to feed from me?"

Nino's chest tightens. "Are you sure?"

Haruka nods against the pillow, his burgundy eyes soft but unwavering. "You have consent."

A new rush of warmth and excitement washes over Nino's body. His heart swells as he moves one hand up to meet Haruka's free hand lazily resting on the pillow beside his head. Smoothly, he slides their palms together. They entwine their fingers as Nino bends down once more, licking Haruka's neck to savor the cool, sweet taste of him before softly biting into his skin.

He exhales a sigh as he feeds, amazed at the sublime pleasure of his blood—of everything they've done tonight. The rich complexity of Haruka's blood is so filling and like nothing Nino has ever tasted. He can feel it coursing through his body and revitalizing him, strengthening him in a way that he has never experienced.

In exchange, he focuses his mind. Pouring his sincere love and desire into Haruka. He thinks about how elegant and intelligent he is, and how much he loves simply talking to him. He thinks about his deep, bubbly laugh and how it sounds to his ears like music or an exotic bird's mating call. He thinks about his wry sense of humor, mesmerizing eyes and how, if he could, he'd be content to spend every single day of his life in Haruka's charming, enigmatic presence.

Nino takes a breath and pulls again, but something happens. He opens his eyes, startled. It feels as if something has jerked or rumbled, but he doesn't know if the shift has occurred within himself or if something happened externally within the room. He stops feeding and licks Haruka's neck. He lifts his head. Haruka's dark brows are furrowed tightly, confused and wary. He felt it too.

"Haru... what was—"

Nino gasps sharply, his voice cut off from the rush of his nature forcefully pouring out of his body in a haze of brilliant golden light. Haruka's body tenses and stiffens beneath him, his eyes blazing red again just before he forces them shut. The haze of Haruka's aura intensifies and brightens, powerfully twisting and moving around their bodies.

His eyes wide, Nino watches as their two energies swirl and intermingle, like two beautiful snakes engaging in an ancient mating ritual. But as soon as Nino discerns what's happening, the two energies fuse in a flash of vivid orange light, then slam back down in a rush of warm air against their naked bodies.

Nino inhales sharply again, feeling the heat of his vampiric nature enclosed within him. It's different—heavy and stiff. He can't move at all. For about five seconds, both he and Haruka are completely motionless, their eyes staring. Unable to speak. The intense thing deep inside Nino is squirming, adjusting. There's a pull of pressure as if he's linked to Haruka by an invisible and heavy chain.

Soon, the thing settles and relaxes, the weight of it becoming warmer and lighter. It felt daunting at first, but slowly, it offers an incredible sense of peace and security as it swells in his abdomen. Nino swallows, taking another deep breath to stop his body from quivering.

Just as he's beginning to unpack what's occurred, fear slices through his mind and down his spine like a machete. Intense fear, disbelief and anxiety flood his mind and heart, and the sudden intrusion of foreign emotions frightens Nino. The sensations are so strong, but unfamiliar to his mind. He knows these feelings, but they're not his. He doesn't feel this way and there's no clear rationale for their existence.

Haruka shifts to slide his body upright, pushing away from

Nino as he sits straight with his back pressed into the head-board. Nino sits up as well, staring at him. He sees the expression in Haruka's eyes and he understands. These unexplained emotions Nino is feeling—this fear and terrible sense of panic—they aren't his. Even though they radiate so severely inside him, they don't belong to him.

They belong to Haruka.

THIRTY-SEVEN

For a moment, everything is silent. Completely still. Nino's body is tense, his mind busy trying to process the wild scatter of Haruka's severe emotions while his body spasms from the unfamiliar energy settling within him.

Haruka's burgundy eyes are manic. He isn't moving and Nino can't tell if he's breathing as he sits against the headboard, his naked frame folded tightly with his knees drawn up.

His hand shaking, Nino reaches out to touch Haruka's fingers against the mattress. "Haru, are you—"

Nino jumps when Haruka snatches his hand away and draws back further, his eyes glowing bright crimson again in the darkness. Haruka shakes his head, and simultaneously the pressure of harsh emotions in Nino's mind pounds violently—an earsplitting crack to his left breaks the silence. Nino slams his palms to his ears, feeling as if his head will explode from the throbbing pain. The glass of the patio doors violently shatters, falling and sliding in large shards across the wood floor.

Haruka's chest is heaving when Nino looks back at him, but

there's another loud crack just beside the bed. The porcelain lamp on Haruka's bedside table violently splits, forming a map of crooked lines across its surface before it bursts as if smashed by an invisible hammer. Nino flinches with his palms still pressed to his ears, the agony in his head intensifying and making his vision blurry.

Something inside him pulls toward Haruka, telling Nino that *he* is doing this and that he needs help. Haruka isn't focused. He's losing control. The crippling fear and confusion he feels are consuming him. Panicked, Nino removes one hand from his ear and takes hold of Haruka's wrist. *"Haru, stop—"*

"Don't—" Haruka snatches his wrist away, but Nino swiftly and firmly refastens his fingers around it, then shifts his body forward. Haruka tries to push him, but Nino grabs his head and presses their foreheads together, concentrating through the intense, painful throbbing in his mind. His eyes water as he clenches them shut, then wills the bright warmth of his energy outward.

His aura doesn't manifest in the way he's accustomed to. Doesn't magnify from within him, glowing warmly in a golden haze like it has for the entirety of his life. When he opens his eyes, a light is slowly radiating and growing from within Haruka. It's the same deep orange light that had washed over them after Nino fed. It's beautiful. It reminds him of the Chilean sunset as it quietly engulfs Haruka's body.

Nino blinks, his fingers still laced in Haruka's dark hair. The mania in his eyes clears, his breathing slowing as he regains sone sense of awareness. The pounding between Nino's ears subsides and the violent emotions calm to a quiet lull.

Am I doing this? Nino scans Haruka's body, amazed. He is manipulating his own nature, but he's accessing it from *inside* Haruka's core. Instead of pushing it outward from himself to calm him, his aura... or at least some part of him is inside Haruka now. Nino is activating it for him, as if Haruka doesn't know how to access it but Nino has the key.

Haruka's body slackens, his breathing deep and even as he closes his eyes. Nino massages his fingertips against Haruka's scalp and takes a deep breath. "Are you okay?"

Haruka is silent for a long moment before he breathes, "Mm." His eyes are still closed, his arms limp at his sides. Nino removes his hands from Haruka's hair. He slowly crawls backward against the sheets, careful to avoid the thick shards of porcelain from the broken lamp.

Standing from the bed, Nino runs both hands into his hair. He exhales a heavy sigh to ease his racing pulse. Haruka is still sitting folded in the same position against the headboard, but now he's rubbing his palms up and down his face.

His emotions are not as intense and all consuming, but Nino can feel that he's deeply unsettled and confused. Like a humming in his mind, he knows that Haruka is grappling with what's just happened between them—with their new reality. Nino doesn't understand it either and he desperately wants to talk about it. But he knows that Haruka's mind is too messy right now. Too distraught.

Suddenly cold from his nakedness and the night air streaming in through the shattered patio doors, Nino shivers. He leans with his palms against the bed, his eyes patient as he stares at his mate.

"Haru."

Haruka slowly lifts his face. He's panicked. Guarded. As if Nino is about to ask him if he can borrow an obscenely large sum of money. He doesn't speak. Only stares at Nino with his fearful burgundy eyes.

"Should we clean up the sheets and sleep in here?" Nino

asks, his voice calm and low. "Or do you want to sleep in a guestroom?"

Blinking as if he's only just realized it, Haruka turns and looks at the destroyed patio doors. He takes a breath. "Per—perhaps... guestroom."

"Do you want me to get a robe or pajamas for you? You'll need to tell me where they are."

"I—I will get them..."

Haruka cautiously moves from the bed like he's afraid his body will completely shatter. He walks across the floor and into his large closet, the glow of light streaming brightly through the door as he quietly rummages around inside. When the light flickers off, he reappears. He's wearing a casual, dark-colored robe covered in a threaded traditional Japanese pattern and he's carrying a second robe in his arms. He hesitantly offers it to Nino.

"Thank you," Nino says, carefully taking the robe. He holds it tightly against his chest, bracing himself. "Last question. Do you want me to sleep in a different guestroom? Would that be more comfortable for you?"

Haruka rubs his hand against his forehead, avoiding Nino's gaze. "No, you—you do not need to do that. I am not upset with you, Nino. And I... I sincerely apologize for... the circumstance, and if I have harmed you—"

"*Please* don't do that." Nino sighs, smiling weakly. "I know this is unexpected, so let's just try to sleep. We'll talk about it when you're ready. Okay?"

Nino wants to touch him. To hold his hand, embrace him, *something* to comfort him and pull him far away from the deep fear looming inside his mind. Nino puts the robe on, wrapping his body up as Haruka nods. "Yes... okay."

They leave the bedroom, then proceed down the dark hallway toward one of the guestrooms. They're silent, but as they walk together, Haruka brushes his knuckles against Nino's. Gently, Nino grasps and holds Haruka's hand.

It is a demure end to the passionate actions they committed to earlier in the night. But to Nino, and more importantly, it is also a loving, encouraging beginning to their bonded life together.

THIRTY-EIGHT

The problem with this particular guest bedroom is the large square east-facing window just above the bed. Because of the window's position, the room is awash with bright yellow sunlight from early in the morning, making everything perfectly clear and visible. It is as if nothing, no shadow nor dark entity, can remain hidden within this space once the sun has risen.

Haruka lies on his back in the bed, his robe wrapped tightly around his body as he quietly stares up at the ceiling. He turns his head. Nino is lying on his side facing him. Despite the bright rays flooding the room, he's still sleeping. Haruka sighs. Nino's lovely honeyed skin is flawless in the unfiltered light. He looks handsome and peaceful, deeply contented somehow.

I envy him. Haruka shifts his head back to stare up at the ceiling just as Nino stretches his body. He exhales a soft yawn and his voice is groggy and low. "Good morning. Did you sleep?"

"No," Haruka says. He turns his head against the pillow,

meeting Nino's lazy amber gaze. "I believe that there is something intrinsically wrong with me."

Nino simply watches him, unmoving. He blinks slowly. "What do you think is wrong with you?"

Shifting his head again, Haruka inhales deeply to calm the block of tension sitting in his chest. "My family has collected data and research on bonding for centuries. In all the accounts I have read and studied, there is not *one* instance of a couple bonding the first time they exchanged blood. *Not one*, Nino—across all forms and levels of intimacy. There are also no instances in *Lore and Lust* of a couple's bond breaking. Again, I am a severe deviation from what is considered normal and I do not know why I am like this."

Haruka drags his palms down his face, distressed. Is he some kind of malformation? Some damned thing that exists outside the formalized lines of vampiric culture? Is he even a vampire? Maybe he is something else entirely.

He loves Nino. Truly. He feels no animosity toward him and none of this is his fault. But Haruka has tried to be exceptionally careful to avoid this. For seventy wretched years he has restrained himself and been cautious, strictly stifling his nature and never offering his blood. The *one time* he allows himself to submit to his desires, he is instantly bound and chained again. It doesn't make any sense.

Nino slowly sits up beside him, pressing his back into the headboard. He relaxes his shoulders, his hands resting in his lap, legs outstretched. "How many times did it take before you bonded with Yuna?"

"Nine." Haruka sighs. He places one palm flat against his forehead and closes his eyes. "With intimacy and mutual feeding every time. And there had been a plan. It had been arranged and discussed so there was much preparation. Nino, we have not discussed *anything*, and now the entirety of our lives and our inherent natures are deeply fused together. We are strictly dependent upon each other now. Does this not frighten you?"

Shifting his head to look over at him with panicked eyes, Haruka waits. Nino seems so calm and unbothered as he sits in the hazy yellow sunlight. Haruka can't understand it.

Nino sighs. "No, Haru, I'm not scared. I don't know... Like I told you last night, something in me relaxed after we made love. It settled me and I hadn't even realized how badly I needed that."

Haruka drops his hand from his forehead and exhales. He supposes it's good that at least one of them is calm.

"Speaking of Yuna..." Nino furrows his brow. "What was she talking about last night?

"She told me that after five years of attempting to bond with Kenta she was unsuccessful. She was tersely suggesting that I might befall a similar fate."

"Well... that certainly doesn't seem to be the case."

"Indeed." Haruka closes his eyes again, taking slow, concentrated breaths. This is unfathomable.

"Why are you scared of this?" Nino asks softly. "What are you afraid of, exactly? Do you think... that I'll do the same thing Yuna did to you?"

"I—No, I don't." He pulls his body upright to sit beside Nino. "My bond with Yuna... It was a very strict and rigid thing. I constantly sacrificed my desires in every way, and being beholden to her... Bonding means the loss of *autonomy*, Nino. My body is no longer exclusively my own. It unsettles me to be so vulnerable and bound this way again. Can you understand?"

"I understand," Nino says, his expression thoughtful as he folds his arms. "But... can I offer a different perspective?"

"Of course."

"What if nothing changes?" Nino blinks, waiting. Haruka's

brows draw together in confusion. In his estimation, *everything* has changed.

"What do you mean?"

"I enjoy spending time with you—you enjoy spending time with me. That's why we're here, yes?"

"Yes," Haruka says.

"I love you." Nino smiles. "You love me..."

"I do."

"The way I see it, now we just get to be together all the time." Nino shrugs. "We were starting to make plans for me to move here anyway. We made that decision. You say that you're afraid of being beholden, but to me, we're *free* now. We're not limited anymore. We can research and help each other. We can be closer and nourish each other without worrying. You don't need to restrict your aura—you can just be yourself."

Be myself? Haruka stares forward, letting the words sink in. It is a paradigm shift in his mind. Being bonded is a means of being free? How? When he'd been bonded before, all he did was sacrifice the things he wanted. This is his station in life— constant sacrifice. He tries to wrap his consciousness around Nino's point of view. It is difficult.

"I've never forced you to do anything, Haru, and you've never imposed anything on me. That's not our relationship. Why would we suddenly start doing that to each other now?"

Haruka sighs. "I... I don't know."

"I'm excited," Nino says, folding his hands in his lap. "Now I can help you with your realm, if you want me to. And I can feed you whenever you want. I can finally tell you how beautiful I think you are, hopefully without you thinking I'm just trying to get in your pants—although I would... *really* like to do that again, but that's not my point."

Haruka closes his eyes and breathes a laugh. He rubs his palm down his face.

"My point is, I'm happy... about this," Nino continues. "And I'm curious to explore what's happened between us. It feels like the energy of our natures has fused together, like maybe we share our innate auras. Two bodies, one essence. We should figure this out. We might be like the Wonder Twins or something."

"The what?" Haruka frowns.

Nino shakes his head, incredulous. "How is it that you know ancient languages and can recite Greek philosophy, but you have a *ridiculous* blind spot for pop culture?"

"This is untrue." Haruka raises his chin. "I know music, particularly from the modal, bebop and free jazz movements."

"Yeah?" Nino's eyes narrow in challenge. "What about outside of that? Jimmy Hendrix, Freddy Mercury, Prince and David Bowie?"

"*Yes.*" Haruka turns his nose up, indignant.

"Bruno Mars? Gaga?"

"What... language are you speaking?"

"What about TV shows, anime and movies?" Nino presses. "*Star Trek, Doctor Who... Cowboy Bebop—Amelie, Kill Bill, Spirited Away?*"

Folding his arms, Haruka sits back. "You are making these things up."

"Jesus, Haru," Nino laughs. "I am not."

"I do not watch television or movies because the motion of it bothers my eyes. We have talked about this. The light of the smartphone you bought me as well. I'm glad that you are here and I no longer need to use it."

Haughty, Haruka shifts his gaze away from Nino. At his mate's silence, he looks back toward him. He's smiling. In a surprise move, he smoothly leans into Haruka and sneaks a quick kiss upside his nose, making Haruka wince.

"I'm glad that I'm here too," Nino says. "I love you, Haru."

Haruka smiles, feeling an undeniable flash of warmth in his chest. "I love *you*. Please do not insist that I watch strange things."

Nino shrugs. "It's your loss."

There is a knock at the bedroom door. Haruka calls out and Asao peeks his head inside. He frowns. "I'm not going to ask why your bedroom looks the way it does. Whatever the reason, I hope we don't make this a habit?"

Nino looks away in a stifled laugh. Haruka straightens from the headboard. "I apologize, Asao. No, it will not be a habit. At least, I don't think it will."

Asao shakes his head before he calls out, "Nino."

Nino lifts his chin in the manservant's direction. Asao's face softens, warm and kind. "Welcome to the family."

"Thank you, Asao." Nino beams.

Asao steps into the room. "We have a lot to talk about. Arrangements, formal announcements, combining finances. We need to think about hiring more staff for the house as well."

"Agreed," Haruka says. They have much work ahead of them. His mind is bending around his new circumstance. Little by little, it doesn't seem nearly as daunting as it had an hour earlier.

Asao continues, "Also, you haven't seen the paper this morning, but apparently Ladislao is gone. Poof. Vanished without a trace."

Haruka draws back, his chest tight. Nino's face also wears a look of panic. Is the Vanishing truly happening again? And what about the purebred he'd briefly sensed in the woods? Is he part of this, somehow? The confounding mystery of the Vanishing is that purebred vampires should *not* be capable of simply disappearing. The innate strength of their auras always makes them discernable to someone, somewhere—especially if they are mated.

"Anyway, I'm not trying to spook you," Asao says, moving back out the door. "I just thought you should know. Let's try not to let this news dampen our exciting morning. I'll start breakfast."

Haruka's brain is already scanning and flipping through all the historical accounts, research and data he's read and studied about the Great Vanishing. Nino's voice breaks his concentration.

"Alright..." he breathes. "Am I allowed to panic now?"

LATE APRIL

THIRTY-NINE

Nino loves the train in Japan. Especially when he misses rush hour on his way back home and it's easy for him to get a window seat. Something about it—the quiet atmosphere, only disturbed by the muffled, smooth sound of the wheels against the train tracks, and the peaceful monotony of watching traditional houses interspersed with green rice fields, cement buildings, bright convenience stores and pedestrians and bikers zipping by like short clips from a movie reel—it gives him a sense of calm. A sense of wonder.

His phone rings. He looks around before discreetly answering the call and bringing the phone to his ear. "Thank God, she's alive."

"Yeah, yeah," Cellina snarks. "Don't be a brat."

"Are they holding you captive in Greece somewhere? Why don't you ever answer your phone, Lina?"

"Because I'm busy," she says. "The museum has some exciting projects going on and I have a lot of responsibility. Everything is alright, isn't it? Are you and Haruka okay?"

"Yeah," Nino whispers. "We're great—I just miss talking to you."

Ever since Nino became bonded a month earlier, Cellina is even harder to get ahold of. He would never say it, but it suddenly feels as if his best friend is a fed-up nanny. She's finally off duty and she's washed her hands of him.

"Sorry," she says. "I'll try to do better, but I have shit to do. Why are you whispering?"

"I'm on the train. They don't like people talking on phones on the train here—or eating. But it's after rush hour and the car isn't very full."

"Got it—so you're happy?" she asks.

"Yes. Very." Maybe this is the happiest Nino has ever been in his long life. He never anticipated this—that within a matter of months, his life would be wholly and wonderfully changed forever.

He is bonded. With another purebred vampire. It's unbelievable.

"Good," Cellina says. "How's Haruka? Is he adjusting?"

"He's much better. I can tell he still grapples with the shock of it though. He's been reaching out to Historians in other countries... his network of dusty vampire-professor nerds."

Cellina laughs at this. Nino smiles as he continues. "He wants some kind of empirical data or logical reasoning for why we bonded so quickly and easily. I tell him it's because we're meant to be. He calls me a romantic and sticks his handsome little nose back in a book."

"Cute," Cellina says. "It's that ancient blood of his—combined with the fact that you both genuinely trust each other. It's a beautiful thing. How's the aristocracy treating you?"

"I had a big meeting with the ranked vampires in Osaka and Kyoto last week. It went well, and I feel good about the role

I'm creating for myself. Everyone is really receptive except for a couple of vamps here and there. I'm going to oversee the major cities in Kansai and Haru is going to take Chūgoku and split it with another purebred in Hiroshima."

"Oh, is that the same purebred that oversaw his realm while he was away? The 'substitute' you mentioned?"

"Yeah." Nino laughs. "He's not popular. So tell me about the museum. G keeps asking me how you're doing. He's been pretty grumpy since you moved to Athens."

There's silence on the other end and Nino bites back a grin. "Lina?"

"You wonder why I don't answer your calls?"

―――――――

IT'S dusk when Nino finally walks into the quiet master bedroom. The light of the newly replaced lamp is soft in the impending darkness. Instinctively, he glances through the open patio doors. The bamboo fence is vibrant and green against the luscious pink of cherry blossom trees. They delicately shed their petals in the stillness, reminding him of snowfall. Haruka is there, slowly sinking his long, naked body down and into the water.

Immediately deciding to join him, Nino walks over to his mate's side of the bed to get the tube of liquid from the night-stand drawer. He rounds the corner of the mattress and is met with a small hoard—stacks of books, shuffled papers and an empty wine glass are set against the hardwood floor. Nino shakes his head as he steps over his husband's miniature nest.

"He has a library *and* an office. Why does there need to be books and papers in our bedroom, too?"

He breathes a laugh, knowing Asao will fuss at him and say the same thing when he finds the mess. Bottle in hand,

Nino swiftly moves toward the master bathroom to quickly shower.

The sun has dipped below the horizon when he's finished and walks outside. The sky is an incredible blueish-purple with clusters of dark, lingering clouds. They slowly drift, as if playing hide-and-seek with the silvery twinkle of stars above.

Haruka is sitting on the underwater ledge lining the inside of the spring. When Nino approaches, he stands, then dips underneath the water's surface. Nino moves further into the spring, only stopping when his mate emerges just in front of him. Haruka smooths his dark hair back. He opens his haunting burgundy eyes. "Hello, my love."

He steps into Nino, wrapping his arms around his naked waist and tilting his head to place a firm kiss against his mouth. Nino returns the affection before lifting his head. "Asao is going to fuss at you for leaving your research stuff in the bedroom."

"He will get over it." Haruka smiles, leaning in to catch his mouth once more. After a moment of indulgence, he pulls back. "How was the first meeting?"

"It was good," Nino mumbles, busy kissing Haruka's face. He moves near his ear, then down the line of his neck to his shoulder. His skin is so soft and damp from soaking in the warm water. He wants to tell him about his day, but the combination of Haruka's muffled scent, the bath and the clean, spring night air is doing a number on Nino's mental capacities. His voice is husky as it passes through his lips. "Can I tell you about it later?"

Haruka laughs, affectionate and deep from his throat. Nino loves that sound. Maybe it is his favorite sound. Haruka kisses him, then grasps Nino's free hand beneath the water to drag him toward the edge of the hot spring.

Once there, Haruka lifts himself to sit atop the underwater

bench, simultaneously pulling Nino between his spread thighs. He wraps his long legs around Nino's waist in the water, bringing their bodies tightly together. Nino leans forward to place the bottle of lube at the edge of the spring, friskily taking Haruka's mouth as he does so. With his hands free, he reaches down and grips Haruka's ass. He lifts him into his body, the weight of him like nothing from the buoyancy of the water.

They cling to each other, their bodies slick and their mouths moving and teasing underneath the dark celestial sky. Just as Nino is building up his courage, Haruka lifts his head from the kiss and lazily looks into his eyes. "My love, if you desire me, you can have me. You do not need to hesitate like this."

"Well... I... I thought we weren't supposed to be intentionally reading each other's thoughts until we practiced more?"

Haruka smirks, unwrapping his legs from around Nino's waist to stand on his own. "Intentionally reading your thoughts is superfluous. You are an open book." Haruka turns his back to him and Nino shrugs in agreement. Fair point.

His mate places one knee against the bench, partially lifting his body from the water to quickly grab the bottle and hand it to Nino. Mesmerized by the sight of his long, creamy back and firm cheeks slick in the moonlight, Nino's eyes glow to life as he steps into him. He presses his chest into his spine and tilts his head to kiss Haruka along the curve of his shoulder. Multi-tasking, Nino makes quick work of lathering his fingers as he indulges in the taste of his skin.

When he's finished, he tosses the bottle back to the edge of the spring, then lays one palm flat against his husband's tight stomach. At Nino's touch, Haruka subtly arches his lower back, making it easier for Nino to reach down and softly caress his fingers against his tight, damp flesh. Haruka's breathing shortens as Nino teases him and kisses behind his ear, nuzzling his face into his hair. Nino finally presses his fingers into him and Haruka groans, lying into Nino's chest.

As Nino strokes and stretches him, Haruka rests his head back against his shoulder, his eyes closed. He grasps Nino's free hand at his belly, then slowly guides him down until their fingers are wrapped tightly around Haruka's shaft. With both hands busy, Nino whispers against his husband's ear, "Tell me when you're ready."

Haruka lifts his head, then bends forward slightly to rest his palms against the edge of the hot spring. He breathes out and Nino can feel him relaxing his body. His warm flesh giving and flexing around his fingers. His beautiful back is glistening and dotted with droplets from the hot, rolling steam of the spring. Soon, Haruka's deep voice is husky in the quiet night air. "I'm ready."

Nino removes his fingers, then slowly replaces them with his shaft, gradually pressing deeper into his tight, slick warmth. His mate is breathing, steadily yielding to him and taking him in. Nino exhales as he moves his hips forward, not wanting this to end prematurely.

He gently rocks against Haruka, driving himself in and out of his body in a steady rhythm. The heated water surrounding them ripples and swirls with his movement. As Haruka pushes back, his breathing is controlled—perfectly calm—and his eyes are closed.

Actually, he's a little too calm. Too polite.

Nino pauses in his movement, then brings his hand back up to grasp Haruka's damp belly. He encircles his navel with his thumb as he whispers, "Tesoro... we would have more fun if you stopped restraining yourself like this. Why won't you let your aura rest?"

"I am deeply enjoying you." Haruka turns his head, smiling seductively. "But when you have done something systematically for seventy years, it is not an easy habit to break."

"I can help you..." Nino breathes, his eyes glowing even brighter against the darkness.

Nino firmly holds his mate's abdomen, willing his own essence within Haruka to grow and expand—to unravel, rest and be free from the strict hold he's imposed upon it. Haruka gasps sharply, his eyes burning the color of fiery sunset and his spine tensing. He grips his fingers around Nino's at his stomach and firmly bucks backward, the water splashing from his movement. His deep voice is hoarse. *"Harder."*

Nino obeys, driving his hips into him. Haruka bends forward again, bracing himself as he pushes back into Nino's body to match his carnal movement. The mist in the air is like a veil around them, making smooth lines of condensation trickle down the center of Nino's spine as he thrusts into his mate, over and over. The sound of their bodies clashing in the water combined with Haruka's grunts of pleasure has Nino teetering on the edge—the pressure of release bubbling hot and low in his groin.

Need and lust are overtaking his mind, but he wants Haruka with him. For them to reach the height of ecstasy together.

In a quick decision, he runs his fingers into the back of Haruka's short hair and pulls him upright. He wraps his palm around his husband's shaft, then bites down into the curve of his shoulder. Nino sucks hard against his flesh, feeling the metaphysical weight of Haruka's aura inside his core. Focusing his mind, he pulls again, filling his mate's body with love and assurance—urging him to let go. Haruka cries out, his voice echoing through the trees as his body trembles.

Nino holds him tightly as the rosy coolness of his aura releases like a dazzling sunset. His scent is divine and Nino moans, slowly rolling his hips into him as his own body finally surrenders. He pulls his mouth from Haruka's shoulder, gasping as the release rushes warmly from within him and into his mate.

When the force of the climax subsides, Haruka is sagging. His elegant body lulled and satiated as Nino supports his frame. The beautiful, hazy glow of their bonded aura surrounds them. Peaceful and dreamlike. Truly, it is the manifestation of something deeply significant between them.

He licks Haruka's neck where he fed. After a moment, Nino rests his forehead against his temple while he holds him tightly, warmly in his damp embrace. "So... have we been too timid? Is this what turns you on, Haru? Diplomacy and rough sex?"

Laughing, Haruka stands straight as they carefully disconnect their bodies. He turns in his arms, then cradles Nino's chin with his fingertips. He smirks, his evocative eyes practically shining. "As I have said before—when you are involved, *many* things arouse me. And I am looking forward to making new discoveries with you."

Nino leans in to softly kiss his lips as he wraps his arms around his waist. He can't believe that this intelligent, beautiful, complicated, messy and seductive male is his mate. His partner, friend, source and lover for *life*. He takes a deep breath to calm the warm pounding of his heart, then grins. "Agreed. I think this is the start of something very good."

-The Beginning-

PREVIEW

Lore and Lust book 2: *The Vanishing*

ONE YEAR LATER | LATE APRIL

Morning. Nino enters the kitchen and Haruka is already there, sitting at the table with Junichi. The doors to the courtyard off the kitchen are propped open, allowing the cool, sweet air and sunlight of spring to saturate the open space.

Moving toward the counter, Nino's objective is clear. Coffee pot. He smiles in their direction. "Hey, Jun."

Tall and dark with warm, almond butter–brown skin, the first-generation vampire lifts his marble-black irises, grinning. As Okayama's local tailor and clothing designer, something about Junichi Takayama is unquestionably suave. In Nino's mind, he's like a male peacock, except his feathers are *all* black. When the light hits him, the darkness of his plumage flashes like liquid iridescence.

"Good morning, Nino." Junichi nods politely, his English smooth and unimpeded by his native tongue like Haruka's. Junichi is also fluent in Spanish. His mother was Dominican, but he was raised in Hiroshima. "Your husband and I are at an impasse. Maybe you help can us?"

"What's going on?" Nino pours his coffee. He has told

Junichi that he can speak Japanese when visiting their home, but the male has coolly refused, claiming it's "more fun" this way.

"This is for the Hamamoto-Iseki wedding in six months," Junichi explains "We're having difficulty deciding whether Haruka should wear a suit or traditional attire. Do you have a preference in his clothing?"

Junichi flirtatiously raises his eyebrow while Haruka sits with his arms folded at the head of the table, his gaze focused on a letter directly in front of him.

"Well..." Nino leans against the counter with his elbows, cradling the warm coffee cup in his palms. "He looks regal in a kimono... but modern and sexy in a suit. I like both. Maybe I prefer the kimono? Oh—you know what's even better? A yukata. He's always naked under those things. Only *one* layer."

Junichi laughs. Haruka shakes his head, his eyes closed. Nino grins, bringing his coffee cup to his lips. Lately, whenever Haruka wears traditional robes, Nino feels as if he's bonded with one of those elegant lounging figures in an ukiyo-e wood-block painting—especially with his hair so dramatically long like this.

"That was a lot of information." Junichi smirks. "Unfortunately a yukata is too casual for a wedding, but your preference is noted. Maybe I'll make a couple new robes for him this month before I fly to Europe? They're easy for me to design and tailor since I know his measurements by heart."

Feeling accomplished, Nino beams. "You'll be traveling for three months, right?"

"Yes sir. My clients abroad demand personalized deliveries."

"You're amazing, Jun. Everything you make for Haruka always suits him perfectly. My favorite was that kimono you designed for his welcome celebration last year... Maybe I should wear a kimono to the wedding?"

Junichi blinks, considering. "You could absolutely do that. I'll have to think about a design that complements you."

"Haru has so many, maybe I can just try one of his?"

"Absolutely not." Junichi frowns, shaking his head. "You two are the same height but your shoulders are broader and rounder. Your physique is slightly more defined from your exercise routine. There's no way I'd let you walk around in a tight, ill-fitting kimono."

Haruka unexpectedly laughs. The deep, throaty sound of it surprises both Junichi and Nino as they shift their attention toward him. Haruka is holding the bridge of his nose with his fingertips. "My apologies. The mental image of that scenario caught me off guard."

"Welcome to the conversation, tesoro." Nino stands straight and walks to the end of the counter. He leans there comfortably with his hip. "What are you reading?"

"A formal visitation request." Haruka's dark brows are drawn together as he takes a deep breath, his previous mirth evaporated.

"From someone you dislike?" Junichi asks.

"From someone I do not know and have never heard of." Haruka lifts his bright burgundy gaze toward Nino. "May I please have a cup?"

Nino nods and turns toward the cabinet to grab a mug. "What's the request for?"

"Introductions..." Haruka folds his arms. "The vampire is Lajos Almeida, which is undeniably synonymous with Ladislao Almeida of Rio de Janeiro... but I have never heard of this particular male within the clan's family lineage."

Tense, Nino walks around the counter with Haruka's coffee. In light of both Gael and Ladislao disappearing last year, having anyone even vaguely associated with the Almeida Clan so close to their home seems like a bad omen.

"Why would someone from the Almeida Clan want to meet you?" Junichi asks. "I hate to say this, but things calmed down in Brazil after Ladislao vanished. He was obviously the root of the problem."

"We have a connection," Haruka says, accepting Nino's offering. "We crossed paths with one of the Almeida Clan's associates last year. There was an altercation regarding my family's research, but then he escaped and I have not seen or heard anything since."

In a fog, Nino sits down at the table beside Haruka. The associate is Gael Silva, a large, domineering first-generation vampire they met in England more than a year ago. He'd attacked Haruka after learning about the *Lore and Lust* manuscript—an impressive compilation of accounts on forming vampiric bonds. The research is invaluable, giving shape to a topic typically shrouded in mystery.

Gael's brutal response had convinced both Nino and Haruka that they should avoid casually bringing up the manuscript's existence. At least among strangers.

Using his fingertips, Nino slides the request within his line of sight, then reads the details. The appeal is for one month from now—the exact minimum amount of time considered proper when making formal requests of purebreds. Nino pushes the letter away so that it sits in the middle of the table, unsettled by the sense of foreboding emanating from it.

Junichi picks up the paper to read it, his black irises scanning. He pulls the letter to his nose and inhales deeply. "Smells strong—like sage. This Lajos is probably purebred?"

Haruka blows out a breath. Concern is etched in his forehead. "So it would seem."

Book 2, The Vanishing, *will be released in the spring of 2021.*

To receive a bonus chapter from this story (Date Night in Milan), *please visit LoreAndLust.com and subscribe!* *Thank you for reading* Lore and Lust.

If you enjoyed this story, please visit Amazon.com and leave a review.

ABOUT KARLA NIKOLE

Karla Nikole has a long-standing love affair with Japan. They have always been very good to each other. Having lived in the country for two years and taken several extended vacations there, she is deeply inspired by the culture, language, landscape, food and people. A trip to Italy in 2018 for a wedding breathed new fire into her writing, eventually leading to the birth of Nino Bianchi and Haruka Hirano—two love letters to these beautiful countries. She has also lived in South Korea and Prague, and currently resides in the USA (although Milan is adamantly calling out to her).

facebook.com/LoreAndLust

instagram.com/karlanikolepublishing

Printed in Great Britain
by Amazon